# Pride and Pursuit

## A Pride and Prejudice Variation

RIANA EVERLY

***PRIDE AND PURSUIT***



*Published by* ***Bay Crest Press 2024***

***Toronto, Ontario, Canada***



*Cover design by Dash at Calliope Covers.*

*Front cover image: Central cover image is The entrance to Llangollen, North Wales, by Julius Caesar Ibbetson, 1792*

ISBN-13: 978-1-7781297-6-6

# *Dedication*

To those still in Wickham's grasp, may they soon be set free

# Contents

# Acknowledgements

This book has been a long time in the making. Other projects, real-life obligations, and plain old writers' block threatened again and again to derail it but I pushed through. I had a great deal of inspiration and incentive to finish this novel and polish it to the best of my abilities. I'll get to people in a moment, but this story is a tribute, in some way, to Wales.

I'm not Welsh, but I've always felt an affinity for that beautiful country, and after a couple of visits there, my love for it just grows stronger. What better place for Lizzy and Darcy to fall in love, after all, than in this majestic and stunning land? *Croeso*—welcome—to my version of Wales, where true love triumphs over all.

I cannot forget to thank people. Oh, what amazing people I have in my corner, cheering me on and offering so much insight and assistance. As always, Mikael Swayze, editor and proof-reader extraordinaire, deserves accolades.

Also, a huge round of applause for Liz Martinson and Trish Henry Green, both fabulous authors in their own rights, for their excellent editorial comments and critiques, without whom this book would not be nearly the creation it is now. I further wish to thank Pamela Willing of the Oswestry Genealogical Society for her patient and kind help in my research.

Thanks also to cover artist HR Swayze at Calliope Covers for her lovely artwork. The central image is *The entrance to Llangollen, North Wales,* by Julius Caesar Ibbetson, 1792.

Cover design by HR Swayze at Calliope Covers

# Chapter One
# After the Ball

*August 1811*

Elizabeth Bennet stifled a yawn as her father's coach bumped along the country lane. Bright sunlight poured through the windows, illuminating tiny motes of dust caught in the beams, turning them into joyful reminders of last night's chandeliers. Her feet ached still from the hours she had spent dancing, but she would have it no other way.

"You were popular last night, Lizzy." Jane's voice filtered through her recollections, and she turned to her sister with a wide grin.

"As were you. I do not believe you sat out a single dance. The gentlemen were lined up to have a turn on the floor with you. You always were the prettiest one in the room." Elizabeth's teasing laugh filled the coach, as Jane flushed a delicate pink and cast her eyes modestly downwards.

Across from the two sisters sat their aunt, with an indulgent smile upon her face. She was closer in age to the sisters than to their mother, and was at once a respected family member, confidante, and dear friend. When she had invited her nieces to spend a week with her in London, both had accepted almost before receiving their father's certain permission. These visits to London were not infrequent, and usually included visits with friends, concerts, afternoons in the park with the young Gardiner children, and outings of various sorts.

This particular trip to London had been somewhat different, for Elizabeth and Jane's four young cousins were now enjoying the vast grounds of their family estate in Hertfordshire, a holiday from the heavy air and heat of the city. But, in compensation for the loss of their exuberant company, Aunt Gardiner had introduced the sisters to a friend, who in turn had invited them to a ball in the grand garden of an estate just past the city's limits.

They had accepted with pleasure and had danced the night away, before returning very late indeed to the Gardiner's house on Gracechurch Street. No, Elizabeth corrected herself, not late at all, but very early this morning. It must have been almost five o'clock before they fell into their beds and had slept for only two hours before rising for the morning's journey back to the Bennet family's home in Hertfordshire.

Their aunt was accompanying them, eager as she was to see her children again, and their uncle would join her at Longbourn for a week or two once his immediate business was complete. Had Aunt Gardiner slept at all last night? For surely, while Elizabeth and Jane took what little slumber they could, she had been organising the servants and seeing to the household and calling for the Bennets' carriage to return them all to the country.

Still, while she must have been quite as tired as Elizabeth, her bright eyes did not show it at all.

"She speaks the truth, Jane. You turned many heads last night, and I know that several young men will be calling at our house in town before long in hopes of furthering the acquaintance. Perhaps at Christmas, you might come for a longer visit to satisfy them." She glanced over at Elizabeth and added, "And I might say the same about you. At least three young men spoke to your uncle, hoping to learn more about you. No, do not put yourself down. You are every bit as pretty as Jane, if in a different way. And you looked very well indeed in that dress we remade for you." She talked on, and Elizabeth tried to follow the conversation, but her smiles were overtaken by yawns and she felt the weight of her eyelids pulling them closed.

"Lizzy? Are you awake? Oh, I am sorry..." Jane patted her arm. "You can rest on my shoulder if you wish to sleep. We have another half an hour before the inn where we will take some refreshments and let the horses rest."

Elizabeth squeezed her eyes for a moment and then blinked herself back to consciousness. "No, indeed, Jane, do not let me sleep. Let us talk of the ball and the handsome men we danced with. And the music! What a fine orchestra your friend engaged. I most enjoyed that new dance they played at the very end of the evening. What was it called? 'The Arrow's Flight'?"

She hummed a couple of notes, and Jane added what she recalled, followed by Aunt Gardiner's melodic voice, and soon the three women were singing the song that had so captivated them the previous night.

*Cupid's bow is magic-touched,*
*His arrow's flight is true.*
*For when his arrow takes its flight,*
*My eyes are fix'd on you.*

"What silly words," Elizabeth laughed between yawns.

"But memorable, for all that!" her aunt teased in return. "Even half-asleep, you recall them perfectly."

Despite these amusements and the cherished company of her aunt and sister, by the time the coach arrived at the inn where they had secured a private dining room whilst the horses rested, Elizabeth could no longer force herself into wakefulness. The very notion of staggering out through the courtyard and encountering a hive of busy and noisy patrons and servants all but made her head swim; and after a very late supper and early breakfast, she had no wish for food. If only...

"Aunt," she said through another stifled yawn, "I would prefer to remain in the carriage and sleep. I can hardly keep my eyes open and shall be no pleasant company at tea. Would you mind terribly? Colin will be keeping watch on the horses, and he can ensure I am not disturbed." She mentioned her family's manservant who tended the horses, and who now sat on the rumble with Peggy, the maid.

Jane's porcelain forehead wrinkled with a frown. "Are you certain, Lizzy? It cannot be very comfortable in here; you cannot even lie across the seat as you did when you were a child. Perhaps we can take a room with a bed in the inn..."

Her aunt looked equally perturbed but said nothing.

"No, I shall be quite well. I can roll the blanket under the seat into a sort of pillow to lean against, and I have my shawl if I get chilled. We shall only be here for an hour; it would be quite unreasonable to take a room, for by the time it was arranged and I lay down, it would be time to rise again. I only need a short rest. Enjoy your tea, and I shall be a far more cheerful person when you return."

Her fatigue must have shown in her eyes, for Jane and Aunt Gardiner looked at each other and nodded.

"Very well, Lizzy," her aunt replied. "I shall tell Colin. Call to him if you change your mind or need anything."

Within moments, the carriage came to a stop in the yard behind the inn, and with a final glance towards her, Jane and Aunt Gardiner alit. There were some noises from above, presumably Peggy and Colin descending from the box, and more sounds as her father's two carriage horses were released from their harness for the time being, to be led to the shade to take water and rest before continuing on for another twelve miles or so to Longbourn. All this

Elizabeth heard but dismissed from her consciousness as she fashioned her pillow, pulled the curtains closed over the windows, and made herself as comfortable as she could before drifting off into a much-desired sleep.

FITZWILLIAM Darcy shifted behind the bale of hay by the side of the stables. He was safe from view for now, but he knew his time here must be short. He had escaped this time, but it would not be long before his pursuers found his scent and tracked him like a fox running from the hounds. And, like the poor fox, if he were caught, he would be torn to shreds. A piece of straw poked through the burlap he crouched upon and scratched his leg through the rip in his breeches. He shifted again and pulled the offending straw away, groaning in dismay as he glanced at his filthy hands. Something in his hair itched and he prayed he had not contracted lice.

What a horrid night this had been. What a horrid week! He ran a dirt-blackened hand across his forehead to wipe off the sweat, dreading to think what dreadful mark it might leave. It hardly mattered, he laughed bitterly to himself. No one who saw him now would think him any more than another addlepated labourer, staggering around England half-dressed in rags and looking like something ejected from the gutters.

He had, somehow, to get home to Pemberley, to gather the troops! But how that might occur, he knew not. He still had his coat, now torn and covered in dust, and the handful of coins and notes he had shoved into a pocket before he had fled, but he dared not take the mail or the stagecoach. Perhaps another farmer would offer him space at the back of a cart, much like the one who had brought him this far. Or, he could set out and walk, somewhere off the main roads where he would be harder to find. But oh, what damage might be done in the length of time that would take. Could he buy a horse? No, not with the few funds he had, and no one would believe him, looking as he did, to take credit. It all began to seem rather hopeless.

The sound of an approaching carriage caught his attention. It seemed a rather ordinary sort of vehicle, not too large and certainly not elaborate, but in good repair and pulled by a team of two sturdy horses, clearly chosen for their stamina and not looks. There was no coat of arms on the door, not that he expected one, and the servants on the rumble wore regular clothing rather than livery. It looked, he considered, to be the coach of a gentleman well-enough off to afford such a luxury, but certainly not one of his own wealth and standing. A country squire, returning, perhaps, from a visit to town.

His estimation was reinforced when he saw two ladies descend from the vehicle. From this slight distance, it was difficult to see precisely, but one looked to be about eight or nine years older than the other, both rather handsome. The younger one might be very pretty indeed if seen from closer proximity. They were well dressed and spoke to their servants rather than ordering them. Yes, minor gentry, the daughters of that vast race of land-holding gentlemen whose tenants fed England.

As they turned towards the inn itself, Darcy heard the older one call out to the manservant. "About an hour? That suits us well, Colin. Send Peggy for us when the carriage is ready again." And off they walked to avail themselves of whatever the proprietor had for their enjoyment.

An hour. They were not changing horses, then, but continuing with the same team. They must not be travelling very far. It was a pity, else he might go down on bended knee and beg passage with them, even with the servants on the box, or next to the driver. He could even offer to help drive, for he had taken the reins before and was said to be adept with the horses.

A thought wormed its way into his mind, which he rejected completely. It would not do! A gentleman did not behave thus, and he would have no part of that foolish scheme. But the thought would not be quiet, no matter how he squashed it. He groped for the apple he had bought from the farmer with far too much coin and took a bite, soothing the gnawing hole in his stomach. It might be some of the last food he would eat for a while if he could not get far away very quickly.

For almost an hour, he sat behind his bale in the shadow of the overhang, watching. He watched the two horses be taken to drink and rest in the cool stables; he watched the manservant and maid flirt and eat their meal, as the driver joked with some of the grooms by the wide-open stable door; he watched as other carts and carriages came and left, none of them promising any sort of help for his dire predicament.

And then, with alarm, he watched as one more vehicle neared. It was not the curricle that set Darcy's heart pounding, but the driver.

Damnation! Wickham had traced him thus far. He crouched further down, wondering if he could somehow burrow into the piles of hay. If he were found... He refused even to think of it.

There were only two men, Wickham and another he did not know. He hoped to maintain this situation. But he was trapped. If they began to search, it would not be long before he was caught. The grooms were now hitching up the horses to the gentleman's carriage that had arrived earlier, and he wished he could somehow become one of those horses and flee.

That unwelcome thought made itself known again, and he ignored it as he heard Wickham call to his companion.

"I'll ask the innkeeper if he's seen him. Then we can have an ale before going on to Edgware. See to the horses and meet me inside."

The other man nodded and waved to the groom who was approaching. In short minutes, their business was completed and the man ambled towards the inn.

That dreadful idea was no longer a silent whisper, but a scream. He had to do it. If he remained, he would be discovered and his life would be over. If he acted, he could see things right later.

The carriage's driver was still gabbing with the other men, and the manservant and maid put away their meal and started towards the inn to call for the ladies who were travelling. It was now or never.

In that moment, when no one was looking, he dashed from his hiding place and leapt onto the driver's seat, grabbing the reins in the process. A tug and a crack of the whip and the horses began to move, then run, as he urged them faster and faster in his desperate attempt to escape.

It was not until his heart stopped pounding with the force of a hundred drums that he realised the banging noise was not only in his head, but was coming from inside the coach he had just stolen.

He had, he realised in horror, abducted somebody along with it!

# Chapter 2

# Runaway

Elizabeth swam back to consciousness as the carriage jolted and then began to move across the courtyard, first at a trot and then gaining speed until she felt the coach were flying. Had she slept through her aunt and sister's return? Surely their entry and the ensuing arrangements would have roused her from her sleep. But no, they were not here with her at all. Could they possibly be on the rumble with the servants? Or sitting by the driver, since the day was fine? It seemed improbable, but what alternative could there be, other than...

Her eyes snapped open and she jolted upright. She could hear nothing above the rumbling of the wheels and the thunder of the horses' hooves, running far faster than a coach ever ought to go.

"Jane?" she called out, her voice still thick from sleep. "Aunt? Who is there?"

Had the horses taken a fright and begun to run, driverless, down the roads? Such things happened, she knew. She had heard a tale once, of a stagecoach team who were so trained to the time and destination of their route that they completed the entire stage of their own accord, their driver still nursing his drink at the previous posting inn. But no, not this fast, this seemingly out-of-control.

The thrum of her heart grew louder in her ears until she felt faint.

"Jane?" she shouted once more, and shifted across the shuddering coach to pull aside the curtain that covered the front windows, expecting to see nothing but flying reins trailing behind the two unguided horses. She took a deep breath in an attempt to steady herself and held firmly to the back of the squabs to stop from falling.

"They know their way home," she whispered to herself. "They will return me to Longbourn. All will be well. They know their way." it was as much a prayer for the running beasts as it was reassurance for herself.

But the look she cast through the windows was anything but reassuring, for rather than the unimpeded sight of the horses she expected, she saw two boot-encased legs descending from the coachman's box, the reins held by some unseen hand rather than flapping loose.

For a moment, her mind failed to make sense of these images, as much from incredulity as from the harsh return to consciousness, but all too soon, she lit upon the only possibility that explained her circumstances.

Somebody had stolen her father's coach, with her inside it!

What to do? Never in her years of reading at her father's side had she come across this situation. Ought she to yell out? To remain silent in the hopes of not being discovered? If the thief knew she was about, might she come to physical harm? But she would surely be found eventually. Better to shout out now in the hopes that the miscreant would abandon his mission and run off into the surrounding countryside, or at the very least, release her so she might walk back to the inn.

"Oy, there! Stop! Stop at once!" She yelled as loudly as she could, banging on the roof first with her hand, then with the handle of her aunt's umbrella that lay on the back of the seat. "Stop and return me to the inn this very instant!"

But the driver either did not hear her, or did not care, for the coach continued along its way, if anything, gaining speed.

*I must not panic,* Elizabeth commanded herself. *I must not panic. I must think!* Soon enough, he would have to stop. The horses would soon tire and would have to rest and drink. He must find an inn, or some other watering spot, and then she could make an escape.

She shifted to look out of the side window now, which afforded a better view of the countryside than the narrow slits at the front, which were blocked by the driver's legs. She knew this area, which brought her some relief. They were still on the main road, heading northward as they had been before the coach was commandeered.

Would the thief stop at Edgware? Surely not. What about the toll houses along the route? He must slow for those, and she could leap from the vehicle, or cry out to the gate keeper.

A hundred different plans formed and unravelled in Elizabeth's mind as she gathered everything she could and packed them into her reticule and the soft bag she had carried with her from London. The trunks with their clothing would be lost, but the bit of coin and some personal effects might still be salvaged. She held her breath and waited, knowing a booth must be coming soon.

In answer to her prayers, the coach began to slow. Perhaps the horses had run their bit and would answer the whip no more. Or was the next gate closer than she thought? She put her hand on the door, thankful that it opened from the inside, and prepared to fling it wide and leap.

But instead of slowing further to pay the toll, the coach veered sharply to the side and began to rumble in a different direction. This was a lesser road, still in respectable condition for a carriage, but narrower and rougher than the main London Road. More to the point, it was not a road she knew, and her hopes for escape began to dim.

Despite her continued bangs on the roof and shouts to stop, the thief continued a fair distance, through several turns of the road, and down one or two smaller lanes yet, until at last, he slowed the vehicle and came to a stop.

Anger now gave way to fear. Along the main road, there would be help. Transports of all sorts were frequent, and there were enough towns and stops that she felt somewhat safe. But here, out in the country, out of sight of any house or farm that she could see, her perilous position settled heavily upon her.

Clammy with perspiration, her hands slipped on the handle of the umbrella she still held, and her breaths came short and shallow. What could she do? Was she to die here, out behind a copse of trees in the woods somewhere? No! That could not be. She would not allow it.

Calming her mind with the greatest of effort, she looked around the carriage once more to see what she could find. A book, the umbrella, the blanket, a deck of cards...

Her hat! More to the point, her hatpin! Armed with the umbrella and the sharp spike, she crouched by the door and waited as the driver leapt from his box and began to walk her way.

DAMNATION! What was he to do?

Darcy looped the reins around the fence post he had spotted and surveyed this disaster he had created for himself. He had stolen the coach with all intention, although he would find the owner and compensate him for the inconvenience at a later date. But what of the person inside? How on earth had he chosen the one conveyance that carried somebody within it?

He cursed out loud.

There was nothing for it but to confront his unintended victim. Perhaps he could let the fellow off at some village or coaching inn with some of the coins he still possessed and an abject apology. The servant—for servant it must be; who else would have remained in the carriage whilst the ladies went to refresh themselves?—could then make his way back home and beg his master's forgiveness. From the high-pitched voice that had shouted at him for the last hour, the lad must be quite young, perhaps his sister's age.

The thought of his sister sent a blade into his soul, and he stood for a moment to steel himself before grabbing for the handle to open the carriage door.

Instead of a meek boy of fourteen or fifteen summers, a screeching hellcat emerged, shooting from the interior like a ball propelled by a cannon, flailing and stabbing with an umbrella as if it were a sword. All arms and wild hair, the creature whirled this way and that like a dervish from the East. Darcy leapt back, narrowly avoiding being skewered by something sharp and vicious, his years of fencing coming through to save him from what could have been a rather unhappy injury.

By the gods! This was a young woman, and she was attacking him with a hatpin! The sight so stunned him that he lost concentration enough for her to score with the umbrella, catching him across the side. Pain bloomed through his ribs and he almost stumbled until he saw the hatpin's end coming all too close. He ignored the throbbing in his ribs and leapt aside, circling around to capture the mad creature from behind. He pinned her arms to her sides, barely controlling her frantic attempts to free herself from his grip.

Had she been trained in the arts of swordplay and pugilism, as he had been, she surely would have succeeded. As it was, Darcy made certain to position himself such that she could not crush his toes with her heels, or crack her head against his nose.

She was quite a handful. Although shorter than him by a full head, she thrummed with vinegar and strength, and it was only when he growled something indistinct but feral into her ears did she cease her valiant struggle.

"Drop the pin and the umbrella. I shall not harm you."

She shifted and stamped down on his foot despite his manoeuvring. But he wore solid riding boots and she soft slippers, and her attack was ineffective.

"Drop them. I give you my word, I mean you no harm."

She let out a curse that no lady ought to know and resumed her struggles for a moment, until she drooped at last, her writhing clearly ineffectual. Darcy retained his hold on her arms; this could be a feint. He had spent too long sparring with his cousin to be deceived by an opponent, even a short, female one such as this.

"Drop them." He tightened his grip, squeezing what felt like a nicely padded bosom. At last, the fight truly seemed to go out of her and she obeyed, letting her makeshift weapons fall at her feet. Without releasing her arms, he kicked the umbrella aside and then shifted, dragging the hellcat with him, until there was no possibility she might reach again for the hatpin. At last, incrementally, he released his hold on her.

Whatever he was expecting, it was not the slap across his face that she dealt him. The sting on his cheek muted the ache that still throbbed in his ribs where the umbrella had struck, and from instinct more than conscious thought, he countered to capture her arm in his hand.

"Consider yourself fortunate that I am a gentleman," he growled. "Now stand down, for I will not harm a lady."

Narrow slits of eyes met his as he peered, for the first time, into the face of his hellcat. She was young, far younger than he had imagined from her initial attack, perhaps no more than twenty. Her hair had long since escaped its pins, and wild wisps and curls stuck out from her once-coiffed head at strange angles. She radiated animosity, her face blotched red and her chin thrust forward in defiance, the incongruous scent of rose cologne at odds with her thorny expression. But she relented at last, and her arm relaxed.

He did not ease his grip.

"Not again, Madam. I shall not receive another of your blows."

"Thief!" she spat at him. "You stole my father's coach! Now take me back at once."

"That is not possible, Madam. To return would be to forfeit my life."

"A life of disgrace, by your actions today. How dare you abduct me thus?"

The hellcat hissed at him, the thin line of her mouth daring him to respond.

"Forgive me, Madam. I had need of the conveyance to escape a man who wishes me dead. I had no notion it carried a passenger. I assure you I shall make amends for my, er, appropriation when at last I am able to return home. Permit me to ask your name."

"Those are grand words for a common thief, no matter how prettily you say them." Her eyes flashed hatred at him. "I had rather ask who you are, that I might have you brought up on charges of theft!"

Tension built in Darcy's jaw and his scowl met her glare. Could she not see and hear that he was a gentleman? Despite his damaged and filthy garb, his very air ought to have proclaimed his superiority to her.

"Who I am matters not, lady. I had not intended to carry you with the coach, which I needed to save my life. But as you stowed along, you must, I am afraid, remain with me until I can send you home safely. Madam." He added the final word as an invective.

"And should I decide to leave at this moment?" Her narrowed eyes threatened him.

"Then you leave. Shall I remove your trunk from the back of the coach? Decide now, for the horses are no longer breathing as heavily and I must be off again."

For the first time, he saw fear in her regard.

"Where are we?" Her head swivelled left and right as she scanned the tree-lined lane down which he had driven. "Are we north or south of Edgware?"

"I cannot say. I do not know exactly where we are, and hope that if I cannot find myself, my pursuers will also have no success in finding me."

"Then where are you going?"

This was an excellent question, and one he had not entirely considered. If he turned northward to Pemberley, Wickham would certainly be lying somewhere in wait, to pounce before he reached the sanctuary of his estate. Nor could he return to London. This was something he had to consider at a better time, when he was not filled with the horror of his near escape and burdened with the realisation of his unwanted accomplice.

"North," was all he said. "I can find my direction by the position of the sun."

She wrinkled her nose. It was, now that she was not attempting to eviscerate him, a rather pretty one. "Then I shall make my own way. Good riddance, thief!"

She reached back into the coach for her reticule and a small bag and began to stomp down the lane. Her umbrella still lay at Darcy's feet, the lethal hatpin a few feet away. He bent to pick both up, storing the hatpin in the seam of his lapel. The coat was in poor enough repair now that another hole in the fabric would render it no greater harm.

He was well rid of that hellcat. When he found himself somewhere safe, he would make inquiries and return the trunk to its rightful owner, but for the present, he could make his escape, free of this encumbrance in a petticoat. Now, where to go? North, he judged by the sun, was that way, where the road seemed to curve. It would take several days to reach Derbyshire at this rate, but if he turned westward at some point, he might make for his school friend's estate in Staffordshire. Even if Julian were not at home, his housekeeper knew Darcy well enough from previous visits that she would afford him accommodations for a time. That would involve crossing the Great North Road at some point, but...

His eyes flickered up to the retreating figure, still pounding her way down the lane. Good riddance, indeed. Let her stumble her way to whatever farm or village might lie on the path of this narrow lane. He had not wanted her and was pleased to see the back of her. His rib ached, and his cheek still stung from her unprovoked attack.

But his good principles protested. She was a nasty creature, but she was, by her speech and dress, a lady. And a gentleman never left a lady in need of assistance. This had been drummed into him since his most tender youth. She had no food or drink that he could see, and with the sun growing ever warmer, no shade other than that offered by the trees that dotted the edge of the lane. Then there were other dangers as well that he did not wish to consider.

Well, she had decided on her fate, had she not? He glanced up at the sun to get his bearings, but his eyes would not leave the small figure that trudged towards the horizon.

With a huff of annoyance, he knew what he had to do.

He clambered back onto the driver's seat and nudged the horses forward at a slow pace, following her down the dusty lane. She did not look back as he neared, but increased her pace.

"Where are you going, lady?"

Silence.

"I cannot, in good conscience, leave you here alone. This road is quiet, and by the surface of it, little travelled. It might be hours, or days even, before somebody comes along with a cart. And then, what sort of person he might be, I would not wish to guess. You might well be lucky to encounter a good and honest farmer, but there are other sorts about who would be happy to do harm to one such as yourself."

She still did not speak, but her gait faltered for a step.

"Allow me, at least, to convey you to a village, where you might send a message to your family. There must be a good woman there, a parson's wife, perhaps, who would offer you lodgings until you are sent for."

She glanced aside to scowl at him, but slowed her steps.

"I promised I would not harm you. Please, lady. Else I shall be forced to walk these poor horses after you all day. I cannot leave you alone."

She did stop now. Her face, when she turned it completely to face him, was streaked with tears. The hellcat was really a very frightened kitten, it seemed. A glimmer of compassion lightened his annoyance. He pulled the horses to a stop and waited.

"Very well." Her voice was quiet, scarcely heard above the rustle of leaves and the calls of the birds.

She walked to the door and fumbled for the steps, then climbed inside, pulling the door closed after her.

Blasted nuisance! He cursed quietly as the horses resumed their steady pace. He needed to run, and fast. Wickham had tried to kill him once, and the anger borne of failure would not soften the man's heart towards him. But how could he flee when he was responsible for this stow-away?

She was absolutely the last thing he needed now, a pampered society miss who was certain to be more concerned about the dust damaging the lace on her fichu or the state of her hair than on the very real danger that chased them. And if Wickham should find her... His heart went cold at the thought. Darcy knew how Wickham treated young ladies when other eyes were turned away. If he thought that the hell-kitten was somehow under Darcy's protection, there was no saying how vicious he might be to her.

Confound it all. Added to his monumental task of staying alive, he now had to protect this unpleasant young woman until he could somehow rid himself of her.

His arms tensed, tugging at the reins, and the horses jerked before regaining their pace.

This was no good road that wound through the countryside, skirting farms and cutting through copses of trees. The parish must be poor, or the residents uncaring of their comfort, for it was uneven and pocked with holes and stones. The carriage bumped and shook, and at times swerved from side to side as he guided the horses around larger obstacles to their travel, such as fallen tree limbs and the remains of what was once a rabbit. He thought.

He kept the pace as fast as he thought the horses could manage for a long journey and, wherever possible, he avoided the villages. The fewer people who saw them, the safer they would be. Thank the heavens this was no elaborate coach to draw the eye, but one much like any gentleman of comfortable means might possess.

Darcy glanced at the sun again and considered the time. Yes, north was that way...

A tap from the inside of the carriage caught his attention.

"Stop!" the hellcat called out.

"Nay, my lady, we have canvassed this topic and rejected it. I cannot oblige."

What did she expect of him? A hot nuncheon under a canopy, with a full staff of servants to cater to her needs?

"Please," she called out again. "It is rather... urgent."

"You might have considered that before remaining in the coach instead of visiting the necessaries at the inn." He had never had such conversations with a lady before. Such country manners as these reminded him of the quality of his own society.

"No, you do not understand..."

There came another sound from inside, and he heard one of the windows being flung open.

Oh.

He pulled the horses to a stop, and the woman all but fell out of the carriage, so quick was she to escape. She stumbled to the side of the lane and bent over for a moment, gasping for breath.

Darcy reached under his damaged coat for the small canteen he had remembered to take as he escaped. He opened the cap and passed it to her. "Here, drink a bit." It was only water, boiled and cooled, but it would help her. It also deprived him of yet one more thing he needed to stay alive. Perhaps a kind farmer would offer assistance at some point.

The woman handed the flask back with a nod. "Thank you." She raised her eyes to meet his. They were rather fine, now that they were not narrowed in fury. "May I... May I sit with you?" She took a deep breath. "My stomach..." The red that infused her face now was not the blotch of her earlier rage. "I have eaten little and am feeling not quite the thing. Fresh air would be welcome."

Damnation. Now he would have to engage in idle chatter with this annoying creature. But, he reminded himself, he was a gentleman. He just hoped she was the sort not to prattle.

"Very well," Darcy replied after a moment's pause. "Allow me to assist you."

Within a few minutes, she was sitting up beside him. The box was not so very wide, but there was sufficient space for the two of them. Darcy flicked the reins, and the horses began their forward march once more. They rode in silence for a quarter of an hour, perhaps more, as the sun climbed towards its peak in the sky.

Eventually, the young woman cleared her throat and announced, "Until such time as we may separate, I suppose we need to know what to call each other. You may call me Miss Bennet."

Ah, the hellcat had a name.

"Fitzwilliam Darcy, at your service, Madam."

"Very well, Will. Drive me to an inn so I can return home."

Will? She called him not even by his proper Christian name, but by this diminutive, like a servant? Miss Bennet needed to learn exactly who he was!

"That is Mr Darcy to you, Madam."

# Chapter 3
# Laneways

Elizabeth scowled at the filthy creature beside her. What sort of man was this, all covered in dirt and grime like a stray dog, demanding to be addressed like a gentleman? There was a large black smudge across his brow under the brim of his hat, and he had not shaved today, although his sideburns bore the evidence of having been carefully shaped to best suit his face.

It would be, she admitted, a rather handsome face at that, if it belonged to a real gentleman and not this rotten thief.

And then there was the smell. Had he slept in the stables? Granted, she would have smelled worse had she not managed to bring the roiling in her stomach under control in time. Still, he smelled more of horse dung and spoiled vegetables than a man ought. But his fingernails, when she glanced at his hands, were neat and buffed, in stark contrast to the grime that encased him.

His clothing, too, was something of an enigma. It was as dirty as the man, as if he had rolled in the dirt in it, and was ripped in places, yet it was the clothing of a wealthy man, and it fit him as if tailored to his form. He seemed a common criminal, having absconded with her father's carriage, but he spoke with the tones and vocabulary of the upper classes. And he had quite taken affront when she called him by his given name. She resolved to do so as much as possible, simply to vex him, annoying creature that he was.

He could hardly be trusted! What a bother that she had no choice but to do so.

He was correct in one matter. She could not set off on foot to find her way home. She did not know where she was and would be an easy mark for somebody up to no good. The scoundrel—Will, she insisted to herself—had been true to his promise not to harm her thus far, and she could only hope that he would continue to keep his word.

Confound it all! What dreadful luck to be in this unhappy situation.

She glanced at him from the corner of her eye. He looked as displeased with this situation as she was, if the scowl that marked his face was anything by which to judge. Insufferable man. If he had not abducted her, he would not have been forced into her company, after all.

Perhaps she ought to have attempted to ride inside the coach after all. Her stomach would have settled eventually. As if in answer to that thought, her insides gave a little lurch, and she sucked in the clear air to settle herself once more. No, riding inside would not do at all. Better to sit here next to this objectionable person than to cast up her accounts all over her father's upholstery.

She let her eyes drift to the side where Will's hands caressed the reins. His fingers were long and tapered, his grime-caked nails smoothly trimmed where she expected them to be torn and rough. Moreover, he seemed comfortable on the coachman's box, his posture easy. Despite his many failings, the man did seem a dab hand at driving the team. He controlled the horses with an economy of movement, keeping them moving at a steady pace, the carriage travelling as smoothly as this narrow country lane would allow.

As he had boasted earlier, he kept glancing at the position of the sun, taking new lanes and country roads in an attempt to head northward. He did not speak for a very long time, only grunting every so often when some new unpleasant thought seemed to cross his mind.

After what must have been an hour, Elizabeth noticed the horses slowing.

"They are tiring, Will." He did not correct her, but frowned at the use of his name. "They have come from London this morning and ought to have been home already."

He frowned at her from beneath heavy brows and let out a long sigh. "You are correct. I have been trying to avoid the villages, but needs must. We require food and drink as well."

Her eyes went wide. "You do not propose to steal it, surely!" Vinegar coated her words.

"What do you take me for?" he growled back. "A common thief?"

Elizabeth let out a rather unladylike snort. "Behold the carriage, which you drive but do not own, and likewise the horses, which dearly need a rest. A common thief, indeed, is what you are."

"Impertinent..." the man started but closed his mouth with a snap. "Very well. Think of me what you must. I shall be rid of you soon enough. If I can somehow procure a saddle, I can ride, which will carry me home faster than these two stalwart beasts can manage with this coach in tow."

"Then why did you not steal a horse? Surely there were ones set for postilions, all saddled and ready for you." She intended the words as an insult, but his response surprised her.

Did his shoulders slump a touch? For a brief moment, the wretched man looked vulnerable.

"I had no time to make such choices," he said after a moment's thought. "When I made my way to the inn, I believed myself to be safe and hoped to send a message to someone who might help me. But then I saw my foe ride into the yard with a crony, and I knew I could not hide for long. They would have turned the place upside down if they thought I might be there. Your coach was ready and untended, and I did not think, but took the opportunity the heavens gave to me."

Elizabeth opened her mouth to protest, but words, for once, failed her. Was this scoundrel really fleeing for his life? It seemed too strange to be true, but something of the man's expression pierced her indignation and she let his explanation lie for the time being.

After a few more minutes, they passed by a farmhouse that looked well-tended and Will directed the horses up the short drive. A woman of middle years, strong and stern, bustled out to see what was happening, and Will made his case. They had taken a wrong turn, he explained, and he had had a mishap, and the poor horses were in desperate need of a rest. The woman did not seem taken by his unkempt appearance, but his excellent manners and the small pile of coins that appeared in his hand eventually won her over. Before long, a youth of about fifteen appeared to water the horses and lead them to a shaded grove, and Elizabeth and Will were invited into the house.

Will had given his name as Will Bennet, which annoyed Elizabeth exceedingly, until she recalled his desperation not to be found. She, then, was assumed to be Mrs Bennet, which bothered her almost as much. Still, she smiled and accepted the appellation, promising herself to castigate her unwanted companion when they were on the road once more.

Will promised to join the ladies shortly and followed the lad with the horses. When he did enter the house a while later, he had clearly availed himself of some fresh water as well. His hair was damp and his skin clean, and he had dusted off his clothing as much as possible, rendering his appearance much improved.

He spoke to Mrs Peters, for that was the woman's name, as if she were a duchess. He did not prattle on as some do, but his few words were elegant and respectful, and he praised the quality of the small repast they were offered. At the end of an hour, when he judged the horses ready to travel once more, Mrs Peters would have done anything for him and pressed a small package into Elizabeth's hands as they left. "Some biscuits and apples for your journey."

With her directions in their ears, they continued their journey, each more at ease with then other than they had been earlier.

"You really did pay for her food and the care for the horses." Elizabeth was not sure what she had expected, but it had not been this courteous display.

"You expected otherwise, Madam? I have not an endless supply of coin, but I would not rob an honest farmwife of the bread and cheese her family must work hard to procure. You wound me, Miss Bennet."

And he truly did sound offended.

"Accept my apologies, Will. You must understand that my first impressions were not positive."

"Madam, if you insist upon using my given name, then I must know yours. It would never do in a parlour, but our circumstances are unusual, and a breach of etiquette must be excused."

Heavens, but the man spoke like an Oxford don! Perhaps he really was the gentleman he claimed to be. He certainly had the manners of the upper set, as stiff as they were, and devoid of the grime that had covered him earlier, he really was rather handsome.

"Very well, then, Mr Darcy," she stressed his name, "you may, until we reach our next inn, call me Elizabeth."

"Elizabeth." He drawled the name as if tasting it. "It suits you."

He lapsed into silence again, as they continued their way to who knew where.

"Why are you running?" She had to know this.

For a minute, Elizabeth heard nothing but the clop of the horses' hooves on the packed dirt lane.

"It is not a pleasant story. Suffice it to say, I am the wronged party."

Once more, the strong jaw snapped shut. His eyes turned cold and his every movement warned her against asking more. But Elizabeth was not one to run from trouble, her courage rising instead in the face of intimidation.

"How can I believe you if you will not tell me?" She laid a soft hand on his forearm, feeling it tense under her light touch. "You might find comfort in the telling, and I shall hardly divulge what I hear, for we have no common acquaintances."

His arm relaxed again under her hand, and he took a long breath.

"The story is not entirely mine to tell. I would not break the faith of another in divulging what she must wish to remain concealed." The words were considerate, but his demeanour stiff, as if he had retreated behind a shield of some sort.

Elizabeth would not be deterred. She was entirely reliant upon Will for the time being; she must know something of his circumstances. "But this man who is chasing you—surely that matter concerns yourself, and most intimately. Something must have raised his ire against you."

He blinked at her before turning his attention back to the lane. "Very well. I can tell you something of the matter, if only to assure you of my character. I am not in the habit of appropriating unguarded carriages and teams for my own use. I am more than able to afford my own." The ice in his voice thawed a bit more.

This tramp was a wealthy man? It seemed hard to credit it, for all that he had the manners of a gentleman. Elizabeth let out a sniff of surprise, to which her companion turned icy once more. It took a great deal of coaxing to encourage him to resume the tale.

"My predicament involves a man who believes I have cheated him out of a great deal of money, and who sought to harm somebody I care about in his pursuit of revenge. I thwarted his plans."

"But surely many men find themselves in similar circumstances, and yet not all roll around in the dirt and steal other men's coaches. And daughters," she added for good measure.

"Indeed, but not many men have come up against George Wickham, who has tried to rob me of thirty thousand pounds."

THE EXPRESSION on Miss Bennet's face almost made Darcy laugh.

"Thirty thousand?" she choked out, her eyes wide and her jaw slack. "That is a great deal of money indeed! But, if this is true, should it not be you chasing him, rather than the converse? Can he be so rash as to expect success?"

Darcy shook his head. "He is angry—no, more than angry—at having been thwarted, and angry men are seldom wise. His aim now is revenge, plain and simple. If he cannot have my money, he would see me dead."

"But did he say as much to you?" A frown appeared on Elizabeth's face, wrinkling the soft skin between her eyes.

"He did not need words. His actions sufficed."

A chill ran up Darcy's spine despite the hot sun as he recalled the previous night. He had completed his business in London by the middle of the afternoon, and made the fateful decision to start early on his journey back to his estate in Derbyshire by taking a room at an inn out of the city. Even the four-mile distance would set him clear enough of the city's busy morning streets that he would save well over an hour of time spent travelling. And thus it was that he enjoyed an early dinner with his aunt in London and commanded his coachman to carry him to The Angel in Islington, there to start their long drive at sunrise, refreshed and unharried by small routine bits of daily chaos.

But matters did not conform to plan. Instead of the quiet and restful night he had envisaged, his dreams became a nightmare.

What woke him from his slumbers at some dark hour, he would never know, but he thanked the heavens above that wake, he did. Perhaps a dog barked out in the courtyard. Perhaps it was the unexpected creak of a plank. He rose from the bed and made his way to the window to look outside, as he was wont to do.

There, instead of the quiet and abandoned stable yard he expected, he saw the shadow of a low gig with a single horse still in harness. As his eyes adjusted to the light, he noticed two men skulking about the perimeter, looking upwards every few minutes. He could not discern their faces in the darkness of the night, but the moon picked out enough of their shapes for him to recognise one of them by his height and his particular manner of moving.

George Wickham!

This did not bode well. He had sent Wickham off only the day before with a flea in his ear and a warning never to cross his path again. "I have bought enough of your vowels, covered enough of your debts," Darcy had warned his former friend, "that I can see you sent to the poorhouse for the rest of your natural life." And Wickham had sneered like a cornered rat and had run off.

And now he was back, and it was not to make a toast to Darcy's good health at the taproom.

Darcy's carriage was in the carriage house, fine and black, gleaming and emblazoned with the family's distinguishable crest. It would take no brilliance to determine that Darcy himself was on the premises as well. What ought he to do? Risk disturbing the sleep of a great many people and confront his nemesis now? Wait until morning and summon the local magistrate?

Then the moonlight picked out something Darcy had no desire ever to see again. The figure that looked like Wickham pulled something long and metallic out of a coat pocket. Was that a pistol that he brandished? The unknown companion patted his side as well, presumably to indicate that he, too, was armed.

Darcy's heart began to race, and he wiped damp palms on the sides of his nightshirt. The window was cracked to allow in some cool air, and he pressed against it, hoping to hear something of the men's conversation, whispered though it was.

"Run him through..." he heard through the otherwise silent air, and, "no mercy." Suddenly, his mouth was as dry as his hands were wet. Were they really planning to kill him? It could not be, for they would be caught at once, and hanged before the day was out.

"...spirit him away from here," Wickham's voice sounded more clearly now. "He will come peaceably enough when we introduce him to this piece." The pistol glinted once more in the moonlight. "Then we can truss him up and use him to practise our swordplay."

There was no time to think, only to act. In a moment, Darcy threw on his clothing and stuffed his money and whatever of his belongings he could into his pockets, then slung his canteen, a present from his cousin, over a shoulder. The rest of his personal effects would be sacrificed to Wickham's greed. With a deep breath, he glanced down from his first storey window, desperate for a means of escape. The building's exterior was rough stone, with a drainpipe leading down to a low overhang that wrapped around the side of the inn. If he could use the drainpipe to get that far, he could crawl along the overhang until he achieved the High Street just a few yards away.

As soon as the dimming of the men's voices suggested they had gone to seek the inn's back door to gain entry, Darcy crammed his hat onto his head and eased himself out of the window, thankful for his customary choice of a dark coat. He reached for the drainpipe and prayed it would support his weight, then shifted until his feet found some purchase on the stones that made up the inn's exterior. His panicked imperative to flee was tempered by the necessity for caution, and when he alighted on the overhang a few minutes later, it was with rapid breath and sore hands, but no injury to himself.

He stopped, perfectly still, and lay flat on the low roof. Here, facing the courtyard, it was silent. Gathering his wits, he crawled along the overhang as it skirted the building, until he was on the side facing the main street through the town. There was more noise here. Towards the east, the first intimations of daylight began to ease the darkness on the horizon, and faint sounds of the town beginning to stir reached his ears. A voice from a room somewhere, a dog barking, the clop of a horse's hooves, and the squeak and rumble of a cart, making its early way through the town.

Darcy raised his head to see what was coming. It looked to be a muck-cart, driven by a man in rags, and pulled by a nag whose pedigree would not turn heads at Tattersalls. Still, it was hope.

The overhang reached far enough over the street that when the cart made its slow way down the road, Darcy would be able to roll from his perch into its putrid embrace. And this he did, watching it grow closer, closer, ever closer, until, with a deep breath and a quick prayer, he flung himself off the overhang.

"Oi!" The driver turned in shock as Darcy landed with a thud and a splat. The smell was alarming, but he could wash later if he remained alive.

"Hush, please, my good man. There's coin in it for you if you take me somewhere safe, and at good speed."

"What are ya?" the driver scowled. "Some toff so far in 'is cups 'e's falling off roofs?"

"Something like that, indeed. All good haste, if you please."

The driver sniffed once more, as if Darcy smelled worse than the contents of his cart, and pressed the nag on, mumbling about 'damned rotten half-wit nobs' the whole time. At any other time, Darcy would have looked down his patrician nose in arrogant horror at this display of crude manners, but a saviour was a saviour, even when dressed in rags and transporting... whatever this mess was. If the man delivered him to safety, Darcy would supply him with the promised coin and not utter a word in defiance of the man's insults.

Luck was with him. The driver was heading towards a market, where Darcy was able to convince a farmer to carry him further out in the back of a hay wagon. Thus, despite the filth and damage to his fine clothing, he made it to the coaching inn where he hid behind the bales until the opportunity of the Bennet coach was given to him.

The gist of this tale he recounted to Elizabeth with an economy of words. It was bad enough to think of, and worse to tell. And now, just as he was on the brink of being able to fly home on the back of some borrowed horse, he was saddled—he grimaced at the word—with this pampered young woman who would be nothing but a hinderance.

She did not know his thoughts, however, and looked at him with a compassion he did not expect.

"You are certain he wished to kill you?" She caught her bottom lip between her teeth.

"Quite certain. I heard those words most clearly."

"How dreadful. I suppose... I suppose, then, that I cannot blame you for wishing to make your escape. But why did you not send for help from the inn?"

"I hoped to clean myself before entering the building, and was still rather worried that I might be found. And, indeed, it was Wickham's arrival at that very moment that spurred me to my rather rash actions."

She contemplated him for a moment, and under her scrutiny he was strangely relieved that he had taken the time to wash off the worst of the filth at Mrs Peters' stables.

"What will you do now?"

"That, Madam, is the question I have been asking myself all day."

# Chapter 4
# A Narrow Escape

Elizabeth found herself lost in her thoughts, the to-and-fro jostle of the carriage a sort of rocking that lulled her and permitted introspection.

Who was this man beside her? His tale of woe certainly explained a great deal—if he could be believed. Who could not feel compassion for a gentleman of means, rousted from his comfortable bed in the darkest hours of the night and forced to escape by any means necessary, even if they involved a muck cart and the theft—borrowing—of another man's carriage? If his tale were true, this George Wickham had a great deal to answer for.

But could he really be believed? Elizabeth was no woman of the world, but neither was she completely sheltered from the harsh realities of life, and she had heard many a story. There was a sort of man, she knew, handsome of face and smooth of tongue, who lived by playing on the credulity of others. They looked and acted the part of gentlemen temporarily down on their luck, who would most certainly repay that loan the minute they were able to speak to their banker and withdraw the appropriate amount from a considerable bank account.

These bankers invariably did not exist, neither did the wealth of funds alluded to, and Mr John James Worthington-Smythe turned out to be the latest in a string of false names used by some worthless sort who had rubbed up against Quality enough to have learned the social niceties that went with the status.

Just like—the thought struck her like the slap of a hand—this George Wickham that Will had mentioned.

Heavens! Could he have misled her so completely? Was it possible that this man driving her father's carriage was, in fact, George Wickham himself, seeking to escape from the real Will Darcy whom he had wronged and who was now seeking him to mete out justice?

She glanced sidelong at him, careful not to turn her head and alert him to her thoughts. Such men could be dangerous! There were even stories of them abducting and selling young women to places she ought not to know about. She almost cried out in alarm. Was that his true motivation in convincing her back onto the carriage after she set off down that lane earlier? He spoke with words of concern for her safety, but was he really trying to lull her into a sense of complacency, to have her learn to trust him before being...

She let out a squeak of alarm and Will turned to peer at her.

"Are you well, Elizabeth?"

She swallowed and nodded. She must make plans to escape once more, but they must be her secret alone. Perhaps if she could encourage him to talk more, she might learn something of use.

"I am well enough, but I am becoming fatigued, and to be honest, worried. My family will be beside themselves wondering what has become of me, and I wish to return home."

He pursed his lips. "Indeed. I cannot say what our destination is, for I do not know exactly where we are. We have been travelling northward, roughly following the line of the Great North Road, or so I hope. We must, at some point, cross that road, for my intention is to head westward. Perhaps we shall find an inn where we cross, or along that path. I dare not stop at the coaching inns along the main route, as I have explained."

Oh heavens! It was true. He was working to keep her from finding a reputable place where she would be safe. She bit her bottom lip to prevent another gasp of distress from escaping and took in a slow breath. "But what, then, am I to do?" That sounded calm enough, she hoped.

He contemplated her as if she had only now appeared on the seat beside him. "You must, I suppose, travel with me until such time as I can be assured of your safety."

Elizabeth swallowed. This fit even more perfectly with her supposition of him being the villain she had begun to imagine. At first, he promised to take her to an inn, but now he had come up with a reason for her to continue as his captive, of a sort.

"And where shall we sleep? We cannot drive all night. The poor horses, at the very least, need to rest."

"We shall find somewhere. Now," he looked back up at the sky, "this road tends westward." He started mumbling to himself, "Wolverton... Birmingham... Shrewsbury... Llangollen... We can avoid these towns. Perhaps some small village near Aylesbury. He will not think to seek us there."

Elizabeth listened with great interest and tried to memorise the places. If she could determine his goal, she could send for help!

It was not too long before they came to the crossroads Will had mentioned, but rather than their lane continuing past the busier road, it ended there, forcing them to turn. Thunder clouded Will's face, but he kept silent and let the horses pick up some speed as they enjoyed the smoother surface.

He drove them for another hour, saying very little. The sun was starting to dip towards the horizon, and they must find somewhere to stop for the night soon. This Elizabeth brought to Will's attention, and he agreed with a scowl and a grumble.

When, a few miles down the dusty road, they saw a large establishment fit for their purposes, he pulled the horses aside into the yard.

"Will this be suitable, Miss Bennet? Let us inquire as to the next coach to return you to your family, and then I shall see to the horses." His words were still everything proper, and still she wondered if his motives were pure. Could this be the location where his... business operated? He had seemed unhappy enough at the prospect of stopping and had approached the inn with a show of reluctance, but it could all be a feint, to put her off her guard.

She must be prepared!

With the excuse of retrieving some of her belongings from the carriage, Elizabeth groped around the inside, looking for a weapon should she need one. Her umbrella had done her good service once today, and now that she had the luxury of a vehicle that was not bumping all over the road, she felt under the seats for the small folding knife that was kept there to effect minor repairs when needed. This she secured against her forearm with the ribbon closing her cuffs and hid it under her sleeve.

Will, despite her fears, seemed true to his word. He escorted her inside and inquired directly of the innkeeper whether there was a stage or mail coach that might help his cousin (so he called her) return home.

"The mail came by just an hour past," the innkeeper answered as he shook his head. "Not another one till tomorrow, same time."

The glimmer of hope Elizabeth had felt faded. Tomorrow! That was far too long to wait. "But my mother... my father! They must be so worried."

Once more, Will surprised her by asking if there was an express rider available. "Write your family a letter," he offered, "and it can go out at once. I shall get you a room for the night, and you can return home safely on the morrow. And perhaps," he whispered to himself as much as to her, "I can find a fast horse and saddle, and ride rather than drive."

A room in a strange inn, with no chaperone and no maid! It was quite alarming, but Elizabeth could think of no better solution, and accepted with as much good grace as she could manage.

She procured some paper and a pen from the innkeeper, and set about writing her missive, whilst Will went out to ensure the horses were being fed and given water, with plans to ride on after a quick meal. They would dine together, and then would say their good-byes, never to meet again.

There was something unsettling about that idea, no matter that she had only known the man for a few hours, and in the most unpleasant circumstances, at that. He was taciturn and, frankly, rather alarming, but there was also something appealing about him when he deigned to speak openly.

With a sigh, she finished her letter and went to find the innkeeper, who would call for the express rider.

A handsome man stood at the counter, leaning against it with one foot crossed over the other. His golden hair shone in a beam of light that filtered through a window, and his blue eyes sparkled with good humour. He straightened at once when he saw her approach, and gestured for the innkeeper to attend to her, suggesting that his business could well wait. A lady, his wink and grin intimated, must always take precedence.

Elizabeth nodded her thanks and then presented her letter, which the innkeeper took from her and sealed with some wax.

"I'll have this off in just a few moments, Miss Bennet," the good man nodded to her. "I've a good fast lad to deliver this for you. Allow me to ensure this direction is all correct: to Mr Bennet at Longbourn in Hertfordshire, near Meryton. I'll make sure it gets there, and likely tonight afore the sun is gone. That's not so very far, now, is it?"

She confirmed the directions to help the rider achieve his destination most easily as the handsome golden-haired man stood patiently by, and then went to sit in the calm public room until Will came to join her for their final meal together in a small private salon off the public.

Their meal was quiet, neither having much to say after their day on the carriage box. Will looked exhausted, and Elizabeth feared she looked little better. The food, when it arrived, was hot and tasty, and after they ate, Will sat back with a beer while she sipped at some weak tea.

"It has been an hour. The horses will be ready for me." He stood to bow and take his leave. "I shall endeavour to return your family's carriage as soon as I am able. Forgive me." He reached for her hand and kissed the back of it before making for the door.

Why should her heart give a little flutter? The man was a thief and a scoundrel, after all, and she still did not entirely believe his tale, no matter that she was not—yet—sold into some form of bondage. Her eyes followed him as he departed the room, but the door was still open when she heard someone holler his name.

"Darcy!"

It was not a friendly greeting.

At once, she was on her feet and at the door. There, standing at a table near a set of windows, was that same handsome man who had been waiting at the counter when she handed her letter to the innkeeper. His eyes were no longer twinkling, but were hard and cold. The public had grown quite busy whilst they had been at their dinner, but the man seemed not to care about the others in the space.

"Wickham!" Will spat out. "What are you doing here?" He stepped backwards, realising too late that he was in a corner, with no escape.

"Waiting for you. We have business to complete."

So Will really was Will Darcy, as he had claimed, and this elegant blond gentleman was not quite what he appeared. Looks could, indeed, be deceiving. But what of the rest of Will's story?

Elizabeth watched as Wickham slid his way through the tables and approached Will's side, facing away from her. The low orange sunlight that slipped through the windows caught on something, sending a glint of light through the space, and Elizabeth stifled a gasp. That was... that was a knife, and Wickham was clearly planning to use it.

"Outside, I said," he repeated, his voice a rumble only just loud enough for Elizabeth to hear. "I have no wish to disturb these good diners with our disagreement."

"Be reasonable, George," Will spoke just above a whisper. His voice was even, but his eyes betrayed his alarm. He really was scared of this man. Elizabeth stood frozen in place, barely breathing, as Will tried to calm his nemesis. "There is no good ending if you try to harm me. Enough people know of our... disagreements. You will be found, and soon. Leave now, and I shall not raise the hue and cry. Just go."

But Wickham's shoulders shrugged off this plea.

"Leave? And go where? You've ruined me, Darcy. You've taken everything from me!"

"You ruined yourself. You were the one who threw away everything you were given. That money—my sister's fortune—was never yours. Go now, or you will regret it."

Wickham spat towards Darcy's face, the spittle landing on the floor by his feet. "You've left me nothing! The debtors are after me... I've seen the bruisers from McLeary's gaming halls crush men's knees into rubble." His voice took on a low, desperate edge that sent Elizabeth's blood cold. "If I'm going down, I'll take you with me, Darcy!"

Wickham began to move forward, but Will held him back—for now—with a gesture. His voice, when he spoke, also held an edge of something Elizabeth had not heard before.

"This is not my doing, George. It's all of your own making. You had a good future; you had a fine prospect. Do not blame me for your mistakes. Those, I could have forgiven, but to try to draw Georgiana into your clutches, no! That was despicable, and you are lucky I did not call you out on it, as my cousin urged me to do."

*Pah!* Wickham spat again, and this time he did not miss his mark. His breath was hard, desperate, although his voice was still low. The growl of a trapped animal, but malicious. This was a man who clearly took pleasure in cruelty.

"You useless sot, Darcy. Your mistake! You were always too soft as a boy, and you are worse now. I'll finish you off, believe me, and then where will your precious Georgiana be? Outside, now!" He flicked his wrist and the blade he held glinted dully in the low tavern light. "Now."

This was a repetition of what Will had told her earlier about the missed encounter last night. Then, too, Wickham planned to force him from the inn and kill him in some secluded place. This confrontation supported everything Will had told her; he had not been misleading her after all. Wickham really did want to kill him. She could not let this happen!

As silently as she could, she slid the folding knife from where she had secured it to her wrist and picked up a heavy metal tray from the table, where the tavern maid had left it a while ago. Whilst Wickham was scowling and making threats at Will, she crept up behind him, praying that Will would not give away her actions with a glance or a word, and as soon as she was within reach, she raised the tray as high as she could and slammed it down on Wickham's head.

This did not have quite the effect she hoped for, as the man was several inches taller than her, but it sufficed. The crack on his pate broke Wickham's attention and caused him that moment's hesitation. Will took his opportunity to step out of the way of the knife and swing a fist at his enemy, causing him to drop his blade.

Wickham stumbled back, knocking over a nearby table and spilling a man's ale all over his clothing.

"Watch it!" that ale-soaked man growled and threw himself at Wickham, who in turn launched himself at the new attacker, hitting another customer by mistake. More and more men rose from their tables, some angry, others seeming to enjoy the prospect of a good brawl, and the confrontation was growing into something quite alarming.

Chairs were pushed aside and fists flew through the air, and Wickham looked to be in the middle of it, being set upon by more men than Elizabeth could count. She stepped towards Will, who put a protective arm around her shoulders, just as Wickham glanced up to see them both. His momentary lapse was met by a fist to the jaw, and the fight continued.

"Now!" Will grabbed her hand and pulled her towards the door. "We have to leave now! He saw us together, and you are not safe from him."

They burst out of the inn and ran towards the carriage, which was waiting as Will had said it would be. "I cannot leave you here, Elizabeth. We have to find another way to get you home."

He threw her up onto the box and leapt up after, cracking the whip to spur the horses into motion.

It was only after they had travelled a mile or more, far faster than the roads allowed, that Elizabeth turned to Will with a tear-stained face.

"He knows. He heard me give my name and where I live. I cannot go home at all!"

ELIZABETH'S words hit Will like a bucket of icy water on a cold winter morning. The first import was that he would not be rid of her within an hour or two. All his plans to find a horse with a saddle and ride for his life vanished in the course of those short words. He was stuck with her until such time as they made their destination, wherever that might be. Instead of being able to gallop cross-country as fast as his steed would allow, he had to keep this slow-plodding team dragging a heavy coach, in order to accommodate a helpless young thing whose only skills in life were probably painting tables and embroidering initials on the corners of handkerchiefs.

She might be pleasant to look upon, with more than the usual allotment of sheer spunk, but she would slow him down most dreadfully.

The second realisation was that Elizabeth was now in danger just as much as he was. Wickham had seen the two of them together and would make the assumption that they were a pair. Indeed, being seen together at an inn far from town would lead the most generous observer to believe them engaged to be married; Wickham would not be so generous. The scoundrel would gladly use Elizabeth as a tool to wreak his revenge and would likely cause her great harm simply as another way to bring Will pain.

He could not send her home. If Wickham knew where she lived, she would not be safe. Will's duty as a gentleman was to protect her.

Although, he now acknowledged, she had been quite efficient at protecting herself. The hatpin still stuck in his lapel reminded him of that. And she had been the one to save him back at the inn when she brought that heavy tray down on Wickham's head. Will had seen the glint of the knife in his nemesis' hand, and knew it would not be satisfied until it ran red with his blood.

"I neglected to thank you." He turned to his unwanted companion and offered his gratitude. "You saved me from serious harm. I cannot repay that."

"Returning my father's possessions unharmed will be a good gesture." Her gaze was sharp, but there was the hint of a smile on her lips.

"The horses and carriage, yes, and his daughter as well. I am sorry, Elizabeth. I never intended to embroil another in my troubles. This burden ought to have been mine alone. All I wished to do was flee until I could summon help."

She cocked her head and faced him. "I see that now. I was uncertain, for a while, whether your story was true, or whether it was only a tale told to elicit my sympathy. But there was no mistaking the blade in his hand, or the hatred in his voice."

She stared at him for a moment longer before asking, "Why does he hate you so? What did you do to him?"

Will let out a snort. "What did I do? As if I were the instigator of this! No, Madam, it is not what I did, but what he wished I would do, but did not. He is the villain in this story, not I."

Her gaze did not waver. "Whether you intended this or not, I have been brought into your dispute. Do I not deserve to know, at least, why we are being pursued by this person?" She straightened her back. "And who is Georgiana?"

Will clamped his jaw and stared at the road, concentrating all his attention on the horses as they cantered along.

"Will..." Her tone brooked no refusal.

He sighed. This was a private matter, a history which would reflect well on nobody, with the exception of himself. His family's name was at stake.

"Will?"

What was it about her eyes, so expressive, that pierced through his armour? He hardly knew the girl, but the touch of her hand on his arm and the glance from under her thick lashes were comfortable and familiar.

She had, after all, accepted her fate with surprisingly good grace. After her initial frenzied attack on his person when she first realised her predicament, after her attempt to walk down that abandoned country lane, she had been the model of calmness. Will might have expected endless weeping, or harpy-like screeching, or fits of nerves, not this resolute determination to do what she must until she could return home. She had castigated him for his crimes, but had not dissolved into the useless puddle so many fine ladies of his acquaintance would certainly have done.

And then, when Wickham had come at him with that knife, she had saved him. She had, at that point, the very real opportunity to be free of him completely, simply by letting Wickham act. The room was paid for, and she had money for the coach the next day. She could have been home within hours. But instead, she acted to save him, thereby throwing her lot in with his.

This deserved more than stony silence, and he chastised himself for his poor manners.

"Very well," he spoke over the rattle of the carriage. "I owe you something, after all. But please, I must rely upon your absolute discretion, for it involves somebody very dear to me."

A shadow crossed Elizabeth's face, but she answered simply. "I give you my word as a lady."

"It involves my sister. Georgiana is my sister."

At these words, her smile grew easy. Encouraged by her compassionate expression, Will allowed himself to speak.

"She is more than ten years my junior, only fifteen years old." He paused.

"I have a sister of that age as well," Elizabeth supplied. "She is half woman, half child, with all the worst parts of each."

Will blinked. Why had he not imagined that she might have younger sisters as well? "Georgiana is a quiet soul. I have been called aloof and withdrawn, but she is far more timid than I. Our mother died when she was young, and our father followed her five years ago. I have been both parent and brother to her since that dreadful day, and I feel most ill-equipped for the role."

"It is a difficult position, I am certain. But how does it relate to Mr Wickham's anger towards you?"

"Allow me to start again. There is more you must know. When I was very young, my father engaged a most capable man as the steward of our estate, this man having a son of around my own age. My father was named godfather to the boy and doted upon him, for he was handsome and lively, where I was quiet."

"You are still quiet," he thought he heard Elizabeth murmur to herself, "but also handsome."

Pretending he had not heard her, he went on. "This boy, George Wickham by name, grew up to be most unlike his father. He was wild and dissolute, much given to wagering and running up debts. His dealings with the female sex were also less than respectable. I hope I need not say more." His face grew warm as he spoke these words and dared not look at Elizabeth.

"I understand you perfectly. He is handsome, and I can see how a lady might fall for his charms."

"Such that they are. Let me recount to you some of our sad history."

Elizabeth sat quietly beside him on the box as Will told the tale of Wickham's refusal of the living he had been offered, of his requests to study the law instead, of how he spent a huge gift of money within a year, and how he then returned to plead for the living he had rejected previously.

"He had found the law an unprofitable study, he told me, and was now absolutely resolved on being ordained. It was rightfully his, he insisted, as my father had intended. You cannot blame me for refusing him, after he had quit every claim to it three years before."

"No indeed. You did nothing wrong." This was shocking. "Such a man ought not to be in such a role. Was he angry?"

Will's face hardened. "Most vehemently. From what I heard tell, he was no less violent in his abuse of me to others as he was to my face. He blamed me entirely for his failings and believed that I owed him some great sum in recompense."

"A fortune in exchange for the legacy he refused? I can hardly account for it!"

They were approaching a crossroads marker, which looked familiar, and Will slowed the horses for a moment to examine it. These names he knew, and despite the setting sun, the air brightened around him. He knew these roads, knew where he must go, and guided the horses onto the new road, heading westward. There was some hope for an easy night, for this evening at least.

He had four miles to travel before they must turn again, enough time to finish his story.

Elizabeth had remained quiet whilst he concentrated on his new destination, but now encouraged him to continue his tale, which he did.

"This is where my dear sister enters the story. I would wish to forget this dreadful circumstance, but I fear I will suffer its consequences for the rest of my days.

"Georgiana was unhappy at school, and I thought it would suit her quiet nature to engage a companion for her. At the beginning of the summer, they went to Ramsgate, where I took a house for them to enjoy the society and the sea air. Unbeknownst to me, Wickham was an associate of this companion, and he too made his way to Ramsgate with the sole purpose of endearing himself to my sister and convincing her into an elopement."

The lady beside him gasped. "At fifteen! How shocking. I understand why you would not wish this spoken of. That is far too young to really know her heart and to consider matters sensibly. And yet I recall being fifteen, when one is entirely subject to one's sensibilities, much like poor Juliet and her Romeo. My sister Lydia, I suspect, would act no differently."

These words of understanding were a balm to his sore heart, and speaking further grew easier with each word.

"My sister's heart is tender, and she recollected George fondly from her childhood, and his task, I fear, was an easy one. She soon felt herself to be in love with him. Luck, and luck alone, was with me, for I joined them unexpectedly just four days ago, immediately before the intended elopement, and Georgiana confessed the entire plan to me.

"You may imagine what I felt and how I acted. I informed Mr Wickham at once that I could not support this plan, that I refused to give my consent for the marriage, and that he would by no means achieve his aim, which was undoubtedly my sister's fortune. Yes, this is the thirty thousand pounds that Wickham believes I owe him, and which he attempted to rob me of at the same time as destroying my sister's happiness forever."

"How very sad! But could he have been sincere?" Elizabeth asked. "Is it possible that he does, indeed, care for her?"

"Not he. I wish it were so, but he admitted it all when I confronted him. His aim was never love. It was vengeance. He wanted to harm me by harming my sister and winning her fortune, and I stopped him. And now he wishes to see me dead."

Elizabeth's eyes were wide with concern. "You poor man! But what happened? Where is your sister now?"

"Georgiana was horrified by the truth and was inconsolable. She needed a mother's love, and the best I could manage was our aunt in London. I took her there, and left her in that good lady's embrace, with a promise to seek a companion of far better character. After seeing to her comfort, I began my journey northward to my estate, and, well, you know what happened then. Wickham learned where I was, and being unable to importune my sister any longer, came after me."

Elizabeth's hand moved from his arm to cover his own as it held the reins. Her touch was light and comforting. "I am truly sorry. I am sorry for your sister, sorry for your trouble, and sorry that I doubted you."

"And I," Will met her eyes, "am sorry that you are now part of this. But I have been thinking and now have a plan. My uncle has a hunting lodge in the north of Wales. I do not believe Wickham knows exactly where it is. We will be safe there until I can summon aid to deal with him."

"North Wales! But that is hundreds of miles distant! It will take days, no, a week or more, to arrive."

Will shook his head. "Longer, I fear. We cannot take a direct path. I am still concerned lest he somehow track our route. But he will expect me to travel northward to Pemberley. Instead, we shall turn south and make our way up through the valleys. It may take some time, but I would not have you come to harm."

"Nor I you." She looked directly at him and smiled.

# Chapter 5

# Missing

Jane Bennet stumbled out of the hired cart, her head a whirl, her eyes barely taking in the familiar sight of her own home. She felt, rather than heard, her aunt follow her off the hired cart and onto the sweep. A glance backwards revealed the older woman's dried tears and pale face, and Jane feared she looked little better. How dreadful this day had been, and how painfully long the journey home. It had been hours since they finally gave up hope and left the inn, and it was now almost evening, several hours after their expected arrival.

"Jane? Maddy? Why are you so late? Where is the carriage? Where is Elizabeth?" Jane's father strode towards them from the main doors to Longbourn, his wife and younger daughters hovering closer to the house. "What has happened?"

"Oh, Papa!" Jane's resolve faltered and she could hold back her emotions no longer. She dissolved into a puddle of tears, bringing her mother to her side at once.

Next to her, she heard her aunt Gardiner choke back her own tears as she approached Jane's father. "Thomas, I do not know what to say. It was... I cannot... I do not..." She looked around, eyes wide and desperate. "My children? I must see my children."

"In the back garden with three servants. They are well. What has happened?" Jane's mother caught her sister-in-law in a fierce embrace. Then she paused and looked around, her frown becoming more pronounced. "Where is Elizabeth?"

Papa sent off the cart driver with an impatient wave. "Is Elizabeth still in London? Is she ill? You look about ready to swoon." He walked back to the house as he spoke, the travellers lagging behind him, until they were all gathered in the family's back parlour. Jane was too agitated to sit, and the others, likewise, remained standing. "Now enough obfuscating. I must know what has happened. *Where* is Elizabeth? The carriage? Tell me your news. I fear it will not grow easier for the delay."

"Papa, they are gone!" Jane burst out through her tears. A wave of despair and guilt flooded her. "We went inside the coaching inn for tea whilst the horses rested, and when we returned..." She could not say the words.

"Lizzy was too tired to join us and said she would sleep in the carriage." Her aunt Gardiner took up the tale with a choked voice. "The servants were there to watch it, and she insisted she would come to no harm and simply needed to rest. After an hour, when we had refreshed ourselves, they came to find us. The horses were rested and harnessed and the carriage ready to complete the journey, but as we exited the building, we saw the carriage drive off at a tremendous pace. Our driver was with us, and Colin and Peggy were standing just a few feet away, but some stranger leapt onto the box under everybody's noses, and made off with it."

"And with Lizzy inside!" Jane wailed.

Jane's father stood unblinking at her side, as if he were trying to understand the words. Her mother collapsed onto the closest chair, eyes fluttering.

"Mama!" one of Jane's sisters called out. Was it Kitty? At this moment, she hardly knew. "Mama!"

"Bring her salts, Mary," their father commanded. "Kitty, see to her comfort. Lydia... help your sisters. Now," he said, turning back to his oldest daughter, "tell me again exactly what happened. And where are the servants?" His voice cracked.

Then, in an instant, his demeanour changed from despair to fury. Jane had never seen such anger on his face, or such pain. Her father was, by habit, laconic and detached, so unlike this fierce man who stood in the middle of the room.

Whilst her mother recovered her senses under Kitty's less-than-gentle ministrations, Jane fought through her misery to relate the events to her father, although she had little more to add. "We left Colin and Peggy at the inn to start a search, although we knew not where to begin looking. We sent out express riders to the next toll house in all directions, and the innkeeper assured us he would do everything in his power to find them. But if the driver left the main roads, they could be anywhere."

By now, Papa's face was almost as white as his wife's, and he reached out for a chair to steady himself.

"Lizzy is a clever girl," he managed at last with a swallow. "She will find a way. If anybody can, it's our Lizzy."

He fell into his chair now, and a tense silence settled over the room. Anxious glances replaced frantic words, and Jane had never felt so helpless in her life. Her aunt pulled her into a fierce embrace and guided her to a seat on the long yellow sofa.

The silence was broken by a tap at the door, where Mrs Hill, the housekeeper, cleared her throat. "Sir, your guest... I have offered him more tea, but..."

As quickly as Mr Bennet had fallen onto the chair, he now leapt up to his feet. "Botheration! I had completely forgotten. What a fool I am. Let me make my apologies and see him off."

"No need for either, sir," came a new voice from behind Mrs Hill. It was smooth and melodic, with a hint of the North, a gentle tenor. "I was concerned when the ladies arrived so late and without the carriage, and I confess to hearing it all. I am most pained, and will offer whatever assistance I can."

A young man slid into the room, more handsome than plain, and with a face that would, under most other circumstances, exude good humour. Now, however, his regard was serious. Jane could not take her eyes off him.

"Mr Bingley," Jane's father sighed. "Your welcome visit must, I am afraid, be interrupted. But please, although these are not the best circumstances, allow me to present to you my daughter Jane and her aunt, Mrs Gardiner, the mother of the scamps tearing up my flower beds.

"Mr Bingley," he announced to Jane and her aunt, "is to be our neighbour, having just now taken possession of Netherfield Park. We have only this afternoon been made known to each other, and I invited him to take tea with us."

There was no expression of joy or delight in the formal introductions that followed. Such sentiments would come at a later time. But the new neighbour made a handsome bow and offered pretty words. He addressed Jane's aunt with suitable salutations and then turned to Jane herself. His glance met hers and he stopped for a moment to take in a deep breath. His eyes, warm honey brown, lingered upon her. "Miss Bennet." He breathed the name like a prayer. Then, almost too quietly for anybody to hear, he breathed the name "Jane," the sound scarcely reaching her ears. She felt her face grow warm.

When he spoke aloud again, it was with all appropriate words and a firmer tone. "I beg you to accept my deepest sympathies on your present concerns, and my best wishes for a speedy and happy resolution. I wish to be of use. Any assistance I might offer is yours. What can I do? I know people in Town, could engage a Runner. Command me."

So sincere was his appeal, so sympathetic his presence, that there was no motion to evict him from this fraught family gathering, and instead of making for his own gig and leaving the

Bennets to commiserate alone, he remained, muttering suggestions and offering words of comfort, his eyes flickering towards Jane perhaps more often than was entirely suitable under the circumstances.

She did not object.

Mr Bingley listened with an attentive ear, leapt up to pour the tea, offered to fetch and carry whatever the family wanted. He was kind, and whilst Jane would otherwise be horrified to share such private misery with a stranger, his company was undemanding and comforting amidst the weeping and helpless lamenting.

Thus it was that he was present when, a half an hour later, there came a loud knock at the front door, followed shortly by the hurried entry of Mrs Hill with a note in her grip.

"An express, Sir, and from Miss Elizabeth, herself." She thrust her hand out to Papa, who grabbed the envelope as if his life depended upon it.

"Oh, thank the heavens! She is alive!" Mama exclaimed, and the room was all at once filled with similar expressions of relief and gratitude. "What does it say, Mr Bennet? Where is she? Does she come? Why is she so delayed? Read it aloud."

No one asked Mr Bingley to leave, nor did he offer, but he sat there near Jane, looking most intent and concerned, as her father read the note.

"It is dated this very afternoon, only two hours past," he began as he scanned the top of the note. "Here is what she writes."

> *Papa, I must be brief. I am well and unharmed, but I do not know when I will be returned home. Our carriage was taken by a man*

*claiming a desperate need to escape a foe pursuing him, in fear of his very life. He promises every attempt to return it when he is safe and is adamant that he knew not that I was inside. He professes to be a gentleman and is not unkind. Not only has he permitted me to send this missive, but has paid for its cost as well. I can only hope his claims are true. I shall remain here for the night, where I have taken a good room. I hope to get the coach tomorrow to St. Albans, and then shall engage a driver to return me home.*

*Should something transpire that disturbs these plans, my unwitting abductor has mentioned a possible destination in the north of Wales, somewhere near Llangollen. He has given his name as Will Darcy, with an estate in Derbyshire. Perhaps you can inquire about his character in London, where he claims to have friends and family. May it please God that I am in your embrace before long.*

*Your loving daughter Elizabeth.*

He glanced through the letter again before folding it and placing it in a pocket. His countenance, recently so fierce, was now returned to its habitual mild indifference.

"There we have it, Mrs Bennet. Our Lizzy is, or was until an hour or two ago, quite well, and we need no longer concern ourselves with this matter. It will be a great adventure for her, and she will entertain us all with her harrowing tales for weeks on end. Shall we now discuss the upcoming assembly, or peruse the latest magazines to determine whether short or long sleeves are the fashion? I, for one, enjoy Latin texts more than Greek."

"Oh, Mr Bennet! How you vex me!" Mama wailed, bringing a lace-encrusted handkerchief to her face. "Kitty, do you have my salts?"

"Very well, my dear. Let us, instead, see to the express rider's needs, and then I shall send somebody to London at once to make inquiries after this fellow. Darcy, she said. Yes. That is the name." He looked at his company, his eyes resting on his guest.

"Mr Bingley, what is that expression on your face? You look quite like a bird who has flown into a window."

Jane turned to look at him, and indeed, their new neighbour did indeed sport a most peculiar mien, eyes wide with shock, jaw loose in amazement.

He blinked his large brown eyes and shook his head, as if to clarify what he had heard. "Darcy? Did you say Will Darcy? No! It cannot be. I know him well, if it is indeed he. Fitzwilliam Darcy is quite the last man in the world I could imagine doing such a thing. Absconding with another man's carriage? Abducting his daughter? Quite unimaginable! He is a close friend, a man I trust implicitly. I have invited him to spend the autumn with me at Netherfield as my guest. Darcy! I can hardly account for it."

Jane's papa frowned. "Could this person who has my Lizzy be using your friend's name? The man you describe hardly sounds the sort to be running for his life from some unnamed enemy."

Unaccountably, Mr Bingley laughed. "My friend, I am afraid, causes offence wherever he goes, through no intent of his own. His manner can seem cold and haughty. But to occasion a nemesis, to infuriate someone who would cause him to flee in another man's carriage? No, not he... unless..." He tilted his head for a moment and screwed up his forehead in recollection. "I did not know Darcy as a youth, but he has spoken more than once of someone from his childhood in Derbyshire, a man who harbours considerable grudges against him. When last we spoke about this man, Darcy had refused him some unreasonable demand, and received threats in response. It could be." He raised a hand to his face and gnawed at a knuckle.

"Will he harm my Lizzy?" Jane's mama sat forward, hands wringing the handkerchief she grasped. "Is he the sort to be cruel to a lady?"

Bingley looked affronted. "Darcy? No, ma'am. Impossible. Quite the opposite. Your daughter is quite safe with him. If it is, indeed, he who has taken her." The young man frowned again, fine eyebrows wrinkling under his sandy-brown mop of hair. Then, with a start, he let out an exclamation. "Now listen. I am acquainted to some degree with his relations, most especially his cousin, who is a colonel in the Regulars. I believe him to be in London at this moment. If there is anybody to know where Darcy might be going in Wales, it will be the colonel. It is almost dark now, too late to travel, but I shall set off at first light and ride to London myself to seek an audience with him. In the meantime, I shall instruct my staff to have the carriage ready, should we wish to travel to this location, wherever it is, if Miss Elizabeth does not return as expected. With luck, I will be back at this time tomorrow and will be able to meet her in this very room."

"You are most kind, sir," Jane's father bowed.

Bingley's eyes caressed Jane once more. "Anything for... for a neighbour." He gave her a half smile, and she felt herself responding likewise. There was no harm in being friendly to a helpful neighbour, after all, and with Lizzy all but certainly safe.

"Mr Bingley," she replied.

Their gazes met and lingered.

Then, as is a spell were suddenly broken, he snapped a bow and made for the door, promising to return as soon as possible.

# Chapter 6
# An Alteration in Circumstances

The sun's last rays filtered through thick trees as the carriage rolled down a long drive. The horses were slow; they were clearly tired and ready for a good rest, and Elizabeth hoped such would be available to them. Will insisted he could provide this, and Elizabeth had no choice but to trust him.

"Where are we going?" she asked for the fourth time in the last ten minutes.

"Milden Hall is the estate of a school friend. We have since grown apart to some degree, but when I was younger, after my mother died, I spent some school holidays with the family. They were very kind to me, and I hold them in affection. I believe Sir Nicholas is still alive. He will remember me. He and my own father were friends from childhood."

The drive swung around a final curve and opened up into a sweep before a large modern house. Built of yellow stone with tall Palladian columns, its proportions were clean and pleasing to the eye. A servant in livery rushed towards them, questions on his face.

"Are we expecting company? Who are your people?" He clearly thought Will was a servant, which, to judge by the man's clothing, was an understandable assumption. Will's face went still and stony, and Elizabeth had to remind him of his circumstances.

"Your clothing, Will," she whispered. "You hardly look the gentleman."

The stony visage eased, and a friendlier expression replaced it, though Elizabeth still heard the echoes of the insult in Will's voice.

"You must be new. My name is Fitzwilliam Darcy, and I am a friend of Mr Julian Strand. My father and Sir Nicholas were likewise acquainted, and I hoped to speak to one of these fine men, should he be available."

Fitzwilliam? Had he given her that name when he introduced himself earlier? Yes, she vaguely recalled, he had, but all she had heard was the familiar Will, to suit his bedraggled appearance. Much like this man in livery. They all had their prejudices, so it seemed.

The servant did not quite sneer at them, but neither did he throw open the gates and welcome them inside. His eyes travelled up Will's filthy body, but stopped when they met his glare. Only someone with a lofty pedigree—or his valet—could achieve so imperious a regard. After a moment, the man condescended to reply.

"Sorry, sir. Neither is at home."

Will's jaw tightened. "And what of Mrs Abbot, the housekeeper? Is she still at her duties?"

The servant's eyes widened a touch. This seemed to be the password he required. "Yes, sir. If you wish to wait inside, I shall see if she is available. Freddy?" the servant called towards some outbuildings. "See to the carriage."

Will leapt down and held out his hand to assist Elizabeth's descent from the box. She placed her own hand in his, and he held it securely for a moment longer than necessary, giving her a squeeze of reassurance. His grip was warm and comforting, something familiar by now in the midst of a day of turmoil.

Freddy came to look after the horses, and Elizabeth followed Will and the servant into the front hall of the grand house.

"Wait here." A footman stepped out from an alcove to ensure they obeyed and ventured no further into the house.

They had been there for no more than five minutes when a diminutive lady with the air of a duchess rounded a corner from some unseen room. Only the chatelaine at her waist indicated that this was the housekeeper and not the mistress of the estate, such was her demeanour. Her eyes were wary at first and she opened her mouth in what looked like the beginnings of a protest, but she took one look at Will and a smile broke her stern expression.

"As I live and breathe, it is Master Fitzwilliam! Or rather, Mr Darcy now, I should say."

If Elizabeth had any remaining reservations about Will's true identity, Mrs Abbot's greeting put them firmly to rest. She had no time to speak, however, for the housekeeper went on.

"Goodness gracious, Mr Darcy, how you have grown. I have not seen you since you were a lad of seventeen. You have put on two inches since, I do believe, and you were a tall boy even then. I was most sorry to hear about your father. He was a good man, and we all miss him. Sir Nicholas talks of him to this very day. Well, well, Fitzwilliam Darcy, and dressed like that! Won't Master Julian be sorry to have missed you. How can I help you, young man?"

Will greeted the housekeeper in words equally effusive and then stepped back to introduce Elizabeth.

"Unfortunate circumstances, the details of which I will not bother you with at the moment, have forced us to travel together for a time. We were hoping for accommodation for the night, and a rest for our team. They have travelled long and hard today."

Mrs Abbot examined Elizabeth as if she were a questionable piece of cabbage.

"Miss Bennet is sadly embroiled in my misfortunes," Will added, when the housekeeper's regard did not soften.

"We only have one room made up for guests..." Mrs Abbot began.

Elizabeth dropped into her best curtsey. "Thank you, ma'am. I would be comfortable in a maid's room, if necessary. I do not wish to cause trouble."

The housekeeper's face cleared up. Elizabeth had passed some unknown test. "That will not be necessary. A sweet girl, you seem, and well spoken. I can have the maids prepare one of the smaller rooms for you whilst you dine. We were not expecting company, but Cook can prepare something simple, if that is acceptable. Some stew, and fresh bread and cheese."

Will raised his eyebrows at Elizabeth in question, and she gave him a subtle nod.

"Thank you, Mrs Abbot. That will be exceedingly welcome. Please convey our gratitude to Cook."

The housekeeper beckoned them to follow her into a compact sitting room at the back of the house and bade them sit. "Somebody will call you when your meal is ready. I shall see to your rooms and ensure the horses are tended to and the carriage secured. Have you trunks?"

Elizabeth looked down at herself in sudden mortification. What must she look like? Her travelling gown was chosen for comfort, rather than elegance, and it was now covered with all the dust of the road and the disarray born from her attempted attack on Mr Darcy. No wonder the housekeeper had taken her for a doxy, if not something worse.

"Yes, there is a trunk at the back of the carriage. I thank you."

But Will just stared at the housekeeper in horror. "I, it pains me to say, have only the clothes on my back."

And as much as Elizabeth must look a fright, how much worse was poor Will, with his torn and still-filthy clothing and no opportunity to change.

Mrs Abbot shook her head and clucked at him. "You poor boy! I must have this story, for I cannot imagine what has brought you to this. Very well. Let me look through the stores. I cannot dress you as a gentleman ought to be dressed, but perhaps I can find something clean in your size. You both sit a spell, until I return."

Off she went, brisk and efficient as any good housekeeper could be, leaving Elizabeth and Will to themselves before the welcome fire.

"What do we do now?" Elizabeth asked once the door was closed. "How long do we stay here?"

Will collapsed into the embrace of the armchair he had taken, his head thrown back on his shoulders, eyes closed. He looked exhausted, as well he must be. If his story was true, and Elizabeth now believed him, he had been awake since well before dawn, and had not had an easy day. He still smelled somewhat of the muck cart despite his hurried wash at the farm, and the shadows under his eyes echoed the dark stubble that shaded his cheeks and chin.

"Tonight, at least. I cannot embroil Mrs Abbot and my friend's home in my plight, but I shall lay it all before her and ask her counsel. One does not attain the position of housekeeper to such a place without a great deal of intelligence and common sense. If I can apprise my cousin of our circumstances, if we can stay until he arrives with help, it might do. I have not had a moment to think further than surviving the next mile. Perchance Mrs Abbot will see me to some paper and ink so I can write to him." He let out a soft groan. "Yes, with her agreement, we stay for tonight, at least."

He fell silent, and Elizabeth was content to let him rest against the back of the chair. She, too, closed her eyes. It was pleasant to sit upon a soft surface that did not jolt and bump, and a rush of fatigue engulfed her. She allowed her thoughts to drift.

How long she sat thus before there came a scratch at the door, she could not say, but when she sat up, a young maid stood before her. "If you please, Miss, there is a bath ready if you wish it." The maid looked at Will, who seemed to be sleeping in his chair. "Ned will be by for him in a moment. Follow me, Miss Bennet, if you will."

The maid led her to a small bathing room near the back of the house where a large copper tub steamed. "Shall I attend you, Miss? I can take your clothes to clean them. Here is a robe, until you select your garments for later."

It was the most welcome bath Elizabeth had ever had, and only the soft murmurings of the maid behind the screen prevented her from falling asleep once more in the lightly scented water. She did not even object to being wrapped in a soft, if old, robe afterwards and bustled down a hallway and up a flight of stairs to a bedchamber looking over the gardens behind the house. Her trunk was there, and she selected a simple gown for dinner.

Will was waiting for her in the breakfast room, where they were to dine. He, too, had bathed and changed, and now wore the simple clothing of a farmer. But the clothing was clean and in good condition, and his eyes were clearer than they had been earlier. He had also shaved, and once more, Elizabeth was struck by his handsome features. In this instance, it appears, clothes did not make the man.

Mrs Abbot was with him, and from the few words Elizabeth heard, he had apprised her of their unfortunate situation.

"Run off with the carriage, and the girl with it? Tut, tut, Mr Darcy. Master Julian will never believe this! Still, I remember George Wickham. That one was trouble. So handsome and charming, but beneath it, I always thought there was something untoward, and the tales I heard from the young maids!"

It seemed, then, that Will's tale was corroborated once more. Whether this was comforting or not, Elizabeth could not decide. The housekeeper was still shaking her head about Mr Wickham.

"I am sorry he has turned out so wild. I had hoped he might turn himself around."

Mrs Abbot clucked her disapproval, before ensuring that Elizabeth had all she needed for the night. They conversed for only a minute, until the food arrived, at which point she bid them both a good night and slipped out the door.

The meal that arrived was simple but tasty, and they ate in relative silence, both choosing to retire almost immediately afterwards. There would be plenty of time to talk on the morrow as they waited for help. Will repeated his intention to send a letter to his cousin at first light, and Elizabeth agreed that another missive to her family would do well to assure them as to her wellbeing. But those would both wait. For now, all Elizabeth wanted was sleep, and the bed in her chamber promised a pleasant night after a rather horrid day. She found her way back to her room, changed into her night rail, lay her head on the soft pillow, and knew nothing more.

Her hopes for a long and comfortable sleep, however, were dashed when there came a desperate knock at her door very early the next morning. The sun was still caressing the horizon, casting that golden light that comes just after dawn, gilding the furniture in her room as it slipped through the partly open draperies.

Mrs Abbot slipped into the room with apologies on her lips and concern in her eyes.

"Hurry, Miss Bennet, there is little time to lose. Put this clothing on, and I will explain as you dress." She held out some unfamiliar garments that turned out to be a simple skirt and blouse, as a farmer's daughter might wear.

"What are these? What of my own clothing? What has happened?" She rubbed her eyes and stumbled out of the bed. Cold water from the basin woke her completely, and she pulled on the borrowed garments whilst Mrs Abbot explained.

"He is here, Wickham, the man from whom your good Mr Darcy is fleeing. I could hardly account for it in the telling, but I see it all now. I knew this fellow as a child and distrusted him then, and I cannot like him any more at present."

"He is here? Now?" Elizabeth's fingers fumbled from a shudder of fear as she buttoned the front of the blouse.

The housekeeper nodded. "He is, and I am not pleased to see him. He has come asking after Mr Darcy and yourself, and we are insisting we have seen nothing of you at all. I am sorry to see you leave, but it is the safest choice. We will delay him as much as we can, of course, keep him here so he cannot follow. Here, allow me to help you with the ties at the back of the skirt. I had the idea from the clothing we lent to your young man last night. With a large bonnet to hide your pretty face, you will look like nothing other than a young country lad and his girl. Are you ready?"

Elizabeth nodded.

"Very good! We must go down the servants' stairs. Mr Wickham is inside the house, by the front door. We thought it best to keep an eye on him, but he will see you if you take the main staircase." She pulled Elizabeth along the hallway to a panel that opened into a narrow set of stairs, and then down into the servants' areas by the kitchen. Will was already there, helping Cook load a basket with fresh buns and some fruit. He looked up at her with serious eyes.

"I am sorry, Elizabeth. I never imagined he would trace us here. Mrs Abbot, I would not have come had I thought to bring danger to you."

"Never you fear," that lady replied. "All will be well. It is only he and one other, and I have twelve strong men in the house should I need them. But I do not think he means ill to this household, only to find you. I can think of no other reason why he should come at so early an hour, other than to catch you asleep."

"As he did," Elizabeth observed.

"He shall find nothing. Mr Abbot is delaying him now with excessive kindness, and in a few minutes, once you have departed, we shall conduct him on a tour of the house to assure him that you are not here. A *very*," she stressed the word, "thorough tour of the house. It will take an hour, perhaps more."

"But our belongings?"

"Your trunk is already stored away in milady's suite, and your rooms are, even now, being turned over. There will be no trace of you."

Will's brow screwed up. "And the carriage? The horses?"

Here, Mrs Abbot sighed. "There is nothing on the carriage to associate it with you, either of you, but you cannot use it, for it is in the carriage house immediate to the house, and he will see you leave. Likewise, your two horses. But here, help me fold this blanket. Jim from the village has just now come with the order of flour for the house, and he will see you back to the village, if you do not mind riding under some heavy sacks for a few minutes. I have sent a note to our stable master. Our primary stables are at the far end of the park, a mile yonder, and he will have a wagon or something ready for you, and a good strong horse as well. You can reclaim your own when you return. Hurry now. Is everything ready?"

Elizabeth turned to Will, who gave a curt nod.

"Then off you go. Here is Jim. He will see you safe."

They thanked the housekeeper with every ounce of gratitude they had and left with promises to return as soon as they could.

Mrs Abbot was true to her word. After a rather uncomfortable ride lying down under a pile of sacks in the back of Jim's cart, they were greeted by a serious stable master, who showed them what he had arranged for their use.

"'Tis not what you are likely accustomed to, I'm afraid," he frowned, "but it's solid and will get you wherever you're going. Dobbin is a good, strong creature, he is, and goes a long way without tiring. Not the fastest horse, but neither the slowest. He'll see you well. Here is the cart we have. I believe it the best for your needs."

He took them to the lane behind the main stables, where a wooden cart stood ready, the horse already in harness. It was long enough for a man to lie down in, and had a frame that supported an oiled canvas as a tarpaulin. The covering had flaps that could be opened or closed at the front by the bench, and reminded Elizabeth of drawings of the covered wagons used in the American colonies.

"It will keep your belongings and the food basket dry," the man said, "and yourselves as well, if you need it."

The implication was clear: It might be the only shelter they would have on some days, and now Elizabeth understood the housekeeper's insistence on them taking the blankets she had prepared. If the weather turned, they would have to wrap themselves up in whatever they had, perhaps even huddle together for warmth.

There was no time to act missish or blush artfully at this. They must be long gone by the time Wickham finished his tour of the house. Will went to befriend Dobbin, the horse, with soft words and an apple, and in a moment, they were set.

With more words of thanks and directions to the best road, they departed Milden Hall for parts unknown.

# Chapter 7
# Whither Shall We Wander?

By the time the sky was fully bright, Darcy and Elizabeth had put five miles or more between them and Milden Hall, and—hopefully—George Wickham. They spoke little, but when Elizabeth reached into the basket and pulled out a soft roll to offer him, Darcy took it with gratitude. Gratitude for Mrs Abbot's thoughtfulness and care, gratitude for another day out of

Wickham's clutches, and, oddly, gratitude for this young lady seated beside him, delicately chewing on her own breakfast.

An added responsibility she might be, and he would certainly make better time without her, but her presence lightened his load, even though it added to hers. He glanced at her now, as if for the first time. He had distractedly considered her somewhat pretty the previous day, but the benefit of a reasonable sleep and a calmer mind now allowed him to refine his thoughts. A few errant chestnut ringlets escaped the confines of the large bonnet she wore atop her head, framing expressive brows over fine, thickly lashed eyes. Were they brown or dark green? Suddenly he longed to know, to see them smiling at him in the glory of full sunlight.

But his eyes lingered on her lips, plump and rosy pink, with a cupid's bow and a curve at the bottom that seemed shaped to smile. Even in repose, her expression was one of concealed satisfaction, and his own mouth began to twitch into a shy grin in response, despite the desperate circumstances under which they now found themselves. It would be too easy to fall into an easy friendship with his unsought companion. But he recalled then those same lips spewing invectives upon him only the previous morning, and he schooled his thoughts.

Still, she was a balm at this moment with her calm presence and soft smile, and when Darcy turned to her and uttered a simple "Thank you," they both knew it was not only for the food.

"Where are we going now?" Elizabeth asked after another mile or so. "You were watching the sun yesterday to head north, but now, from what I see, we are travelling west, and perhaps a bit south."

Pleasant company, and observant. He was pleased once more that she was here. What would he have made of her, he wondered, had they met in more conventional circumstances? Perhaps over tea, or at a ball. But no! He scoffed at the very notion. She had said her father was a gentleman; therefore, they might be equals in official rank. But in the eyes of society, he was as far above her as a bishop to a church mouse. She, from what he had seen and heard, associated with minor gentry and wealthy tradesmen in a small market town near nowhere. He, on the other hand, dined with dukes and bishops, and called an earl his grandfather.

He doubted he would ever have found himself in company with her, let alone lower himself to form an acquaintance. The loss, he realised with a shudder, would have been entirely his.

Perhaps there was something to crawling out of inn windows and hiding in a muck cart that put new perspectives on one's place in the world. Considering how he appeared yesterday, it was a miracle that Elizabeth had deigned to speak to him at all!

But speak to him she did, and she was now awaiting his answer to her question about the direction of their path.

"You are correct; we are heading southwest. I have been considering what I know of George Wickham, and what he expects me to do. He remembered Julian Strand as well as I did and judged that his home might be my first attempt at refuge. He will likewise guess that I deem heading northward to Pemberley in Derbyshire too predictable, and therefore will consider other places I might go. Of course, that makes Pemberley an option after all, but it is still too risky, for he may have his minions lying in wait along the route."

Wickham had his fingers in many pies, most of them rotten. He knew the sort who would set upon a stranger for the pure pleasure of it. Darcy shook off that thought with a mental shudder.

"My other chosen destination, he will consider, and the one which is my ultimate goal, is my uncle's hunting lodge in the north of Wales. It is there that we are going."

Elizabeth gave him a look that, had she been his governess, would have sent him back to his desk to repeat his work. "As you mentioned yesterday. Then why, sir, are we travelling south?"

"You are too clever for me, Miss Bennet. Wickham will assume we will take the most direct route there, and will wait for me along the way, I am certain. But as a young man I spent some summers tramping through Wales with my cousin before he took his commission, and this, Wickham does not know. I learned to love the countryside and I found my paths through the hills and the vales. If we go south now and come up through the valleys, he will not find us. Therefore, instead of passing by Birmingham, I propose heading towards Gloucester and then towards the Brecons before turning northward again, perhaps at Abergavenny."

Elizabeth blinked. "That will take us a great deal of time."

"I can think of no alternative. There are lesser-travelled paths and diversions that we will take, and he cannot watch them all; therefore, knowing him, he will watch none. I would not have you come to harm." He spoke more warmly than he should—indeed, he was often said to be cold and aloof—but something about her warmed his soul. It must, he reckoned, be their joint peril. "You are no wilting daisy. You are made of tougher stuff than that. I will do what I can to keep you comfortable."

"And I will not complain as some do when my creature comforts are less than I would like to expect. I suspect I may surprise you, Will. Very well. We have no choice, so let us ride."

They travelled with grim determination that day. The borrowed conveyance was surprisingly agile on the rough country lanes. The wagon was lighter than the carriage and held almost no cargo other than Darcy and Elizabeth and the few belongings they could carry out of Milden Hall. Dobbin seemed to have no problems pulling it along, one tireless mile after the next.

They found small inns in smaller villages to take refreshments and allow the horse his rest, and avoided the busier roads. It was not the fastest Darcy had ever travelled, but he was willing to sacrifice speed for security, and Elizabeth was of the same mind. More than once, he offered to send another missive to her family, but she declined.

"If we send a letter, they might be able to trace our route, and if Mr Wickham finds out about it, we will none of us be safe. I must leave them ignorant for a while longer, as much as their certain worry pains me."

Once more, her clear thinking and sensible nature impressed him where, had they met on the floor of a ballroom, he would have deemed her of too little consequence to offer more than the coldest of nods.

Their conversation, still very much that of strangers, was sporadic and essentially limited to the practicalities of their situation, but Elizabeth proved not unpleasant company, and the day passed without incident.

The first real difficulty along their journey came that evening.

They had been sitting under a tree near a stream, allowing Dobbin to rest and have some water. It was starting to grow dark, and the discussion concerned where to sleep that night. They had seen no villages for a while, nor was there any suggestion that one might be near. The lane they travelled was all but deserted, and Darcy began to fear he had chosen a road that somehow avoided all places where they might find accommodation for the night.

"If we turn northward, we are sure to come across a more important road." He scanned the horizon, willing the rumble of distant carriages into existence, but to his disappointment.

"Is that wise?" Elizabeth asked. "If you wish to travel southward to avoid Mr Wickham's notice, should we not go that direction instead?"

Darcy consulted a map he had in his mind, wishing he had paid more attention to his schoolmasters so long ago. "If we go too far south, we will end up in Cornwall rather than Wales. Our direction had best remain westward, until we come to Cheltenham or Gloucester." He took a deep breath, but it failed to provide the answers he sought.

"Shall we continue onward, then, and hope to find a village?" Elizabeth asked. "Oh! Here comes somebody down the lane. He might help us."

Indeed, a farmer was approaching, one of the few people they had seen since turning onto this country road. At their call, he pulled his pony to a stop, and dismounted from the cart it pulled.

"'Evenin'," he greeted them. "Help you? Fine night 'twill be, at that. No rain."

He walked over and leaned against one of the trees, clearly expecting some conversation.

Reserved by nature, Darcy was ready to say a coolly polite word to the man and send him on his way, but Elizabeth was a different sort of person, fashioned for society, and she met the farmer's greeting with a wide grin and introduced herself.

"I'm Lizzy," she said with a winning smile. "This is Will. We are travelling to..." she paused for a moment, "We are off to visit Will's uncle over in Wales."

Darcy allowed himself to smile. Every word was true, no matter how the man would understand them. Clever lass, she was. He sat back and allowed Elizabeth to conduct the conversation, praising the beautiful countryside, lamenting the long journey ahead of them, and wondering if the farmer had an idea of where they might spend the night.

He was as friendly as men get, and before long was chatting with them as if they had been friends these last twenty years.

"Follow me, then," he said after a while. "You're nice folks, and we don't get much new company. My wife will like to meet you, and we can find you a place to sleep. 'Tis not too far, only around those trees."

Such words were music to Darcy's ears, until the farmer—who had introduced himself as John Neeler—added, "The barn is nice and warm this time of year, and there's a couple of cots in the loft if you don't like sleeping on the hay."

Darcy stared at the man as if he had grown three heads. What was this? Fitzwilliam Darcy, invited to sleep on the hay? He, the master of Pemberley, grandson to an earl, and one of the wealthiest men in Derbyshire, offered a cot in a barn? Did this man not know who he was? He was about to open his mouth to utter something that would certainly cause the greatest offence, when once more Elizabeth laid a gentle hand upon his to still his words, as she gratefully accepted the kind invitation.

"Our clothing, Will," she whispered to him while his mouth still hung open in shock.

At that, Darcy did glance down to see himself as he looked now, not as he imagined himself. Clad as he was in rough trousers, an old linen shirt, a long loose neckcloth more akin to a scarf than a cravat, a shapeless waistcoat and equally shapeless loose coat, and wide-brimmed straw hat, he looked much like Farmer John, a man of the fields rather than of the town. Elizabeth, likewise, wore the simpler garb of a country lass: a yellow blouse, a dark petticoat, a short apron-like garment over a billowing skirt, a colourful kerchief, and a straw bonnet, with a scarlet cloak tossed onto the bench of the cart. How different this was from the elegant pale gowns of society. It quite completed the picture of a field hand and his lass out for a drive. What John Neeler made of their upper-class accents, Darcy could not guess, but the man likely thought them to come from nearer London, where all manner of strange things could be imagined.

Elizabeth still held Darcy's hand in hers, and she gave it a squeeze before releasing it, a gesture that Farmer John noticed by his grin. "Well, follow me, then, folks. Just a half-mile that way, and we turn."

They were met at the entrance to the small stone farmhouse by the farmer's wife, as friendly as her husband.

"Company!" she exclaimed with a broad smile. "There's always good food in exchange for good conversation. I've pie ready to bake, and I can make another as easy as it comes. Welcome."

Darcy followed John around to the barn to tend to the horses for the night, and when they returned to the house, it was to find Elizabeth chatting happily with their hostess as she rolled out pastry and chopped vegetables.

Hmmm... he had thought her rather lacking in practical skills, but she seemed to know what she was about. Perhaps she had one or two more accomplishments than painting tables.

They were soon joined by four young men, all wide and tall like their father, just now coming in from the fields. Each was pleasant and polite, but the house was full. This, then, explained the invitation to sleep in the barn. This was no fine inn at a busy crossroads, nor a wealthy man's sprawling house in the midst of his parkland. There, in another time and place, Darcy would have expected some youngsters of the family to give up their rooms for the guests in favour of smaller quarters; perhaps the poor cousin could sleep in the nursery for a night or two. But this was no such establishment. These were hard-working people who lived off the sweat of their brows, with no luxuries to offer to the strangers they had generously offered to house for a night, and they likely considered the barn to be perfectly acceptable accommodations for two others of their class.

The barn would do, and he would be grateful.

And, he decided, he was. When one has everything, one expects so much. When one has nothing, the slightest gift is a luxury. How quickly his attitudes had changed.

Soon enough, it was time to retire. Farmer John showed them the ladder up to the loft, said his goodnights, and departed.

Darcy had never felt so awkward in his life, despite a childhood of never quite finding his place in society. The magnitude of this situation was staggering, and he did not quite know what to do. He and Elizabeth had been alone, for two whole days, as they drove along silent country lanes. But that was different. They had been in an open carriage—or cart, to be precise, although the distinction was immaterial—and that breached no boundaries of propriety.

Now, for the first time, they were truly alone, in a quiet and private place, away from the eyes of the world. No matter that there was no one around to observe and chastise them. He knew. Everything he had been taught shouted at him from the depths of his conscience.

There was no chaperone, no beneficent guardian ensuring that decorum was preserved along with everybody's reputation and virtue. Now, for the first time, they *felt* alone together, or—rather—he did. A glance at Elizabeth showed her discomfort as well, for she was fussing with something in the corner and decidedly not looking at him.

There was, he considered, something particularly intimate about sleeping, that was not a part of sitting on the box of an open carriage. At night, when the sun had set and there was no light, the protective armour of everyday clothing was stripped away, leaving the soul as bare as the body.

Would Elizabeth sleep in her clothes, or change into a shift? What would he do? Mrs Abbot had shoved an old nightshirt into the sack she thrust at him, and he wondered if Elizabeth had taken along a night rail as well. Now, it seemed, was when he would find out. If he dared do anything other than stand here, paralysed into motionlessness.

Elizabeth broke the silence. "I suppose I ought to go up and see what we need. It is almost dark and we have no light, nor would I want an open flame in a barn." Her voice was flat. Without another word, she climbed the ladder with sure and practised movements.

"There are three low cots," she called down from the loft, sounding a bit more her usual self, "with straw-stuffed mattresses. They might be used for field hands during harvest, for they look quite abandoned for now. We will need the blankets from the wagon."

"Blankets. Yes. Of course."

Grateful for something to do, Darcy went in search of the necessary items and managed to pass them up to Elizabeth before attempting the climb. When he hoisted himself into the loft, Elizabeth was already under her blanket on the cot the furthest away. She must have made herself ready for bed whilst he was at the cart. Of the two other cots, she had laid the blanket on the one closest to where he now stood, leaving the middle one empty. He could not see what she was wearing, but now he had his own decisions to make.

It was dark enough that he must look, to her, like nothing but a moving shadow, as she was little more than a shadow to him. Still, he felt as if he were standing on a stage, being illuminated by a thousand lamps. His face burned hot, and had he a mirror, he knew his reflection would glow red with embarrassment. He must, at least, remove his coat and boots, and he wished desperately not to have to sleep in these trousers. He stood motionless with indecision and anxiety.

"I shall roll over and stare at the wall whilst you undress." Elizabeth's voice filtered through the growing darkness. "I believe I can trust you to be a gentleman. We might be forced into further, similar proximity over the course of our flight."

In quick motions, he slithered out of the least comfortable items of clothing and hurried under the blanket. What was he to do now? Engage in pleasant conversation? Pretend she was not there? Sing a lullaby?

Again, Elizabeth settled his worry with her quiet words. "Do not be uneasy, Will. It is strange, I know. We will grow accustomed to this."

"You deserve better than this, Elizabeth. You are a gentleman's daughter, not a farmhand." And it was true. She had offered not one word of complaint. What other woman of his acquaintance would have borne so willingly these rustic conditions?

Her response confirmed his estimation of her. "We are warm and safe, and our bellies are full. A great many people cannot claim even these comforts. And after we leave, should Mr Wickham chance by and inquire after us, our host will remember only a farmer and his wife out on a drive to visit an uncle in a distant village."

Wife? They thought she was his wife? That momentary panic subsided in an instant. Of course, else they never would have offered this space to them. And, as he contemplated the matter, he found the notion did not bother him quite so much.

"Sleep well, Will."

"And you, Elizabeth."

But although he slept long and deep after the exhaustion of the day, he was always aware that she was so very close.

# Chapter 8
# Fear

The following day began far more gently, with no alarmed awakening, and no panicked flight under a pile of bags of flour. Instead, they rose when the sun lit their loft, slowly and with a sense of relief at having spent a peaceful night. Elizabeth announced she would stare at the wall whilst Darcy dressed, and he scurried down the ladder to see to the wagon whilst she prepared for the day. They filled their bellies with hot porridge in the Neelers' kitchen, and departed when the men were just heading off to the fields, the sun still low in the sky. Mrs Neeler had filled their basket with some bread and fruit, and Darcy had thanked them for their kind hospitality with a handful of coin to compensate them for the food for themselves and for Dobbin. Armed with directions and landmarks, they moved with more confidence this time, knowing how to find their way without venturing onto the better-travelled roads.

They continued west and slightly south, using the sun to guide their way. The countryside, always green and lush, grew hillier, their narrow lane darting through thick growths of trees, then breaking into wide fertile valleys, sometimes edged by ancient stone walls or wooden fences, other times running along well-tended farmland or through the occasional village, cradled between river and hillside.

In one such place, they stopped to allow Dobbin to rest and eat and purchased some more bread and cheese and some early apples. Darcy counted out the coins from his purse. Each one was precious.

"Have we enough?" Elizabeth asked when they returned to the cart. Darcy did not miss the import of the word we. They were in this mess together; she was no longer his adversary, but his companion. It made the awful situation a little less dreadful.

He tested the weight of the purse in his palm. It was not as heavy as he would have liked.

"I cannot say. I know not how long it will take us to get there, or what obstacles we might meet along the way. If we are lucky, if fortune smiles on us and we—" He swallowed at a dreadful thought. "If we avoid encountering our foe and eat sparingly, we might manage. But whilst I am prepared to forego a meal or two, we cannot ask the same of Dobbin. He must eat well."

"And rest well," Elizabeth added. "It will slow our progress."

"That might help us. The longer we take to arrive at the lodge, the more likely Wi—our adversary is to believe us elsewhere. I hope, I pray, that a delay will be to our advantage."

He tried to keep his voice dispassionate, but Elizabeth must have heard something in it.

"You are afraid."

"I? I was raised to face anything with no fear. It is unbecoming to a gentleman, to an Englishman, to be a coward." He straightened his back and thrust out his chest.

"It is not a disparagement. Fear is natural, for it shows that you are a thinking man. Only a fool would not be afraid of someone making such dreadful threats against you. Furthermore, fear does not make you a coward. It makes you a man."

She reached out a hand and let it fall gently atop his own. That small gesture of compassion was a seed that planted itself within his soul. Once more, like her observation about the dwindling coins, it told him that he was not alone.

His heart tightened at the thought. When last had someone looked to him not to lead or to provide, but to offer comfort? When last had someone given, rather than taken? Elizabeth could not offer a fast horse or a pocketful of coins, but she could offer her presence, and it meant more to Darcy than he would ever have imagined. He turned his hand over, so their palms touched, and he laced his fingers with hers for a brief moment before turning his eyes away. But he did not miss the small smile that touched her soft lips.

They set out again on their path, one plodding mile after another. Dobbin, as promised, walked steadily onwards, stalwart and seemingly untiring. The silence between them was comfortable and unforced, but the thoughts churning through Darcy's mind eventually forced their way out in words.

"I am afraid," he said, as if the hour between Elizabeth's statement and this continuation of the conversation were merely a second. "I am afraid for myself, of course, but also for everybody relying on me. My tenants. My sister. They depend upon me." He lapsed back into silence.

Elizabeth's hand covered his own again. She said nothing, but her silence was compassionate.

"I have been called proud," he said after a moment. "It is not always intended as a compliment, but I take it as such."

Now he noticed her eyebrows flicker upwards on her smooth forehead.

"Indeed." It was half-statement, half-question.

"Pride is often conflated with vanity, but I see them as very different things. I am proud of what I have achieved on my estate. Pemberley has always been prosperous, but its stewardship was thrust upon me at the age of three-and-twenty, most unexpectedly. My father, an excellent man, had a weak heart, although we did not know it. I thought... I hoped he would live another twenty years, that I could take over management of the estate slowly, as I learned more about it. But one moment I was carefree and enjoying a house party with an old friend from university, and the next I was responsible for the lives and welfare of thousands of people.

"And," he added after another pause, "a ten-year-old girl."

Elizabeth's voice was as soft as the breeze that riffled through his hair. "It must have been terrifying. I am sorry your inheritance came upon you so tragically."

"This is the double-edged sword of wealth. The cost of my fortune was tremendous. People look at me with envy and whisper about my great luck. But I would give it all up in an instant to have my good father back."

They rode in silence for a few minutes longer. Dobbin strained up a rather steep hill, and the two travellers dismounted to walk beside the horse and lighten his load. How much like this horse he was, Darcy thought. Struggling against the unseen pull of the earth, hoping that somebody would act to lighten *his* load. Like Elizabeth did without a conscious thought. The notion buoyed him, somehow.

"I learned to manage the estate, and with my improvements, it is more prosperous now than ever," he said at last. "Changes are coming, and I hope to balance industrial development with agriculture, so we can prosper into the future. I shall not bother you now with these details, but I am proud of what I have done. I, and my advisors and tenants. We are all partners. That, I believe, is not vanity. But they depend upon me and my management of the estate. At the moment, Georgiana is my heir, with my cousin as her other guardian. What does a fifteen-year-old girl know about managing Pemberley? What does a soldier know? Without me, I do not know what will happen. That is the weight of my pride, if such it is."

Beside him, Elizabeth nodded her head. "It is pride, indeed, but not misplaced. I commend you, sir, on your achievements."

"And for them, I am afraid. If I... if I do not return, what will become of them? What will become of my dear sister? She is fragile, still, and so young. My aunt is a good-hearted woman and will keep Georgiana's body and soul together, but her spirit will be destroyed. If the man who tried to misuse her ends up killing me," his voice broke, "it will utterly destroy her. I am afraid for her as well. No. I am not afraid. I am terrified."

All Elizabeth did was squeeze his hand once more, but it helped far more than she could ever have imagined.

With these melancholy thoughts, they continued their journey. The heavy skies matched Darcy's mood, and even Elizabeth's comforting presence could not keep the blue devils from tormenting him.

At last, with the sun ready to kiss the horizon, they happened upon a small village, somewhere beyond Gloucester. They were sore at heart and exhausted, and the modest inn was as welcome to their sight as the finest palace. They begged a stall for Dobbin at the stables, and then proceeded to the inn itself to find accommodations for the night. It was easier to procure shelter for the horse than for themselves, for the inn's proprietor looked askance at Darcy's request for a bed.

"Don't see I've room for ones like you," he muttered. "This here's a respectable establishment."

For the third time in as many days, the once-esteemed Master of Pemberley was taken for nothing more than an itinerant ne'er-do-well. The Neelers, to give them their due, had not looked down on him, even though a plate of stew and a cot in a barn was nothing like what he had learned to expect. Now, this innkeeper was sneering at him, eyeing his less-than-pristine clothing and judging him as unworthy of taking a room for a night.

A glimpse in a cracked mirror by the stairs told him something of the truth of the matter: two days unshaven, two days unwashed, and looking more than impecunious in his old borrowed clothing, his appearance quite belied the essence of the man he knew himself to be.

How different this was from Darcy's accustomed treatment, when he arrived in a grand carriage pulled by a matched team, and descended in his fine London clothes, his liveried servants already having made the arrangements. On those occasions, he was treated almost like royalty, rooms cleared for his use, and food prepared to his liking. How unlike those days this was.

Was this how he treated others? The notion hit him with force. Did he look at a man poorly dressed and judge him accordingly? Did he take the measure of a stranger based more on what he saw on the outside than on the man's character? He sent a glance towards Elizabeth, herself looking quite as disreputable as he, and wondered once more how he would have regarded her if he first saw her dressed as she was, looking nothing like a gentleman's daughter. He had been forced into company with her now; he was beginning to discover her true worth. With no such requisite upon him, he might well have turned up his nose at her muddy skirts and put her entirely from his mind.

Once again, he began to understand how much the loss would have been his.

Now, that supposedly inconsequential piece of trouble he had unintentionally acquired stepped up to save him once more. She gave the suspicious innkeeper a dazzling smile and, in the sweetest words Darcy could imagine, she told him something of their plight, rather embroidered at that. A runaway carriage, a need to visit an uncle, such a pity about the loss of their trunks. It was a grand tale, and eventually, she coaxed the proprietor of this small inn into accommodations for the evening. The flash of good coin from Darcy's dwindling supply helped matters considerably, and at last, the man agreed to show them to a small room facing the stables at the back. They signed their names in the register as Mr and Mrs Williams, which seemed to surprise the innkeeper simply because he clearly did not expect them to be able to read and write at all.

He walked them to the room, handed over the key, informed them that there was food in the public, and left.

Darcy cracked the door open and stepped inside. The room was plain but it seemed clean, with one bright window illuminating the space with the last rays of the sun. Then he stopped in horror. There was only one bed.

Elizabeth seemed to read his thoughts. "He does believe us to be a married couple," she soothed, "and we could hardly tell him otherwise." Her eyes betrayed her discomfort, however, and Darcy was struck by a need to comfort her. Until this moment, he realised, she had been the one reassuring him, despite the unhappy fact that her predicament was his fault.

He took a step towards her and opened his arms so she could fall against his chest as his sister always used to do. But as she accepted the tacit invitation, he acknowledged that the sensation of having her pressed against him was nothing like Georgiana's affectionate hugs, and that his feelings were far from fraternal. He fought his rather alarming and not entirely unpleasant inclinations. He would not frighten her. He scolded himself severely, but their predicament remained.

Swallowing the lump in his throat, he tried to sound dispassionate. "I am a gentleman. You have nothing to fear from me. Your name, too, will remain unblemished. They know us as Mr and Mrs Williams, and will never associate Lizzy Williams with Miss Bennet from Hertfordshire." His eyes flickered to the single bed, taunting them from its place near the wall. There was no chair in which to sleep, and little space on the floor. Still, the floor would have to do. He was, as he had insisted, a gentleman.

She nodded against his chest and stepped back. His arms felt so empty without her in them, although their embrace had been seconds long at best.

"I trust you," was all she said before she drew her one night rail out from the small bag she carried and laid it on the bed.

They went to the public for their dinner—simple stew and bread and ale—and returned to their room to prepare for the night.

Darcy excused himself to check on Dobbin before joining Elizabeth, to give her time to change, but like the previous night, his re-entry into the room was fraught with uncertainty. Once again, she was under the covers, a soft shape in the faint light from the moon and lamps around the stable yard.

"My eyes are closed," she assured him again. "I, too, promise never to divulge that the great Mr Darcy has arms and legs like the rest of us." The shape on the bed shifted, presumably as she rolled to face away from him, and he slid off his coat and changed his day shirt for the nightshirt he had, before fumbling with the buttons at the sides of his trouser flap.

The previous night he had removed his trousers, since he had his own cot and blanket in which to sleep. But if he were to lie on the floor, and possibly need to rise at any moment, such a shocking state of undress would be... awkward. On the other hand, how long could he remain in this same item of clothing? It could be days, possibly over a week, before they arrived at the hunting lodge and he could beg for new garments.

Modesty won out, and he started to roll his coat up to make a sort of pillow on the floor, as far away from the bed as the small room would allow. They had brought in the blankets from the wagon, and these, too, he began to arrange for his undoubtedly uncomfortable night.

"Will," Elizabeth's voice whispered through the dark room. "This bed is large enough for two. You cannot sleep on the floor."

"I can, and I must. My honour demands it."

"You need to sleep. That cannot be comfortable."

"I have slept in worse places," he lied. Even his tramp through Wales with Richard several years past had taken him from one friend's estate to the next, with a carriage trailing close behind them should the walk grow too tiring.

"Will...? Oh, very well. Good night."

He eased himself onto the floor and kneaded his folded coat into shape under his head. Heavens, but the floor was hard. Perhaps if he shifted this way, or if he padded the blanket differently. He stretched out and willed his muscles to relax, but an uneven nail in the wooden floor kept irritating his arm. He moved a bit, but now every time he shifted, his foot hit the leg of the bed. He forced himself to lie very still and breathe slowly and deeply, hoping sleep would follow.

This he did for perhaps a quarter of an hour, growing less and less comfortable with every moment, until he heard Elizabeth whisper once more. "Come to the bed, Will. I shall not molest you, this I promise. It is wide enough for two, and if you feel safer, we can roll the blanket into a barrier between us.

By now, his back was aching and his head starting to throb, and the twinge in his shoulder was nagging all the more loudly. He could ignore them no longer.

"Thank you," he murmured, doing as she suggested.

The bed was nothing to his fine mattress at Pemberley, but it was a marked improvement to the floor. He rolled onto his side as far to the edge of the bed as was comfortable, and once more closed his eyes, hoping for sleep. But now a different distraction intruded, for all he could hear was Elizabeth's soft, even breath, and all he could feel was the slight sag of the mattress that betrayed her presence, so very close. He could, if he desired it, reach out and touch her, and he had to force his arms to remain as they were.

It was a very long time before he finally slept, but these were tortures of the most pleasant kind, and he could not regret her presence.

# Chapter 9
# The Search Begins

Jane Bennet could not begin to count the number of times she had walked the hallways of Longbourn or the perimeter of the gardens. Waiting was agony; not knowing what had become of her dear sister was worse. Two days... it had been two days. She longed to leap onto the fastest horse they had to go in search of Elizabeth... but where? Where could she go that the riders from the posting inn had not? Being idle was never Jane's choice, and now, when so much action was needed, it was akin to torture.

And Elizabeth was out there, somewhere, possibly in the direst of circumstances, needing help! She had not returned the day after her disappearance, as she had said she would do, which meant that something had gone terribly amiss. Where was Lizzy? What could she, Jane, do to find her? Not knowing, not being able to do anything, was the worst agony she could imagine. Pain stabbed through Jane's hands, and she released the clenched fists that had driven her fingernails into her palms. She took a shuddering breath and set out to pace the garden once more.

Furthermore, where was Mr Bingley? He had promised to return the previous evening, but there had been no word from him at all. He had seemed sincere in his offer to be of service, but perhaps, like with so many frivolous young men, the intention had died the moment he was out of sight of the house. She must have imagined the depth of feeling in his large brown eyes as he proclaimed his shock at events and his intentions of doing what he could to be of service. As he'd looked at her in a way that, even under the duress of her sister's misadventures, Jane had sensed was beyond mere neighbourliness.

Indeed, her own heart had given a skip at the sight of his open, friendly face and the attentions he had given her. Or, rather, that he had appeared to give her. For after his departure, there was nothing left but the memory of an affable smile and the uncomfortable notion that she really ought not to have been drawn into his gaze when poor Elizabeth was out there...somewhere. Somewhere unknown and almost certainly in peril. She chastised herself for even thinking of Mr Bingley when all her thoughts ought to be focused on dear Lizzy.

No, she had been imagining things, her fancies caught up in the horror of the day and the shock of the moment. It was all nothing.

The garden revealed no secrets, and in time, Jane's anxious steps took her into the family's back parlour for the twentieth time that day. She glared at the clock on the mantel, daring it to chime another hour, which would bring Lizzy closer to returning home, but it stubbornly refused and insisted on still reading half-past ten o'clock in the morning. Where, oh where, was Mr Bingley?

Providence heard her silent plea and, as she passed the window, a flash of movement caught her eye. It was a grand carriage, first turning from the lane onto the drive, and then quickly approaching the house. The matched team came to a stop by the main entrance, and two men emerged. One was Mr Bingley—he had kept his word, after all, thank the heavens—and the other was a man Jane had never seen before. She could not discern his exact features from this distance, but he carried himself like somebody rather important, and curiosity widened her eyes.

Her mother, still in a state of great nervous agitation, lay half-strewn across the chaise, a cup of tea neglected at her side. Beside her, Kitty fidgeted with some needlework, while Mary was attempting to read from some edifying volume.

"A carriage, Mama! It is Mr Bingley, returned, and with another." Kitty's voice broke the stifling air. In a moment, the room was awash in a flurry of activity, preparing for the imminent arrival of these two guests.

Mrs Hill led them into the parlour, with Jane's father on their heels. Introductions were made at once.

The stranger stood tall and proud, and bowed smartly. His garb was mufti, but his bearing all military, and when he was announced to be Colonel Fitzwilliam, nobody was astonished.

The colonel was most gentlemanlike and, if not quite handsome, very appealing. His manners were everything that a man's should be, and he greeted Jane's mother as if she were a countess, immediately endearing himself to that lady as a new favourite. He bowed individually to each sister as she was introduced, and when he turned to Jane, the smile on his face broadened.

"Miss Bennet." His eyes met hers and he bestowed her with a slow blink. "My friend Bingley's praise is not exaggerated. My pleasure." He took her hand in his and kissed the air a fraction of an inch above her skin.

Delicate heat flooded Jane's cheeks, and she lowered her eyes and dipped a curtsey. Whose words affected her the most? Colonel Fitzwilliam's gallantry, or Mr Bingley's comments that the colonel repeated? Then the blush was replaced by the red fire of shame. To be thinking of handsome men now, when Elizabeth was in peril, was unforgivable! She swallowed a lump of gall and replied to the kind greeting.

This, however, was no time for idle chatter and flirtations. The men were here on a mission, and this was the first war counsel. The colonel took charge. He accepted the offered chair, but leaned forwards with his hands on his knees as he spoke in crisp tones.

"Mr Bingley has apprised me of this sad situation in which you find yourselves, and I am moved to offer my assistance. I believe I can help. Darcy, you see, is my cousin and a man I am proud to name as a friend."

"Your cousin!" Mrs Bennet burst out. "Then you believe he could really do such a thing?"

The colonel turned his serious face towards her. "I have learned, Madam, that in the most trying of circumstances, all men are capable of the most unimaginable things. But my cousin is not a man to act rashly, and if he has, indeed, done as your daughter's letter suggests, I can only believe it was under the utmost duress. Darcy is a man given to serious thought and hides his passions, even from himself. He has the finest principles, and I can assure you without hesitation that if your daughter is with him, he will move mountains to keep her safe."

Jane's spine sagged in relief at these words, the first she had heard in two days that offered any hope that her sister would be returned in good health. Until now, it seemed that worry alone had kept her upright. But another dreadful thought soon left her back rigid once more.

"But why would he have done this?" Her voice trembled in her ears. "If he feels such fear that he must steal our carriage and dear Lizzy, is she not in terrible danger as well?"

Colonel Fitzwilliam contemplated her, his dark brown eyes meeting her own blue ones. "What Miss Bennet says has merit. But matters may not be quite as dire as we all fear. I believe I have some notion of the cause of my cousin's alarm. I also believe I know exactly where he is going."

There was an onslaught of sound in the parlour, as everybody called out at once.

"Let me explain," the colonel said when he could be heard. "I cannot divulge the entire story, but allow me to say this. I have heard a rather alarming story from somebody most intimately involved, that a certain person we know from our youth believes my cousin Darcy to have done him out of a great deal of money. He is quite mistaken, but in his misapprehension, he attempted to both steal the money and destroy somebody of great importance to us all. Darcy foiled this scheme, rendering this man furious.

"Wickham is his name, and he has always been something of a scoundrel, but has never been violent. Until now. The... person from whom I had the story recounted hearing him utter threats to my cousin of the most alarming nature."

He stopped as another wave of exclamations swelled and ebbed in the room.

"I made some inquiries in Town yesterday and requested leave from my general until we find your daughter. We also made a stop this morning as we travelled northward from London, hence our delayed arrival."

Jane's alarm grew as the colonel told of Mr Wickham's mounting debts in Town, and of how he had been heard uttering vile threats against Darcy in his usual haunts. Then, Mr Bingley interjected, they had stopped at the inn at Islington where Mr Darcy had said he would stay the night before Lizzy disappeared. The place where Mr Darcy was last seen.

"The innkeeper told us a dreadful story," he blurted. "It was in the small hours of the morning, when the world was still asleep. There came a great noise that drew everybody from their beds, and it transpired that somebody had broken in the door to Darcy's room!"

"But how," Mary asked, "did that somebody know which room was his?" Mary always kept a cool head.

The colonel took up the tale again. "You have a clever daughter, Mrs Bennet. I asked the innkeeper the same question. He told me that a window was broken, allowing somebody access to the property, and the register was discovered and left open. It appears that Wickham, for Wickham it must have been, discovered the room number and made his way up the stairs to attack whoever was inside.

"The room was quite ruined. Whoever had broken in there must have been fuelled by rage, for everything was destroyed. The innkeeper took us to see it; it was terrible. The mirror, the bedding, all shattered and ripped, the walls damaged in places, furniture in pieces. But of Darcy, there was no sign at all. The window was open, and we found some scraps of clothing where he must have ripped his shirt as he climbed out. If he knew Wickham was coming, he was quite right to be afraid."

"And, with these words," Jane's father observed, "we are to forgive your cousin for relieving us of both our carriage and daughter. And what do you propose we do now, sir?"

"Ah, there I can help." Colonel Fitzwilliam leaned forward again. "May I see the letter from your daughter, Mr Bennet?"

Jane's father pulled the missive from a pocket and handed it over. The colonel read it slowly several times before returning it.

"This gives me hope. Llangollen is exactly where I would expect him to go, rather than Pemberley. That, I ought to explain, is Darcy's estate in Derbyshire. Wickham grew up there; he knows the area intimately. All the back roads and hiding places are an open book to him. It might have been Darcy's first thought, but he would not risk returning there. With Wickham around and seeking him,

Darcy would not be safe there. But Wickham has never been to Coed-y-Glyn, our hunting box in Wales. He knows it exists, but knows nothing of its exact location, or the land around it. Darcy is a smart man, and I am certain that is where he is headed. He knows the land, the towns, and where to hide if necessary."

"And?" Mr Bennet asked, bushy eyebrows raised.

"And thither we go, at first light, in Mr Bingley's carriage. Do you join us, sir?"

"I shall call now for my belongings to be packed!" He leapt from his chair and called for Mrs Hill.

This was too much for Jane to take in. From aching idleness to this sudden surge of action, how could she contemplate it all? And although she knew she had done nothing wrong, the guilt of having somehow caused her sister's plight only added to her agitation. If only she had convinced Lizzy to join them inside... if only she had stayed with her sister... if only they had come out of the inn a few moments earlier...

She had abandoned Elizabeth once.

She would not do it again.

"I am coming with you," Jane announced. It was not a question, but a statement. She was firm. All eyes turned to her.

"No," she continued as she rose to her feet, "I shall not be put off, not this time. I know I am more often the one to rush to the bidding of others, but now I know my mind and shall act on it. Lizzy needs me, and I need her, and I am coming. Is there room in the carriage? Else I shall ride on the rumble outside. But I will come."

"There you have it, Mrs Bennet," her father shook his head at her mother's stifled gasps. "Your eldest daughter has something of

Lizzy's spirit, after all. Well then, Jane, you had better speak to Hill as well."

After two days of pleasant weather, Elizabeth woke up to the sound of heavy rain hitting the window. Will was still asleep, or feigning such, and she took the opportunity to dress quickly and step out of the room so he, too, could rise and prepare for the day. He joined her under an overhang in the stable yard a few minutes later, his face freshly scrubbed and his hair damp from where he had tried to coax it into some sort of order. He had no shaving kit, and now sported another night's worth of beard. It somehow made him look gentler than that stern man who had first alarmed her by absconding with the carriage.

They checked on Dobbin and dodged the raindrops to return to the inn for some food to start the day.

The damp weather did little to brighten their spirits, and they fell into an argument before even leaving the inn. Will insisted upon Elizabeth riding in the cart under the tarpaulin, and she refused.

"You are a lady, and it is my obligation as a gentleman to keep you from harm." He pulled himself to his full, rather impressive, height, and crossed his arms over his chest, glaring at her. She, in turn, straightened to her full and much less impressive height, and glared right back, craning her neck to do so.

"I am not some delicate flower that can withstand neither heat nor rain, Will. The weather is wet, not cold, and I am as able to survive it as are you."

"No." His face went cold and stony. "I will not have it. You must ride under the canopy. You will take ill."

"And I will not be treated like a helpless incompetent. Coachmen and servants sit out in the rain all the time."

"You are neither a coachman nor a servant."

"And neither are you. Do we spend another night here and wait until the sun shines once more? Your Mr Wickham is unlikely to look this far from his estimation of our route."

The icy scowl turned angry. "The longer we remain in one place, the greater the danger. We must ride, and in the wrong direction, at that."

He was stubborn, this strange and proud man. Elizabeth felt a thread of pity for him, being forced into such a dire position as this. "Will..." She softened her voice and reached for his arm.

His eyes fluttered closed for a moment, and he let out a sigh. "Are you always this determined to have your own way?"

"Only when I am told what I should do for my own good."

In the end, they reached a compromise, where Elizabeth sat right beside him on the bench, holding her umbrella over both of them. They draped an extra length of the tarpaulin over their shoulders for more protection and managed to stay relatively dry. If Dobbin objected to being the only one of the party fully exposed to the rain, he said not a word in complaint.

The roads grew narrower and rougher as they travelled, and villages fewer and fewer as the terrain became more and more hilly.

It would become even worse once they found the tracks through central Wales, Will explained. At times, Dobbin slowed to a pace that a moderate walker could match with ease, and sometimes patches of mud almost brought the cart to a complete stop. They ate the last of the buns they had purchased at the inn under the canopy of the tarpaulin, and stopped only long enough for the horse to take rests when necessary.

Although they had departed the inn shortly after dawn, it was almost full night when they arrived at Abergavenny, both in low spirits and wanting nothing more than a hot meal and a quiet bed, without even the pretence of dismay at having to share a single room.

In another lifetime, Elizabeth would have loved to spend some time in the small Welsh town. It was a charming place, gifted with beautiful scenery and friendly people, but now she could not wait to leave. The pretty high street with its interesting shops, the Mediaeval priory, and the old ruined castle would have to wait for another time.

# Chapter 10
# Questions at the Inn

Jane stifled a groan as she stepped out of Mr Bingley's fine carriage. The vehicle was well sprung and the seats adequately cushioned and as comfortable as such could possibly be, but after a seemingly endless day of travel, she had little desire ever to go further than the end of the drive again. Her back ached, her legs were stiff from sitting, and her knees hurt when she walked.

Any excitement she might have felt when they began this journey had long since faded into misery. Their travels had been slower than she hoped, and their inquiries either fruitless or distressing.

They had left early in the morning after Mr Bingley and Colonel Fitzwilliam's arrival at Longbourn, their trunks minimally packed to keep the carriage light and the horses quick. With no word from the posting inn where Elizabeth had been taken, other than the regretful return of the two servants left there, the colonel announced they would go directly to the inn where Elizabeth had written her letter. He had assumed command of this operation, and the others, for lack of anything better to suggest, had tacitly agreed.

*At least,* Jane had thought, *somebody is capable of making decisions and doing something.* The colonel had ridden postern for this first part of the journey, leaving Jane inside the carriage with her father and their new neighbour. Nobody seemed inclined to conversation at this early hour, and she was grateful when they arrived at their destination some hours later.

The colonel strode into the place and requested in polite, but firm, terms to speak with the innkeeper. The man might have been awed by the colonel's flashing brass, or by the silver in his purse, or perhaps only wished to help, but he offered up what information he could whilst the travellers took a quick meal.

"Aye, I remember them, of course I do. The lady was pretty enough to catch the eye, if you'll forgive me for saying so..." His eyes flickered to Jane and his mouth narrowed in appreciation. "Kin to this lovely lady, I'll wager. Hard to forget. And the request for her to have a room alone and then get the coach on the morrow was out of the usual. But 'twas what happened next that stays in the memory."

The man gave a very definite nod and folded his arms across a thick chest.

"Do go on, sir," the colonel requested. "And perhaps another cheese pie? Thank you, my good fellow."

The innkeeper made a gesture to someone for the pie and resumed his tale.

"This is a busy tavern, being at the crossroads and all. The post comes through, and we have horses and good rooms, and ample ale. Your lady was with a rather rough-smelling man, all filthy and ragged, but he talked like a nob—like you, come to think about it—and she did not seem afraid of him. Friendly-like, rather. They had their tea and were about to set off when another gent walks up to them with a knife, trying to push the nob out the door."

Jane could not stifle a gasp, but the innkeeper paid her no heed and kept talking. He seemed to relish this audience.

"The next thing I know, the young lady grabs a tray and cracks him—the one with the knife, that is—a good blow on the head, and then fists are flying and ale is splashing everywhere, with shouting and cursing and all manner of bad behaviour, and in the middle of it all, your two fly out the door and are gone, before the other cove gets himself off the floor and out of the ruckus."

"Do you mean to say," Mr Bennet asked, "that our Lizzy started a tavern brawl? Her mother will be most put out."

Beside Jane, the colonel barked out a guffaw whilst Mr Bingley stood quite still, only his eyes blinking rapidly. Oh heavens! What must he think?

"Then your daughter, it seems," the colonel replied in a calm voice, "was quite well, as were your horses when they left. Well, we know they were here. The question now remains where, exactly, they went afterwards."

The innkeeper could offer no more information, and he was compensated from the colonel's pockets for some of the spilt ale. Neither could any of the stable hands say where the carriage went, only that it tore out of the yard faster than any driver ought to go, and disappeared around the curve before they could see which way it turned at the crossroad.

"Now we know why Miss Elizabeth did not return home as planned," Colonel Fitzwilliam stated as they reclaimed their own carriage. "And so, our search continues. Onward, friends, towards Wales."

Thus, the journey progressed. The colonel bade the coach driver to stop at every inn and toll house they came upon, there to ask whether there had been anyone passing through answering the description of Elizabeth or Mr Darcy. But none had seen a gentleman in torn clothing, or a young woman in distress, or a carriage that might have been the Bennets'.

"I do not hold much hope for anyone to have noticed the carriage," Jane's father protested after one such stop. "It is black and neither very old nor very new, and is quite unremarkable in every way, other than that it holds my Lizzy. Ask away, young man, but I do not expect you will find much joy in the answers."

Similarly, asking after Mr Wickham seemed fruitless. Who, after all, would take notice of a single man riding through on horseback, or in some sort of conveyance, when the entire business of these establishments was to cater to exactly such men. Likewise, if he had a companion with him, so did hundreds of others each day. He would have been perfectly unexceptional.

"What does he look like?" Jane asked. "Would it be of any help to describe him?"

Colonel Fitzwilliam scratched his head. "He is said to be handsome, but I never saw it. His features are, I suppose, of the sort that many women appreciate. He is just above average height, with light hair and blue eyes, exactly like so many other men in England. He is about thirty years of age, so remarkable neither for being very young nor very old, and he is likely dressed in presentable clothing suitable for a long journey..."

"Exactly like so many other men passing through these inns." Jane sighed. "Yes, I see the problem. A man, looking much like many other men, alone or in company, travelling through busy posting inns. It is the proverbial needle in the haystack."

"And my Lizzy," her father added with a sigh, "is no closer to being found."

By the time the sad party arrived at Northampton, where the Colonel proposed they spend the night, Jane was exhausted. Conversation in the carriage had been sporadic, neither lively enough to keep her interest nor sparse enough to allow her to drift into her thoughts and focused on the sole topic of how to discover and rescue Elizabeth and Mr Darcy. Few personal topics had been touched upon, and Mr Bingley and Colonel Fitzwilliam were almost as much strangers to Jane now as they had been when their journey began. It had been an uncomfortable ride in every manner of the word.

At last, the coach rattled into the hotel's courtyard. Colonel Fitzwilliam had sent a rider ahead to secure rooms and arrange for someone to care for the horses, and a stable hand and servant were both standing ready to greet them, along with a tall man in military garb.

"We are frequent guests here," the colonel explained. "I will vouch for the quality of the accommodations."

If his family hunted often in Wales, they must come this way regularly. But how odd to have a receiving party waiting. They must be good customers, indeed!

But this was no time for musing. Jane was far too anxious to move after a day confined in this small rattling cage, and they finally rolled to a stop, not a moment too soon.

They all but tumbled out of the carriage, each more eager to move than the other.

The colonel leapt out first and shook the hand of the tall soldier, and then clapped him on the shoulders in a much more familiar manner. The soldier gave Colonel Fitzwilliam a momentary grin before turning a more serious face to greet the others.

"My assistant, Major Hawarden," the colonel explained, forgoing formal introductions for the moment. "I asked him to meet us here. He might be of use."

Jane was pleased enough for the lapse of perfect propriety. She only wished to move her aching feet.

Still, she had not gone three steps when her foot began to tingle, and then exploded in a blizzard of irritated pain. She gasped and stumbled.

The colonel, who was only a step behind her, was at her side in an instant.

"Miss Bennet! What is wrong? Are you injured?"

Oh, so much ado for so inconsequential a problem. She started to laugh before another jolt of pain seared her foot. She sucked in a rush of air to keep from crying out.

"No, I am perfectly well. Just my foot seems to have gone numb, from sitting still for so long, I think. It is only pins and needles. A few minutes are all I need, and I shall be quite back to normal."

"Minutes? No, you cannot stand out here in the middle of the yard for minutes. You must be inside, on a soft chair, until the tingles end. Allow me."

"But sir!" Jane began to protest.

At her side, Mr Bingley sputtered some unintelligible syllables, before he, too, began to gush concern for Jane's plight.

"My poor Miss Bennet! Can you hop? Lean upon my arm. No, let me support you like a crutch."

"A crutch? My good fellow," the colonel protested, "we cannot have Miss Bennet hop through the courtyard like a one-legged rabbit. Unthinkable. Now..."

And in a moment, without a by-your-leave, Colonel Fitzwilliam had swept her up into his arms and carried her across the width of the courtyard and into the inn, as if she weighed no more than a light coat, her protests nothing against his insistence that she sit.

"I know it is no severe injury, but this is something with which I can help; please allow me to do so. Here," he said as he settled her on an empty chair in the front vestibule. "Sit until your foot has stopped hurting, and we shall say nothing more of it. Your good father and our friend Mr Bingley will attest that this is the best course of action."

Her father let out a resigned sigh and rolled his eyes. "Very well," he stated after a moment. "The colonel is correct. You will be fine in a minute or two. Ten if you wish for more attention. I can call for salts if you desire."

"Papa!" Jane let out an indignant exclamation, and her parent tutted in response.

But Mr Bingley just glared at the colonel, for no reason that Jane could imagine.

ELIZABETH and Will departed once more at dawn, the weather no better than the day before. They followed a level path along the River Usk through the Beacons to the town of Brecon, where they took a mid-day rest, and then began their slow journey northward. The mountains should have been beautiful, but too many long days and poor meals, and too few hours of sleep, rendered the splendour of the countryside meaningless. The rain grew harder as the hills grew steeper, and all too soon, Dobbin declared, in his own way, that they could go no further that day.

Will tried to coax him forward with their last apple, and Elizabeth too climbed off the bench to talk to the exhausted beast and lead him along, but it was clear they would make no more distance that day. There were no villages that could be seen ahead, and once again, no other traffic on this quiet lane that wound its way northward.

"Trees. All we see are trees." Will's voice was as tired as Dobbin's legs. "I am sorry, Elizabeth. You deserve better. Let us try to lead this fellow off the road and under some of these many trees. We have some food left, but it will be an unpleasant night."

The rain had lightened a bit, and the roads were hard packed enough not to be mud at this high point on their route. Elizabeth pulled her make-do canvas cape about her and walked down the road a few paces. Something caught her eye, and she called to Will.

"I think I see a path here, leading into the woods. It might be just wide enough for the cart. It will get us off the road, at least. Shall we see where it leads?"

Will did not answer, but grabbed the reins and managed to lead the weary horse in her direction.

The path led a few hundred yards into the trees where it opened up into a small clearing, at the back of which stood an old wooden shack, seemingly abandoned. A rough shelter leaned against it, the roof providing some protection from the rain, the two walls sheltering the space from the wind. It would do very well for Dobbin if they had to spend the night here, and there was even enough room for the cart if they pushed it up against the side.

The burble of running water suggested a stream very nearby, and a short walk behind the shack proved this to be so. It was not Milden Hall, but after two days of driving in the rain, it looked beautiful to Elizabeth's tired eyes.

Will knocked at the door, and then, when there was no response, pressed upon it. It swung open, revealing a single room, larger than

Elizabeth had expected, with a table, two chairs, and two cots against one wall. There was a fireplace along the side wall closest to the door, and two shuttered windows, one facing the front and the other the back of the hut. From the dust on the floor, no one had been in the place for several months.

But what caught her attention was not the little set of shelves beside the door that held some tin plates and knives and two iron pots that would fit over the fire, nor the rough trunk by the beds that, when opened, revealed some heavy blankets, but rather, the assortment of tools lying against the corner between the window and fireplace.

"It's somebody's hunting box," Will exclaimed when he followed her gaze. "Look, a small axe, a bow and some arrows, and some traps. Rabbits, probably. Nothing dangerous, thank the heavens. We shall be safe in here until Dobbin decides to walk again. Why do you not see if you can make us comfortable for the evening, whilst I see about feeding the horse. I believe we have enough hay if he cannot find suitable grazing. Ah, there is a bucket as well. I shall try to get some water from the stream."

He took the metal pail and set off to do his chores.

There was little enough to do. The rain had, by now, stopped falling, and weak sunlight slid through the cracks in the shutters. Elizabeth threw them open to allow fresh air and light into the room, dispelling some of the dampness and the scent of old dust. There was a flint and steel knife on the shelf with the implements, and a few minutes work set a little fire burning in the hearth. The wood was a bit wet and it smoked, but it burned steadily enough for now, and they could find more logs later.

Then she shook out the blankets and draped them over the backs of the chairs to air out, before further examining the hunting equipment in the corner. This was something she knew about from time misspent in the woods (according to her mother) back at Longbourn. The bow was old but still strong and flexible, and the string needed only a bit of tightening. She fingered the few arrows and tested their tips, a smile on her face.

When Will returned a while later, it was to find her sharpening one of the knives, with the bow and arrows on the table.

"Elizabeth? What are you doing?"

She turned a beaming smile towards him. "Preparing dinner, of course."

The look on his face was enough to widen her grin. He did not seem the sort of man to be often perplexed, but the expression was eloquent.

"We have a few pieces of bread left," she explained, "which we might wish to keep for breakfast. For dinner, I hope you like roasted rabbit."

# Chapter 11
# An Accomplished Lady

Darcy gaped at the young woman before him.

"Roast rabbit? Elizabeth, we have no rabbit. What can you mean?"

Her bright eyes flashed at him. "We have no rabbit *yet*. I intend to remedy that." She picked up the bow and arrow and started for the door.

"What can you mean?" Surely she was not... She could not possibly... "You do not think to shoot a rabbit! Do you?"

She turned to face him. He could not decide, in the light of the cabin, if her glance was teasing or exasperated. "I do, and I shall."

"But it takes a great deal of practise to shoot accurately with an arrow. Have you ever picked up a bow before?"

Exasperated. Her expression was most certainly exasperated.

"You may come to observe, Mr Darcy," she exhaled slowly, "but I beg you to remain absolutely still and silent. I will not have you frightening off our dinner."

Not quite knowing what he was doing, he followed her from the cabin, feeling a bit like a dog blindly following his master. She walked a way into the trees, and then, from a pocket, pulled out the ends of two of the carrots they had eaten as a sort of nuncheon. These she laid on a patch of moss on the ground, and then, to Darcy's astonishment, began to climb a tree.

She had slung the bow over one shoulder somehow, and strapped the quiver with the arrows onto her back, and made her ascent. One hand reached for a branch, one foot found a grip on the trunk, and so on, until she was quite hidden in a veil of leaves.

"Stay behind that bush there," she whispered, "and do not make a sound."

All astonishment, he could only do as she commanded.

They waited for some time in absolute silence. If Darcy had not seen Elizabeth climb into the branches with his own eyes, he would not have believed there to be anybody else near. Faint sounds tickled his ears: the distant burble of the stream, the rustle of leaves in the slight breeze, the sporadic peeps and calls of the birds, and his own breathing, which now sounded inordinately loud.

Of Elizabeth, there was no indication whatsoever.

Just when he was about to slink back through the trees to the shack, there came another sound, the scurrying of small feet through the underbrush. A nose poked through a low shrub, followed by a head, long ears, and a furry grey body. The creature approached the carrot tops, sniffed once or twice, and then—

Darcy hardly heard the arrow as it sliced through the air. There was a faint vibration, and the rabbit was dead, pierced cleanly through.

If he had been amazed at Elizabeth's agility in climbing the tree, how much more so was he at her marksmanship. This was no accident. She was a skilled archer.

He was still gaping at the dead creature when she leapt down from the branches and walked up to him.

"Dinner. I believe rabbit is being served."

"Indeed! Shall I rename thee Robin Hood for thy skill? I must beg, however, that in this instance, you do not rob from the rich."

She went to pick up her prey and pulled the arrow from its back. "I have seen the size of your purse, Will. Rich you might be in other realms, but now, you are down to a handful of coins. You are safe from me. For the time being."

She started back towards the shack and he followed.

"When does a gentleman's daughter learn to hunt rabbits?" He tried to imagine his sister hiding in a tree with a bow and arrow, and failed completely. It would be quite inconceivable.

"When one grows up in the countryside with nobody important to impress with one's fine manners and superior airs, one learns a great many things. I was always up a tree as a child, to my mother's despair, and archery is a fine activity for a lady, is it not? How difficult is it, then, to combine these two? I went out more than once with some of the village children when the rabbits were becoming a pest on my father's lands."

They had reached the shack by now, and Elizabeth left the rabbit on the ground for a minute whilst she went inside to find the knife. Then she set about beheading and skinning the creature, before chopping the meatiest parts into smaller pieces.

Soon she had the meat cooking in one of the pots about the hot fire. While it cooked, she went out again and returned a while later with a handful of what Darcy would have considered weeds. She washed them in some water from the stream and chopped them up much as she had the rabbit.

"Sorrel, yarrow," she pointed to some of her treasure, "and Jack by the Hedge. You can tell this one by the little white flowers. My efforts here will not rival what your cook at Pemberley can do, I am certain, but these greens will help render our rabbit a bit more tasty."

She added them to the pot along with a bit of water and smiled as the aroma filled the air.

"Do you assist in the kitchens at home? I had thought your father's income more than that."

Her laughter filled the small space. "We have a cook, and a good one at that, but simply because I am not required to be in the kitchens does not mean that I do not sometimes go for my own purposes. You might not wish to eat one of my pies if others are available, but neither will you starve if mine are all that is to be had. Or," she gestured to the sizzling mess in the pot, "my rabbit stew."

Another of Darcy's preconceptions burst as a bubble of soap. Everything he had been taught led him to expect certain things of an accomplished lady. She must speak French, and preferably Italian or German as well, be proficient at the pianoforte and be able to sing. She must embroider a pretty hem and paint charming landscapes, and assist in arranging the flowers in the church. And these were, all, admirable skills indeed.

But Elizabeth Bennet was quite a different sort of creature. Her accomplishments included climbing trees, killing rabbits, and preparing a meal from bits of nothing in the woods.

Whether she spoke French or sang Italian songs was nothing to the fact that, because of her, they would eat well tonight.

This—this—was an accomplishment indeed.

Perhaps it was not ill luck at all that she had been in the carriage he had appropriated. He might ride faster without her, but he would do no good arriving at the hunting lodge starved and exhausted. And speed, now that he had time to consider it, might not be in his favour. The longer he took to arrive at Coed-y-Glyn, the more likely Wickham was to believe he was heading elsewhere and would be off his guard. If, that is, Wickham was even there.

No, it was really quite fortunate that the fates had blessed him with this unusual creature named Elizabeth Bennet. Now he only had to ensure that she arrived at their destination unharmed!

JANE APPROACHED the carriage with an internal groan. Yesterday's drive had seemed eternal, and today's did not bode any easier.

They had risen early and taken a quick breakfast, all anxious to be off as soon as possible. The sun's first rays were still threading through the trees; even the birds were surely still asleep in their nests. It had been an uneasy night for Jane, the first time she had stayed in a room in an inn by herself, with no sister or mother to reassure her, and no maid to assist her, and she had slept very ill. Every noise from the courtyard, every creak of the floor in the hallways denied her the rest she so desired, and she felt more exhausted upon waking than when she had retired the night before.

She took a last, long breath of fresh air before allowing the colonel to hand her up into Mr Bingley's coach for another day of confinement and worry. Once again, she sat beside her father, with Mr Bingley and Colonel Fitzwilliam across from them. The colonel's assistant, who had nodded politely at dinner the night before and then vanished to tend to some unnamed tasks, had been sent ahead to arrange for a change of horses at the next suitable inn. He would be of no assistance in mitigating the awkwardness in the carriage. With no expectation of pleasant conversation, Jane rolled a shawl up to fashion into some sort of pillow, in the hope of sleeping the first leg of their journey away.

At once, Mr Bingley raised his voice in charitable concern.

"Are you comfortable, Miss Bennet? Would you like me to roll up my coat for you? There are blankets under the seats, if you are cold. Surely, we can pull the pillows out a bit for you."

"Let the poor girl sleep, Bingley," the colonel huffed, sending his glance momentarily skyward. "She can manage without fussing."

"Well, yes, but... It is my carriage and I feel accountable for her comfort. After all, it was also in this carriage that she injured her foot only yesterday."

"I was not injured, sir. It was only pins and needles. They lasted but a moment. I was perfectly well."

Mr Bingley frowned. "I am, nonetheless, most distressed. Perhaps if we all move, we can prevent this from occurring again. Mr Bennet, if you do not mind, we three men can sit on this side, allowing Miss Bennet the use of the entire bench."

"No, Mr Bingley, I beg you! That is entirely unnecess—"

"I say," Colonel Fitzwilliam now interjected, "I have a splendid idea. If we ask the driver to stop the coach, we can ride on the rumble, or on one of the horses to chase after Hawarden, or on the roof like the mail coach, which will give Miss Bennet the use of the entire carriage. Shall I knock?"

Jane was about to take the colonel to task for his foolish jest, but from the horrified look on Mr Bingley's face, it seemed the younger man believed the suggestion to be in earnest.

"Of course! I was a fool not to think of it. I shall alert the driver at once."

"Might I request permission to sit with the driver?" her father now asked. "I get rather ill on the rumble. Will he mind if I read?"

"Sir..." Mr Bingley looked quite alarmed. Did he not understand her father's attempt at a joke?

"Please, gentlemen!" Jane forced herself to speak over them. "I neither require nor wish any such thing. I only hoped to lean my head against the squabs for a few minutes. That is all."

"You heard the lady, Bingley," the colonel now said. He took the shawl and rolled it up before handing it back to Jane. "Madam. I have experience with such things from my days fighting on the continent. Sleep well."

Mr Bingley glared at the colonel. "I do not mind being laughed at, sir, but I would mind if I could provide my guests some comfort but did not. If I am to have faults, which I do not deny, may my weaknesses be those of concern and compassion."

To his credit, the colonel bowed his head in respect. "That is no weakness. I cannot laugh at that."

The colonel then passed Jane his outer coat as well. His manipulations had made the shawl suitable for resting against, and his coat was warm. Jane muttered her thanks to both men, but even with this momentary truce, disquiet permeated the air. She nestled her head on the makeshift pillow and tried to sleep.

As the day progressed, so did the tension between Mr Bingley and Colonel Fitzwilliam, until it was almost palpable. If only one of them had chosen to ride, rather than travelling in here all together. Had she only now met the two men, she would have believed that they did not like each other at all. But she had seen them as they arrived at Longbourn two days before, and both had seemed well pleased with the other's company. There had been a seriousness to their demeanours, to be certain, but that was due entirely to the circumstance. Otherwise, they had been polite, even friendly, speaking in animated voices about some shared acquaintance, or some happening in town, and both had been deeply concerned about the events that conspired to make Mr Darcy—the friend to one and the cousin to the other—act in such an uncharacteristic manner.

What had brought their previous easy companionship to this barely civil state? Was Mr Bingley so earnest that he could not understand the colonel's sarcastic comments? But she had seen the young man smile before; he seemed perfectly formed to laugh. But now, at every jibe and jest from the colonel, his jaw stiffened, and his eyebrows lowered.

Perhaps, Jane reckoned after a great deal of thought, it was entirely due to the unhappy purpose behind their journey. The friendly banter between the two would surely reassert itself once Mr Darcy and Elizabeth were found and seen safe and hale.

Jane tutted, not as quietly as she hoped, and tried to disguise it as a stretch.

"A penny for your thoughts, Miss Bennet?" The colonel leaned forward, resting his arms on his knees. "You appear ill at ease, and I would beg to be of service."

Mr Bingley scowled at him from the corner of his eyes.

"No, I thank you, Colonel. All is well. I am merely... pensive. I worry for my sister, that is all."

Mr Bingley shifted to face her directly. "If there is something I can do," he stressed, "you must inform me at once. Is this carriage not to your liking? Perhaps, at our next stop, I can inquire about another cushion for the seat, or different draperies for the windows if you prefer another colour."

He blinked his large brown eyes at her and gave a tentative smile, almost begging for her approval. If she did not know better, she would imagine...

Oh!

She returned his smile and watched as Mr Bingley glanced back over at Colonel Fitzwilliam with a curt, small nod. The colonel's eyes narrowed just a bit, and Mr Bingley sat back in some sort of victory. Chin high, shoulders back. For the moment, his posture shouted, he was triumphant.

Oh no.

So enrapt was she with this silent battle for supremacy that Jane scarcely noticed her father beside her. His expression was bland and his smile that of polite indifference, but his eyes sparkled with that look she knew so well, and his left eyebrow twitched, almost imperceptibly, in what Jane knew was the greatest amusement.

This was the very last thing she wished for right now. Perhaps it was her imagination at play, but despite having been lauded all her life for her beauty, Jane did not hold herself higher than any other young woman. She did not see preference where there was none, and she was not the sort to imagine every young man in love with her. But now, it seemed, there were two such eligible men, both fighting for her attention. This was terrible.

Not knowing what to do, Jane feigned a yawn and pretended to fall asleep, although she was aware of every bump and jolt of the carriage as it continued its slow progression from Heyford to their next stop, wherever that might be.

THEY SLEPT in the shack that night. The blankets had aired out whilst they ate the surprisingly tasty meal, and the cots were not as dreadful as Darcy had expected. Or, perhaps, he was so exhausted the state of the mattresses did not matter. They were warm and dry, with full bellies, and there was almost no danger of their sleep being interrupted by a madman out for his blood.

For the moment, at least, he could pretend that all was well with the world.

He was not even horrified any longer at having to change and sleep in the same room as Elizabeth. They had found their pattern: he would step outside whilst she prepared for bed, and she would turn to face the wall whilst he did likewise. It was now only slightly awkward, and he found he did not mind it quite so much.

What was becoming more awkward, however, was his constant awareness of her. He felt more than heard her gentle breath as she slept, that soft and regular change in the air that would not let him forget she was inches away. She slept quietly, but the sporadic wisp of sound as she shifted a limb or rolled over intruded on his thoughts. Even when he closed his eyes, all he saw were her bright teasing eyes and that pert nose, her expressive brows that took him to task without a word, and her determined chin, refusing to be cowed by anything.

And those lips, soft and pink, so tempting even when parched with the dry dust of the road or pinched together in a line of frustration, quite consumed him. When, in the darkest hours of the night and he allowed himself to release the strictest bonds of self-regulation that he could fashion, he even imagined himself kissing them, before he reprimanded himself for his caddish behaviour and forced his thoughts to something else.

But she kept returning to his dreams, and by morning, he had come to the realisation that he was starting to care for her. He briefly wondered if she might ever feel something similar for him.

But no, such dreams must remain hidden away in the farthest reaches of his mind, only to be let free when the moon cast its feeble light upon the earth and there were none to admonish him for his thoughts.

He was Fitzwilliam Darcy, master of Pemberley, and there were expectations. He must marry brilliantly. The second daughter of a middling squire of no great name and less importance was not a suitable candidate for the future Mrs Darcy. His brain insisted, although his heart protested.

It can never be, he reminded himself when his thoughts escaped their strict control. After all, she will want nothing more to do with you once she is returned to her family. And his heart wept a bit at the notion.

Morning came too soon. They rose, as usual, with the sun, and reversed their nightly routine. Elizabeth slipped out of bed while Darcy pretended to sleep, and then stepped outside as he rose and dressed in his rough country garb. What a fright he must look, with nearly a week's growth of beard and only the water from a basin or stream to wash in.

He began to press his thoughts towards their destination, thinking, planning, wondering.

Would Richard be at the lodge once he finally arrived? Surely somebody had heard of his disappearance. Elizabeth's letter home must have included his name. If Richard had the news, he would know where Darcy would go. And hopefully, he would have considered the reasons behind this most ill-conceived flight and would have taken some measures to protect both Darcy and the lodge from Wickham's rage-fuelled schemes.

What of the staff there? His uncle kept a small staff on the premises, but no more than absolutely necessary. The housekeeper lived there, and there must be one or two others to ensure the property was maintained. But how would they accept his unannounced arrival? Would they even know him, or let him in?

There seemed too many things that could go wrong.

It was in this pensive, somewhat maudlin mood, that he fed and watered Dobbin and harnessed him up to the cart once more to continue the slow, plodding journey northward.

Elizabeth was likewise in a quiet mood. She had no teasing words or arch comments, although neither was her disposition as gloomy as it had been the previous two days when the rain fell so heavily. Like the clearing skies, she seemed to have rid herself of some sort of burden and was pensive rather than sad. He wondered what she was thinking, but was consumed enough with his own thoughts to ask.

Dobbin was much more his old self and led them happily along the narrow lane, wending its way ever northward. They made good time and were able to spend a few of their remaining coins on some supplies and food in a bustling town that spanned the River Wye, and with their basket full of enough to feed them all day and into the morrow, and with some wood and a flint, and hay for Dobbin under the cover of the cart, they set off once more.

Elizabeth's mood grew lighter as the day progressed. She had mentioned her family in passing before, but now spoke of them more intimately.

She talked about her sister Jane, older than her by two years and by all accounts the loveliest young woman in all the neighbourhood. "She is not only beautiful, but also possessed of the kindest nature I have ever known." Elizabeth smiled as she mentioned her dearest confidante, and that smile rivalled the sun. Darcy would have driven this simple cart from Land's End to John o'Groats and back, if only Elizabeth would sit beside him and smile. "Some say her nature is too tranquil, and that she shows no real passion for anything or anyone, giving that same sweet smile wherever she goes. But those who know her understand her better. Her heart is good and her feelings run deep, even if the surface of the river appears smooth."

"And you? Are you placid like her, when times are normal?" Darcy could not help but ask the question.

Elizabeth's smile turned to laughter, bubbling and incandescent in the fresh sunshine. "I, sad to say, have never been accused of being placid! No, my feelings are too strong and my tongue too sharp to be placid. I am made for laughter more than melancholy, but I cannot pretend acceptance or ignore a slight when it is offered.

"What of you, Will?" She turned to him. "I pride myself on sketching characters, but yours perplexes me. You chafe at being thought a farmer, but do not object to eating a foraged meal from a single pot. You steal an entire carriage, but insist upon compensating the kindness offered by strangers with good coin.

You are, in turn, proud, cold, and considerate, and I cannot decide which makes up the better part of you."

"I? Proud and cold?" His voice filled with ice, and for a moment, he was indignant at her accusation. Then he reflected upon what he had just heard himself say and he laughed. Had he ever laughed at himself before? "Yes. Yes, indeed, I suppose I am. You have the measure of me, it seems. Do I often sound like that?"

She raised her eyebrows and looked sidelong at him. "Not infrequently, I am afraid."

"I see." He paused for a while. "We spoke of this the other day, but it forms a large part of who I have learned to be. I do not consider myself proud in the way of vanity, but I admit to a well-regulated satisfaction in my accomplishments and my position. I have worked hard to form myself into the sort of man I wish to be, and of that, I am proud indeed. I have maintained my father's estate and have added to its wealth and the prosperity of my tenants. I have also done my best to provide a good upbringing for my sister. Although there," he realised with slumping shoulders, "I appear to have failed. I am not proud of that."

"Young ladies of fifteen summers are seldom the wisest creatures in the world." She reached over once more and let her hand rest upon his. "You have done your best, which is more than many can say."

He answered her gentle touch with a squeeze of his own hand and released it.

Elizabeth let the silence reign for only a moment before speaking on.

"I have told you something of Jane. Tell me more of your sister. I know her sad story, but what is she like? What sort of a person is she? What are her likes and her interests?"

Darcy contemplated this for a moment, his heart touched by the question. Nobody had asked about Georgiana in such terms before. Her classmates at school, her companions, the matrons and their daughters who sought her attention in Town, all asked after her lineage, her noble relations, her wealth, and her prospects. Certainly, Wickham had cared little enough for anything other than her thirty thousand pounds. But Elizabeth wanted to know about the girl herself and not the heiress.

"She is a private creature," he said at last. "Some call her proud, but she is, in truth, extremely shy."

"Like her brother?"

"I... that is..." He fumbled for the words he wanted. "I have worked at being more comfortable in society, but it is quite against my nature. I prefer smaller gatherings of familiar people, with whom I can be... with whom I do not need to play myself as in a theatrical performance."

Her eyes caught his again. "Am I such a person?" A trace of a smile tilted her lips. Those soft, pink lips.

Now he returned her smile. "You are, indeed, Elizabeth. I have seldom felt so easy in company. Perhaps it is our... unusual circumstances. I hardly feel the need to perform for others here, on this horse-drawn cart. Without the trappings of society, I can be myself. And you are easy to talk to."

She beamed back at him. "I will accept that compliment. Thank you, Will. Now, tell me more of your sister."

He swallowed the grain of disappointment that she did not confess similar comfort with him, but obliged her, nonetheless. He loved his sister and was pleased to talk about her. "She is quiet, as I mentioned, and loves to read. I have tried to guide her reading to the more serious tomes that a lady of good breeding ought to know—the classics, philosophy, moral writings and the like—but I cannot break her of her love of Gothick novels and other sensational works."

"I can only approve of a young lady who wishes to improve her mind by extensive reading. I, too, find great enjoyment in a good novel."

"Perhaps when you meet, you may discuss your favourites..." He stopped, realising what he had implied. "Forgive me, Elizabeth. I did not mean..."

"You have no need to apologise. I understood your intent. What else does she enjoy?"

The soft tones of fine music filled his ears. "She is a fine musician and performs on the pianoforte with great skill. She took to it as a young child, listening in on my own music lessons. Soon, Mother relieved our music tutor of having to suffer through my poor scales in favour of my sister's sensitive and nimble hands. There, I see you smiling again. Do you play, Elizabeth?"

She nodded. "I do, but rather ill. Still, if the music is not too challenging, I can acquit myself without excessive embarrassment."

"I can scarcely believe that of you. I suppose you sing as well."

In response, Elizabeth produced a few bars of a popular melody. Her voice was lovely. Not, perhaps, the highly trained voice of a star of the opera stage, but a sweet and pleasing voice that would brighten any musical evening.

"Indeed you do. Do you know this one?"

He hummed a section from Mozart's Don Giovanni, and Elizabeth joined in.

*Là ci darem la mano,*
*Là mi dirai di sì,*
*Vedi, non è lontano,*
*Partiam, ben mio, da qui.*

*Vorrei, e non vorrei,*
*Mi trema un poco il cor*
*Felice, è ver, sarei,*
*Ma può burlami ancor.*

*Give me thy hand, oh fairest,*
*Whisper a gentle 'Yes',*
*Come, if for me thou carest,*
*With joy my life to bless.*

*I would, and yet I would not,*
*I dare not give assent,*
*Alas! I know I should not...*
*Too late, I may repent.*

Whether they had the proper key, he knew not, but their voices swelled together and his heart soared. Did she know the meaning of the words? Did she think anything of them? For now, he would just rejoice in the music, and in Elizabeth's sweet company. And with such impromptu musical accompaniment, they continued through the day until it was time to stop once more for a rest..

# Chapter 12
# The Duel

If Jane had hoped the morning's discomfort with respect to Mr Bingley and the colonel would ameliorate as the journey progressed, she was most disappointed. Rather than matters between the two men easing, they became, rather, even more fraught with each passing mile. Her father was of little help; he seemed to delight in this little drama, as if it were being played out entirely for his amusement, and when it seemed that matters might resolve themselves, he said something to set the two adversaries off again. It was most troublesome.

As Jane feigned first sleep, and then a marked interest in the various crops in the fields that drifted past them outside, she strove to understand what might have occasioned this strange animosity. It seemed to her, inexplicable as it might be, that the two men were both vying for her attention. That she had somehow given each to think of the other as a rival. It was quite unaccountable.

She tried, for a time, to lighten the mood with conversation, but knew not what to say. Lizzy would have known. She had that gift of speaking the right words at the right time to liven the spirits and bring a smile to each face. But this was not Jane's gift. Oh, she knew how to carry a conversation in a parlour, as every young woman of her class was expected to do, but this was no parlour. These men, both really still strangers despite their enforced proximity, would have no interest in hearing of the village or the latest *on-dits* from her aunt's card parties.

Had it been Lizzy across from her, they would have laughed and talked about the children at the village school, or what Charlotte had discovered about the Longs' new puppy, or about their aunt's latest letter.

But Mr Bingley and Colonel Fitzwilliam were not such familiar acquaintances that such topics were suitable, or of any interest, for what could the colonel care about her young cousin's attempts to write his name? And to gossip about neighbours with Mr Bingley, himself new to the neighbourhood, would be highly inappropriate.

Were this a ball, where one is expected to meet and converse with strangers, the conversation would be different still. There, they might talk about the music, or the crowd in the room, the quality of the band, or one's favourite dance. But here, crushed together in a rolling, jolting carriage, there was no music, no band, and no room to move one's feet, let alone dance.

Perhaps she could speak of a book she had read. She opened her mouth to ask if the gentlemen enjoyed poetry or histories, but the colonel was resting his head against the squabs and his eyes were closed.

It would not do to disturb him.

After a while, when he stirred, she thought to try again, but now Mr Bingley was peering at a volume, although he did not seem to be turning any pages. The two men seemed determined not to say an unnecessary word to each other. And so, Jane closed her mouth once more to contemplate her company.

In the midst of these uncomfortable ruminations, the carriage hit a rut along the road, and it jostled, sending Jane sliding against her father's side. There was no damage, no injury, and the coach driver up on the box might not even have noticed, but all four passengers gasped at the sudden jolt.

"Are you well, Miss Bennet?" Mr Bingley asked in alarm. "That was rather rough. I do hope you are not injured."

His words broke the strained silence.

"I thank you, sir. I am quite well. My father kept me from any harm."

"I have my uses," that man intoned.

But Mr Bingley continued in his expressions of remorse. "This being my carriage, I would feel quite dreadful if anything happened to cause you discomfort. This was recommended to me by my sister's husband, and until now, it has always offered me the smoothest and most comfortable passage."

"One cannot blame one's carriage for the state of the road, sir," the colonel replied.

Bingley glared at him before returning to Jane. "No, no. Of course not. But, Miss Bennet, if you are in any distress, I shall ask the driver to stop at once—"

"Please, I beg you, do not, Mr Bingley. We are seeking my sister—and your friend—and I believe time is of the essence."

The young man went an alarming pink, a colour that quite clashed with his sandy hair and light brown eyes. "Oh, dash it all, you are quite correct. How could I think... that is, I am most concerned for your sister, but also for you... that is..." He went redder still. "If you are quite well, we can continue to our next planned stop."

What was that strange glint in the colonel's eye? Why, Jane considered, he was trying not to laugh. Irksome man. She forced her accustomed smile onto her lips and agreed, before turning to stare out the window once more to contemplate the passing scenery.

It was not until they stopped to rest in the afternoon that Jane felt she was able to breathe. The colonel took himself off to find Major Hawarden in regard to some matters about their mission, and her father declared that he needed a room to rest until they were ready to continue, leaving Jane and Mr Bingley alone for the first time.

They decided to take a walk around the area of the inn, to stretch their cramped legs and breathe air that was not filled with the dust of the road. The sky was grey and heavy with cloud, but the streets of the small town were nonetheless busy, and Jane was pleased for the distraction.

Out of the confines of the carriage and the looming presence of Colonel Fitzwilliam, Mr Bingley was excellent company. The happy disposition she had glimpsed in Meryton, even through his concern for Elizabeth, came to the fore, and he proved to be charming and pleased with everything in a way that spoke of a generous nature, so in accord with her own. He humoured Jane's wish to look in every shop window they passed and bantered with her cheerfully over the wares they saw displayed. At times he agreed with her comments, and at times put forth his own thoughts, all with excellent humour.

"You cannot really like that hat," he exclaimed upon seeing one flower-encrusted bonnet set out for display. "It has far too many ruffles and frilly bits. I believe I should not know the person under it, and should spend the entire evening sneezing if ever a lady were to wear it in my presence." He rubbed his nose as if already so afflicted.

"But it is a charming colour," Jane countered, uncertain whether to tease the young man or let him be.

Mr Bingley peered at the offending item again.

"It is, I suppose, if one likes yellow. A soft yellow rose is charming enough, of course, and a small spot of bright colour can enliven a room, so my sister tells me, but this hat is very... vibrant. Although," he turned to Jane as he spoke, "with your lovely hair and blue eyes, it would look quite well. Everything would look well on you."

Jane laughed at him. "You are a flatterer, sir. I was mistaken. It is rather dreadful."

And Mr Bingley laughed with her.

"What of this one, with the feathers?" He pointed out a headpiece on the far side of the window display.

Jane bit back a laugh. "It is... it is elaborate. Perhaps a bit too much so for me."

"My sister would like it," the young man countered, "and has always told me that my tastes are lacking, but I do believe that hat looks about to take flight!"

"And cluck its way out through the door!" Jane returned with a smile.

He let out a gentle chuckle, which sound pleased Jane more than she could have imagined, and she tittered along with him. This set Mr Bingley chuckling more, and then Jane, until both were laughing so hard that passers-by stopped to stare at them.

This, thought Jane as they made their apologies and turned back towards the inn, was much more the sort of companion she preferred to the sullen men in the carriage.

THE RESPITE of sunshine was short-lived, and soon after their afternoon rest, the rain started again. Now it became cold, despite the time of year, and heavy clouds blanketed the surrounding mountains. Elizabeth tried not to shiver, but wrapped the blanket tightly around her shoulders and fought to hold the umbrella steady to keep Will as dry as possible.

"It is of no use, Elizabeth," he sighed at last. "The rain is too heavy, and the very air is wet. Keep yourself dry under the cover. I am already as wet as a drowned rat."

It was true. His handsome face did not look quite so noble or haughty now, with a heavy shade of beard and rivulets of rain plastering his hair to his forehead. He had removed his hat earlier, explaining that the rain would surely destroy it, and that it was more useful against the sun and as a disguise of sorts. His skin was pale and his knuckles, as he held the reins, were white.

Dobbin, too, was most unhappy, moving steadily onward, but at a slow and halting plod rather than a crisp trot.

"We cannot go much farther. Will there be a village ahead, do you think?" Elizabeth peered into the distance, hoping to conjure up a nice, warm inn. Something tickled the back of her throat and she coughed.

Will turned to her in alarm. "You are not taking ill, I hope! This rain is most unwelcome. I cannot have you become sick."

Elizabeth tried to smile back. "I am made of stern stuff. And even if it is a trifling cold, I shall be fine. Still..."

"We need to find shelter. I am wet through and will be of no use to anybody if I am laid low as well. Let us see what we can find."

But no village appeared through the mist, no welcome mile marker pointed to an obliging inn.

The rain grew heavier, and turned to hail.

"There, down by the river? What is that?" A misty shape wavered through the dismal rain, foreboding and dark, but possibly promising some sort of shelter.

Will nodded once and found a track, down which he directed the increasingly recalcitrant Dobbin.

The shape began to take a more definite form as they approached. This was no farmer's cottage with a bright fire, or convenient hunting shack with a fireplace, but rather, the ruins of an old and crumbling church of some sort. There were three standing walls, the remains of a window casement on the fourth, and a partial roof over one end. It was beautiful.

"It will not give us much protection, but it will shelter us somewhat." Will's eyes scanned the structure and led the horse and cart through the missing wall to that blessedly dry area at the far end. There was enough of the roof left to provide a reasonable covering for the cart and some room for Dobbin to move about if he wished. It was more, frankly, than Elizabeth had hoped for.

"This will do well." She tried to sound cheerful, but the words came out more as a sob.

"Aw, Lizzy, do not cry. We will manage quite nicely. We have food and blankets, and the rain cannot last forever." Will's eyes belied his cheerful words, and despite her every effort, Elizabeth burst into tears.

"I am sorry," she choked out. "I am not a watering pot, nor am I so miserable. These are tears born of exhaustion and not despair, but..." She squeezed her eyes closed, trying to regain control over her leaking eyes.

A tentative touch to her shoulder alerted her to Will's proximity and when she did not flinch, the touch became firmer, more sure. She leaned into it, and before she knew, he had encircled her with both arms and pulled her close, holding her against his chest.

Momentary alarm rippled through her at this unexpected intimacy, but it faded almost at once. This was Will. She could trust him.

Had she been of brighter spirits, she would have laughed at the notion. This, the man who had stolen her family's carriage and who had abducted her, who had brought her into his nightmare of certain danger, and who was now leading her through the most remote side lanes in northern Wales, was her rock in this storm. He was the one she felt she could trust completely. What delicious irony.

But he had, over the past several days, proven himself. Had he been of a less gentlemanly disposition, there had been a great many occasions for him to take advantage of her perilous state. They had been alone, out of sight of any other eyes, for long days, and had slept in the same room—no, the same bed—and not once had he given her the first cause for alarm.

Were he another man, one not so high in society and well connected, with such expectations that must be placed upon him, she could even consider herself fortunate to be in company with him, for he would make some woman a caring and considerate husband. A pang of regret now replaced her trepidation. He would, were he another man, make an excellent husband for her.

But now she must take what comfort could be found, and she welcomed his embrace and fell into it, letting her own arms wind about his back in reciprocity. They stood thus for several minutes until her eyes dried and she felt the dampness from his coat start to soak through her own rustic dress.

"You are wet..." she began.

"We are wet."

"Look there, Will. Against the wall. Is that an old hearth? It is stone and will not burn. Might we build a fire, do you think? Did we bring enough wood?"

Whether they had enough for the fire to burn through the night remained to be seen, but it was enough for now. With the flint they had purchased and some kindling, they soon had a little flame going. Another examination of the overhang proved that they were not the first to take shelter under the remains of the roof, for there was a pile of twigs and branches that some other soul had left at some point, now suitably dry to burn. Elizabeth made a note to find some similar wood before they departed for the next traveller in need of such.

The problem of their wet garb remained. Neither had any alternative, save their night clothes. But they could not stay as they were, else they would surely become ill. Will must have been thinking something similar.

"If you wish to change and dry your dress by the fire, I can go out..." His hands dropped to his sides, palms facing forward in some sort of appeal.

"No. Then you would become even more soaked, which would benefit neither of us." She took a fortifying breath. "We have been together in our night clothes before—"

"Whilst hidden under blankets in our separate beds!"

"—and there is no reason why we should not do likewise now. We have blankets to cover ourselves. There is no shame in it. If you will avert your eyes whilst I change, I can do likewise for you. Our blankets should be tolerably dry under the canopy. It only makes sense."

A slow nod signalled his agreement. "Very well. We can move the cart thus," he pulled the front to shift it to a different angle, "to make a screen. Please, change. I must look after Dobbin, anyway." His face flushed pink, which was endearing in so self-regulated a man, and Elizabeth's smile came more naturally. As he retrieved what he needed from the cart, she slipped behind it and shucked out of her wet garments and into her night rail, before throwing the blanket over her shoulders as a protective cape.

As Will did likewise a few minutes later, Elizabeth went to work laying out her clothing close to the fire, using some of the branches from the corner as a drying rack. It was not perfect, but it would do.

Dobbin seemed content in his corner, munching on hay and drinking water from the metal pail they had brought along. His large equine presence did not help to improve the smell of the place, but it did provide a bit of extra warmth, for which Elizabeth was grateful.

They ate a quiet meal of cold pies and some cheese, and huddled against the wall, waiting for their clothing to finish drying.

Will was the first to broach the question Elizabeth could not form into words.

"Where are we to sleep?"

She glanced down. The earth beneath their feet was rough stone, damp and covered with small rocks and pebbles. It would not do.

"The cart," she ventured, "will not be very comfortable, but it has room for both of us and is dry. If we spread out some of the remaining hay, it might be serviceable."

His eyes flew open. "Both of us?"

"Unless you prefer to sleep on the rocks over there. I cannot think you will get much rest, though. And the ground, even with this shelter, looks quite wet. If you must, you can take the cart and I can sleep tomorrow as we drive."

Something of his former hauteur came over him and he looked rather offended. "I cannot allow a lady to sleep—or not—on hard and wet stone whilst I rest on a mattress of sorts. It goes against my every principle."

"Then we must both sleep in the cart. I repeat my promise that I shall not compromise you, Will."

His back stiffened with alarm before his handsome face cracked into a smile. "You tease me, Miss Bennet! Very well. After all this time we have spent together, it can hardly cause any more damage."

*Damage?* Is that what she was to him? Damage?

She blinked back unexpected tears and turned away with the pretence of setting up the cart.

Of course he would consider this "damage." With his strict principles, he would feel himself honour-bound to offer her marriage. They had been alone together for several days, had slept in the same room, and now in the confines of the same narrow cart. Many a young lady had been ruined for far less. That she and he both knew that the extent of their impropriety was using each other's given name, but society would not judge their proximity kindly.

If he were to walk away, he would be able to go on with his life, this adventure commanding little more than a raised eyebrow in places, and in all likelihood, a clap on the back in others. In time, he would marry somebody eminently suitable and forget her, the "incident with that chit from Hertfordshire" nothing more than a half-remembered joke.

But she would always be tainted. Her lot would not be sly winks and nods of wordless approval, but the scorn of matrons, the derision of young men, and shunning by her contemporaries. Her name would be destroyed in society, and she would drag her family with her. Her dear Jane, her younger sisters Mary and Kitty, and even silly, flirtatious Lydia, would all be tarred by association with her, never to marry, except to those far beneath them in society, never to be accepted into the homes of their friends again.

Her mother would suffer a fit of nerves that might well carry her off, and her father... well, he would be satisfied to live out the rest of his days in the solitude of his library, never to be bothered by visitors again. But her mother and sisters... they must be thought of with compassion!

And Will, of course, would know this. If his story about his sister were true, he would be suffering the same concerns about her. Thank heavens he had interrupted Mr Wickham's vile scheme, but should the story get out, even Georgiana Darcy's reputation would be damaged.

With this in mind, Will would almost certainly offer her marriage. And she would almost certainly refuse him.

It was not that the thought of marriage to such a man was distasteful. Indeed, quite the opposite. Although they had known each other only a few short days, and despite the inauspicious manner of their meeting, Elizabeth had come to esteem the man. No, that was too cold. She more than esteemed him.

She liked him.

His rough country garb and unkempt growth of beard could not disguise the fact that he was a gentleman in every way that mattered. He was kind and considerate, had a fine and well-educated mind and a good understanding, possessed a variety of interests that she claimed as well, and above all, he treated her with respect.

When she had clambered up that tree like a hoyden and shot the rabbit, he had not turned in disgust and disparaged her unladylike behaviour, but rather, he had watched in awe and then lauded her skills. He had not snubbed her admittedly poor musical skills in favour of his sister's superior abilities, but instead had joined her in song. He listened to her, conversed with her as an intelligent person, and treated her like a lady, no matter the circumstances. This was a man she could well come to love.

And this was why she must refuse him.

He deserved better than to be leg-shackled to a country lass he had only just met, and by such dire accident. She would bring him down, for how could he move in his own circles if the chatter behind closed doors was always about his low-bred wife? Her father was a gentleman, it was true, but she could never match the manners and elegance of one born into such exalted circles and raised to be an exemplar of her sex.

This, she could come to manage. She could attempt to refine her manners and how she held a teacup. She could live with the wagging tongues and the disdainful huffs. But she could not force Will to marry somebody he did not love. She would always be an obligation rather than a passion, and he would, in time, come to resent her.

Instead, she decided, she would ask him to tell her family that she had died along the journey. Swept away by a raging torrent, perhaps, or tramped under the hooves of a thousand sheep. Her family would mourn her, of course, but they could then continue with the respect of their neighbours and her sisters could marry well. Maybe there would be a position for her at this hunting box they sought, an assistant in the kitchens, or maybe a schoolteacher in the village.

But she could never be Mrs Darcy.

The tears flowed freely again, although she could not quite understand why, and she busied herself with the cart until, at last, they ran dry.

# Chapter 13
# Confessions

What had he said? Darcy shook his head at Elizabeth's sudden change of mood. Was she crying? She had dashed off at once towards the cart, but he thought he had seen the mist of tears in her beautiful eyes. He made a move towards her to offer comfort and to apologise for whatever he had said, but then recalled his sister, just days ago.

"Leave me be, Will," Georgie had wept. "When a girl's heart is broken, she sometimes wishes for solitude, not for the presence of the man who broke it." At the time, Darcy had been alarmed that Georgiana believed him to be the cause of her distress, rather than that vile Wickham, although Georgie had corrected herself later. But now, when it seemed that he had caused Elizabeth's present unhappiness, the intent asserted itself on his brain.

He would refrain from intruding upon her misery for now, and hoped that she might condescend to confide in him at some later time.

He stretched and went to see once more to Dobbin's needs, allowing Elizabeth some privacy whilst she spread the hay into some semblance of a mattress and prepared for sleep. He stoked the fire and checked the clothing, which would hopefully be dry by morning, and arranged the smaller damp canvases around the area as best he could to guard it from any winds.

There were no more tasks to delay the inevitable. It was time to join Elizabeth in the cart. He was already in his nightshirt, so all he needed to do was crawl into the cart under the canopy and try to pretend she was not there.

But the sounds emanating from the cart were not reassuring. Elizabeth seemed to be moving and rolling over again and again, clearly not comfortable.

"Is there a problem?" he whispered through the growing darkness. "I hear you shifting. Is something amiss?"

There was a long space of silence, then the sound of her moving around again.

"The hay," she breathed at last, "is not what I had imagined. It is rough and irritating to my feet and head, where my blanket does not cover. I have tried to arrange the blanket to cover it all, but then there is not enough to cover me! If only we had thought to purchase some other lengths of cloth. I would take down the canvas canopy, but we need it to keep us dry. Oh, bother! I might be better trying to sleep on the cold and wet stones."

She sounded quite miserable. Darcy could picture her, brows drawn close, bottom lip quivering, and he wanted to do nothing as much as pull her into another comforting embrace. But that was impossible.

She shifted again, a restless sound from under the canopy. He had a thought.

"We could..." Darcy started, but then went silent.

"Yes?"

He chastised himself for his foolish notion. "No. It would never do. I cannot believe I even thought of it."

More shifting, then a frustrated short from the cart. "What is it, Will? Just say it. This is no time or place for your elevated social niceties."

She was correct. He should, at least, make the suggestion. "I was thinking... That is... We have two blankets. We could spread one atop the hay for both of us to sleep upon, and use the other to keep warm."

He expected an outraged exclamation from within, followed by a string of unladylike invectives against his scandalous idea, but instead, he was greeted with a low hum.

"It is quite shocking," she said at last. "But we are hardly models of propriety. You have shown yourself to be a gentleman. I agree."

This was done with a minimum of ado. As Darcy watched, Elizabeth laid her own blanket over the mattress, covering almost the entire length of it. The sun had long set, and only the barest glimmers of firelight flickered through the canvas cover, rendering

Elizabeth as a faint shadow against the darkness. He wondered what she looked like, clad in a long white linen shift, her hair wound into a single long braid behind her back. His imagination refused to stop there, and he scolded himself for allowing these images to infiltrate his thoughts.

He slid into the cart, keeping as far to the side as he could, and draped the end of the blanket over his shoulders. It was not the most comfortable bed he had ever slept in, but neither was it the worst. Forcing himself to pretend Elizabeth was not so very close, he fell into a light sleep as the sound of the constantly falling rain provided the lullaby.

How long he slept, he could not say. He drifted to some sort of consciousness in the middle of the night, most uncomfortable. The sky was dark, the clouds obscuring the moon., rendering the air utterly black. He had lost part of the blanket and he was shivering. Only half-awake, he rolled to his other side and was greeted with a sense of warmth. He moved towards it and was met by a warm shape, which pressed itself to him as he pressed towards it. Now he could wrap the rest of the blanket around himself and, with the shared heat from the warm shape, he drifted back into a deep and restful sleep.

When next he roused, the sun was starting to lighten the sky and by what he heard, the rain seemed to have stopped. He drifted into awareness, warm and comfortable, his arms around...

His eyes snapped open.

Elizabeth!

What was he to do? She was nestled against him, her head resting on his shoulder, and his morning affliction was making itself known. He gulped in horror. As lovely as she felt, curled up against him, this would not do. He had to extricate himself without waking her. She must never know that they had slept the night thus. She would be most alarmed.

Her breathing was still and regular; she must still be asleep. He shifted an inch or two and listened. There was no change in her breath, so he tried again. Shift, wait, listen. Shift, wait, listen. Slowly, one tiny movement at a time, he slipped out from her too-pleasant weight. It would be far too easy to grow accustomed to waking like this, her soft and pliant body nestled against him, the scent of her hair in his nose. His arms felt strangely empty now, as if something had been ripped away from him, and he longed to fill them once more with her. But no, it could not be. He rolled to the far side of the cart, for all that it was two feet away, and began to crawl out. It would be best if he were dressed before she woke.

The crack on the back of his head took him by surprise and he choked back a yelp. It was enough, however, to cause Elizabeth to roll over and gaze at him with liquid, sleepy eyes.

"My head..." he began. "The frame for the canopy. I am sorry." He rubbed the ache at the back of his head where he had banged it. "I did not intend to wake you."

Her smile almost undid him. "I have been awake for some time."

Bollocks.

"You were being so careful, I hated to render your efforts moot."

His face went cold, then hot, as if he could not decide whether to be mortified or embarrassed.

"Please accept my apologies, Elizabeth. I must have moved whilst asleep. I had no notion, no intention of importuning you. It was unconsciously done."

The smile became a laugh, light and slightly husky from sleep, and he felt it from his toes to the ends of his unruly hair. "I, too, welcomed the warmth in the middle of the night. You have done me no harm."

But she was doing him a great deal of harm, and he believed his heart would never be the same. As for the rest of him, he dared not consider that.

Instead, he slid the rest of the way out of the cart without embarrassing himself any further and stepped away from the ruins of the church to take care of his personal needs before returning to examine their clothing.

Although the fire had gone out during the night, Elizabeth's dress was quite dry, as were his clothes, with the exception of his coat, which was still slightly damp. If it did not rain, he could leave the coat stretched on some part of the cart, and use a blanket if he grew cool. He dressed quickly and then went to see to the horse, allowing Elizabeth to dress behind the screen of the cart.

They ate their scant breakfast quickly and set about restoring the shelter to how they found it. Darcy cleaned up Dobbin's area and Elizabeth went looking for suitable logs and branches to replace the firewood they had used, in preparation for the next needy traveller. Before long, they were on their way again.

The space between them on the driver's seat now seemed both far too wide and too narrow. Darcy ached to pull Elizabeth close to him once more, to feel her warmth against his side, to allow his arm to drape across her shoulders. She would fit nicely there, her bright spirit easing his soul when the troubles of the world grew too heavy. How, he wondered, would she get along with Georgiana? They might rub along very well indeed. Then his mind wandered further down the path, imagining Elizabeth at Pemberley, sitting with his sister at the pianoforte, or laughing together as they attempted a watercolour of some object no one could identify.

He would have to offer her marriage. This he knew, and he had known it from the moment they fled the inn after Wickham attacked. She would have to accept him. The damage to her name and her family would be irreparable should she not. And this broke his heart, not because marriage to this spark of light would be painful to him, but because it would be painful to her. He had a choice; he could be the cad and abandon her to the slings and arrows of society, with little detriment to himself. She had none.

She should be allowed to choose her own husband, to marry a man she loved. And that choice had just been removed from her. And he was the ultimate cause, and she would resent him forever because of it.

With this gloomy thought, he pushed away the dream of cuddling her close, and wished the bench were wider so he would not be so tempted.

He glanced over and wondered what she was thinking. She had woken with a great smile, but had grown quieter over breakfast, returning to the melancholy of the previous evening. Did she, too, realise what must happen? Was she contemplating the necessity of a life with the man who had ruined all of her hopes?

Was there a beau she had left behind in Hertfordshire? He did not believe so, for why, then, would she have gone to London to enjoy the balls and soirees she had mentioned? But there might be somebody about whom she had hopes, now all dashed.

He could not offer her the sort of life she had imagined, but he could offer her something. He was a wealthy man, with a great estate and fine home. If he emphasised her material gains in accepting him, it might lessen the blow. He gritted his teeth and swallowed. Yes. This is what he would do. He would speak rationally about their predicament and about his wealth and status, and not cause her more grief by professing an affection she could not hope to reciprocate.

The thought saddened him, but he could see no alternative, and soon was quite decided.

AT LAST, the occupants of Mr Bingley's carriage arrived at their final stop of the day, a comfortable coaching inn near Wolverhampton. Despite his much happier disposition whilst walking with her in the village earlier, Mr Bingley's mood had soured again as soon as they all climbed back into the coach, and the last leg of the journey had been as uncomfortable as the first. Not for the first time did Jane wish one of the gentlemen had chosen to ride beside the coach for a while. She quite envied the stalwart major, free to amble beside them on his own horse, quite removed from the awkwardness inside.

She had even dared such a remark, opining that had she the choice, she would enjoy a canter on horseback, better to enjoy the scenery. Mr Bingley had looked quite aghast at her words. "I would not wish to arrive at our next lodgings smelling of horse and all the more covered in dust."

The colonel had just glanced outside to where Major Hawarden's form was silhouetted against the shifting landscape and opined that he found the view from inside to be perfectly adequate.

The discomfiture, it seemed, would enjoy no abatement.

Thank heavens they had, at last, come to the end of the day's travels.

Major Hawarden had once again ridden ahead and was waiting for the carriage with a servant for the trunks and a groom for the team. Colonel Fitzwilliam leapt out at once to confer with them and see to their rooms, and after entering the establishment, the group separated almost immediately. Jane had already proposed dining quietly in her own chambers this evening, which sentiment was now echoed by her father and Mr Bingley. The colonel concurred, stating business he needed to attend to with Hawarden, and offering his apologies. But nobody seemed too put out to spend the evening alone. They had, it seemed, exhausted their desire for each other's company after the day's travel, and Jane was thankful for the reprieve from this silent duel that was playing out.

Her father kissed her goodnight and disappeared with his books, leaving Jane to do likewise. She wished for the company of the happy Mr Bingley, but what was more than appropriate in the busy streets of a market town in the brightness of the afternoon was quite unacceptable in the confines of an inn after sunset, and thus Jane retired alone to her room.

This night, she slept somewhat better than the last, being more accustomed to the noises of an inn and less concerned at having no assisting maid. Knowing her father was in the room right beside her calmed her worries as well, and she woke in the morning feeling much improved from yesterday.

They took a quick breakfast together before climbing once more into the now-dreaded carriage for another interminable day's travel. There appeared to be some unspoken détente between Mr Bingley and the colonel at breakfast, and Jane prayed it would continue once they resumed their journey.

There must be some sort of pleasant conversation to break the gloomy mood, although so many topics had been attempted and abandoned. The weather, the state of the roads, and the latest novels had all been canvassed and examined, and the men, so Jane imagined, would have little interest in London fashions and they, in turn, seemed to have reached some unspoken agreement to avoid all topics deemed unsuitable for a lady's ears.

She asked Mr Bingley about his sisters, to which he replied in short and unflattering sentences, and then she canvassed the colonel about some of the places he had seen on campaign. He graced her with a grin that made his eyes shine and spoke on for a time of Paris and Italy, as Mr Bingley's pleasant face grew stormier and his curt responses to questions sullen.

Oh dear. This was not helping. When the colonel finished his recitation and the company in the carriage lapsed once more into silence, Jane was almost relieved. Still, the silence was stifling. She must try again.

"Can you be certain, Colonel," she asked at last, "that there will be enough room for us all at your hunting lodge?"

Mr Bingley leapt to Jane's topic. "I would be very pleased to procure rooms for us all at some local establishment." He puffed out his chest. "No expense is too great for Miss...er, Miss and Mr Bennet, my new neighbours. I would be honoured to be of use."

The colonel was not to be outdone. "There is no worry about that, my good fellow. Rest assured; we shall find a bed for each of you with little difficulty."

Jane wondered at the size of the place. She had visited a hunting box with her father once whilst travelling that he had pronounced very fine, with two separate bedrooms on the ground floor, and a loft above where three or four others might sleep if they did not mind sharing the space. If that was considered comfortable, the colonel's family's lodge must be even larger still. She envisioned an entire storey above the main hall and kitchens, rather than only a loft. A grand hunting lodge, indeed!

Her father seemed to direct his thoughts along a similar line. "Are you certain the lodge is of sufficient size?" he asked at last. "We will be six once my daughter and Mr Darcy are retrieved."

No one dared correct his words to '*If* they are retrieved'.

"I shall share with Lizzy," Jane announced with determination. "We have shared a bed in the past, and I am so anxious to see her safe, I would gladly do so again." *I might beg it, even.*

"Your sisterly affection does you great credit, Miss Bennet." The colonel bowed as best he could in the confines of the moving carriage. "Be assured, you will have the choice to sleep where you will."

Once more, Mr Bingley cast a malevolent glare at his rival from the corner of his eye.

Oh dear. This was a most unpleasant journey!

*WHAT WAS he thinking?*

Elizabeth had tried to approach the new day with a brighter mood, but the further they travelled, the more Darcy seemed to sink into melancholy. He said little, responding to her questions and comments with few words, seeming sad more than angry. Could it be worry, that the closer they came to their destination, the closer he came to a possible confrontation with Mr Wickham? Surely, though, he would talk about that. They had achieved a degree of intimacy that would not allow barriers to such a conversation.

But it seemed more internal, more personal than that. She felt as if she were somehow the cause of his distress.

It must have been because of the previous night, when they had ended up asleep in each other's arms. He seemed most embarrassed, and in any other circumstance, she would have felt likewise. To sleep not only in the same room as a man not her husband was bad enough, but in the same bed, and then in such proximity that a grain of sand would not have fit between them, well, that was quite unthinkable!

But it had been cold, and he had been warm, and—she had to admit to herself—his arms felt good around her. They felt right. Perhaps she should have rolled away when first she opened her eyes, but it was too comfortable to lie like that, cosy and protected, and she had not wanted to move.

And now, she recognised, he must be scolding himself further, for with each growing intimacy, he would have less and less choice but to offer for her. And, from the look of gloom on his increasingly dear face, he did not cherish the idea.

She would have to assure him soon that she expected no such offer, and that he was free to pursue his own wishes. She would not hold him back. The smile she forced herself to wear grew heavy, and before many more miles had slipped beneath them, she had given it up entirely.

Despite the clear skies, the roads were still soft and muddy from the rains, and progress was achingly slow. When they passed through a village—something rather rare on these back lanes through the mountains—they replenished their supplies with the dwindling contents of Will's pockets. How many more days would they have to travel? Perhaps, Elizabeth thought, she could snare another rabbit or two to extend their money. If only they could find another well-supplied shack along their route.

As the hours passed, however, the skies grew leaden once more, along with Will's mood. Whatever he was pondering, he spoke not a word of it, but his shoulders sagged more with each passing mile, and his replies to Elizabeth's occasional comments shorter.

"'Tis the weather and the weight of my plight," he responded to a pointed question, before lapsing once more into heavy and brooding silence.

Still, it did not escape Elizabeth's notice that not once, during the worst of his blue devils, and despite the very real threat of both more rain and Mr Wickham, was he rude to her or impatient or cruel to Dobbin. Instead, his few unprompted remarks were concerned with her comfort and the wellbeing of their stalwart horse.

Foul mood and perilous circumstances aside, Mr Will Darcy was a good-hearted man. It made Elizabeth's own burden easier to carry.

Eventually, luck was with them when they took shelter from another sudden downpour in an old barn. This one was not abandoned, but the farmer, also biding his time under the leaky roof, was welcoming and cheerful. The man was a ruddy fellow with a deep voice and a great laugh that seemed to take the edge off Will's black mood. The farmer spoke little English, but he smiled a great deal and the bright fire in a grate and the hot fragrant broth that simmered in a pot above it needed no translation. When the man produced two more small bowls to pass over, Will's temper eased even more.

What surprised Elizabeth the most, however, was Will's passable command of the Welsh language. He paused and stumbled a bit between words, and often attempted sentences a second or third time, but the effort was clearly appreciated and the farmer grinned and laughed all the more. Between the two languages and many smiles and exaggerated gestures, the travellers were offered space in the barn to sleep for the night.

"I am not sure..." Will began. "We must move on. I wish to arrive at Coed-y-Glyn as soon as possible, and we have hours before dark."

The farmer understood that much, and gestured to the sheeting rain that poured down past the open doorway.

"We cannot travel in this, Will." Elizabeth noticed her hand was once again resting on his forearm. It seemed so natural now, this gesture of intimacy, that it was reflexive; he said nothing but covered her hand with his own. "You might tolerate the rain, but Dobbin..."

"No. Of course. I cannot expect the poor creature to slog through this. Perhaps it will ease in a while."

The farmer waved his arms again and said something that Will clearly understood, and a short conversation in Welsh ensued.

"Very well," her companion breathed at last. "I accept defeat. Another night it is, and this place is as comfortable as any we shall hope to find."

And the deal was done, with great expressions of gratitude and more well-meaning smiles and exclamations.

They continued their journey the following morning under somewhat brighter skies and with lighter moods. The roads were still muddy and progress slow, but the small bag of food the farmer had given them made the journey less onerous and they travelled with little complaint for some hours.

"How much further is it to your cousin's hunting lodge?" Elizabeth asked Will as they took a mid-day stop to allow Dobbin to rest. They had found a log by a meandering stream on which to sit and ate some brown bread and hard cheese as the horse drank his fill from the clear water. "We have been three days on these roads, and have seen hardly another soul. I am beginning to doubt that this mythic lodge even exists. Is it, perhaps, in the land of the fairies, to be discovered only at midnight on a single day of the year?"

"And guarded by a fierce red dragon, perhaps?" Will's laugh was a welcome change from his sombre mood of the morning. "Fear not, milady, for I shall slay the dragon for thee. In truth, Elizabeth, I had hoped to be there by now. The rains have made the journey a great deal slower than I expected, and I had forgotten how steep the mountain paths could be. But these are parts I have seen before. If we make good time, tonight we sleep in a village called Llandrillo, about ten miles from our goal, and tomorrow we shall achieve lands surrounding the lodge."

He did not look relieved, and she inquired about this.

"I confess, I am concerned. I must consider our approach carefully. If Wickham guesses our intention, and I feel certain he must, he will have the place watched. He knows the lodge exists, and I now consider it would take no great effort to discover its exact location. A joking question at a tavern, or a coin in some footman's hand, will give him everything he needs. All the roads leading to Coed-y-Glyn, I am certain, will be under some sort of surveillance by some men in thrall to his charm and his purse. My purse, rather, since he must surely have stolen everything of mine he found." He gave a great sigh as he began to pack the rest of the bread back into the basket.

"Then all of this, this long and miserable trip, has been for nought!" Elizabeth cried.

"No, not at all! I had considered this. Listen: all the roads will surely be watched, but I know the area well. There are ways into the park that do not rely on the roads. If we do not pass through the village, but come around from the woods at the back, there are tracks. I shall explain as we come closer, when you can see what I mean. But trust me, please."

He peered into her eyes, and she could not refuse him.

Why were his eyes so appealing? What was it in his countenance that allayed all her doubts? She would not have taken her own father's assurance so readily, but such was Will's beseeching expression and calm manner that she found herself accepting his every word.

"Very well. But what of this village where we hope to sleep tonight? Thlan..." she tripped over the unknown name, the foreign sounds fitting ill on her tongue.

"Llandrillo. Let me teach you how it is said."

They spent a few more minutes on their fallen log, watching the stream bubble past them, as Elizabeth attempted, with uncertain success, to pronounce a sound she had, until listening to the farmer the previous afternoon, never before heard.

The short lesson further brightened both of their moods, and when they harnessed Dobbin back to the cart and started off again a short time later, it was with smiles that did not seem forced.

They would have to have their discussion soon, but after yesterday's gloom and Will's fragile mood, Elizabeth was content to leave it for the time being and enjoy the cheerful afternoon's travels through the beautiful hills and mountains. But all the while, some part of her was painfully aware that this strange episode of unexpected companionship would soon come to a sad and bitter end.

# Chapter 14
# Nearing the Target

The air in Mr Bingley's carriage was, if anything, growing tenser by the minute. Jane had never been so uncomfortable in society in all her life. Every time Colonel Fitzwilliam paid her attention or offered to assist her with any matter, large or small, Mr Bingley became agitated and surly, and strove to outdo the colonel.

If the colonel complimented Jane's frock, Mr Bingley showered praise upon her shoes. If the colonel offered a hand over a muddy patch or an uneven bit of path, Mr Bingley offered to carry her across it.

What had, at first, seemed to be gallantries borne of good breeding and excellent manners, had become something of a competition. The colonel could not have missed Mr Bingley's jealousy—for jealousy it must surely be—and was playing to his opposition, whilst Mr Bingley seemed oblivious to the amusement he was engendering and proceeded to act the green-eyed lover, with or without cause.

All the while, her father sat by, watching with more than his usual sardonic expression, seeming most highly entertained. He said not a word, other than what was required, and kept his nose in one of the several books he had brought on the journey, but Jane knew that he saw all and was as much amused as she, herself, was not.

It was vexatious.

As much as her younger sisters rattled on about the romance of being fought over by two handsome and eligible men, the reality was quite different to what was set forth in novels. There was no heady rush of excitement, no thrill at being so admired. It was uncomfortable, awkward, and put plainly, most unpleasant.

For they were both, when properly behaved, fine gentlemen, so different from one another as to make a judgement all but impossible. How could one possibly set Mr Bingley's sweet and good-natured charm against the colonel's sophisticated confidence? It was like trying to decide whether one preferred fresh strawberries or a beautiful painting. They were not comparable.

Further, Jane liked them both, but wished to give encouragement to neither. They were both new acquaintances and they were not pushed together in the best of circumstances; it was far too soon to really take a measure of each man's character. Nor did she wish to respond to the colonel's elegant gestures or assuage Mr Bingley's jealousy, for what would bring pleasure to one must surely bring pain to the other.

Oh, how troublesome this was. She wished, for a moment, to be as plain as their friend Charlotte or as insipid as her sister Kitty, so as to occasion no desire on the part of either man to engage her attention.

Consequently, she gnawed at her bottom lip and stared out the window, occasionally asking meaningless questions about types of wheat and breeds of sheep, troubled all the while.

They were, at this point, almost at their destination. After spending the previous night at a fine coaching inn in Wolverhampton, they now were approaching the town of Oswestry. There, Colonel Fitzwilliam informed them, they must stay an extra night, for he had business to attend to with the local colonel, which was the condition of him being permitted to take the time to search for his cousin. They would complete their journey the following morning, a full week after Elizabeth had disappeared.

"Our final journey should not require more than a morning's drive," the colonel had offered. "I would prefer to get there sooner still, as would you all, but needs must. The local militia might be of assistance to us, and arrangements must be made. I shall also send a message to the staff at Coed-y-Glyn, informing them of our arrival."

Jane hoped that these staff, whom she imagined to be an older lady and her daughter who lived in the village and who dusted the house once a week, would be able to find her a bed in some area of the lodge separate from the main room where the men would most likely sleep. She voiced her concerns to the colonel, who smiled and assured her that she would have some privacy. Mr Bingley, in turn, opined once again that should he ever purchase a hunting lodge, it would have at least three guest bedrooms for his sisters' friends, but that Netherfield, which he had just now let in Hertfordshire, had good enough hunting that he need not look elsewhere for his manly entertainments. To this, the colonel gave an enigmatic grin and said nothing, and that same tense silence reasserted its reign.

It seemed hours later when the carriage at last stopped at the inn they were seeking and the four passengers alit, spilling into the courtyard to gulp in the early evening air. The day's rain had ceased for the time being, and Jane was thankful to take a minute to stand outside whilst the colonel went to speak to the proprietor. They were expected once more, and within minutes, the inn's menservants were busy carrying up their trunks, allowing the coachman to walk the team to the stables and carriage house.

"May I command a private dining room and order some tea, Miss Bennet?" Colonel Fitzwilliam strolled back towards them, all solicitude and sincerity. He seemed, once more, a master in control of his demesne. "This inn makes a very nice lemon tart, if such is to your tastes."

"Or, perhaps, I can request a meal sent to your room," Mr Bingley blurted. He thrust out his arm to allow Jane to lean upon it as they walked the few feet to the main doors to the establishment. Still stiff and aching from the long and jolting journey, Jane stumbled and let her weight settle upon his offered hand for a moment, which brought a triumphant smile to his lips.

"I think, rather," she mused, "that I would like to take a short stroll. I am not so great a walker as Lizzy, who loves being out in the sunshine, but I am also accustomed to walking into Meryton several times a week. It is only a mile's distance, but these long days of travel have reminded me how much I rely on that exercise. And this seems a rather pretty town. Papa," she turned to her father, grinning his amusement beside them, "have you any objections?"

Once more, Colonel Fitzwilliam puffed out his chest, a knight gallant come to rescue the damsel. "I can vouch for the safety of this town, sir," he declared, "and would be most honoured to accompany Miss Bennet on her wanders. I can show her the little church, which is most worth a visit, and some of the nicer shops, should she wish to look into any tomorrow."

"A walk sounds the very thing!" Mr Bingley interjected. "With both of us at her side, Miss Bennet will be perfectly safe. If you wish to take my arm again, Miss Bennet, I will provide my strength should you tire."

Her father gazed at them all over the tops of his spectacles. "Yes, yes, off with you all. Call by my room when you return for dinner. Off you go." He turned and entered the inn, leaving Jane and the two men at the door in the courtyard.

She accepted Mr Bingley's offered arm and they set off. The colonel did not seem at all put out by his rival's transitory victory, but spoke a bit about the town and gave something of the history of the church of St. Oswald, which had been on the spot, in some form or another, for nigh on a thousand years.

"The church was damaged during the Civil Wars," he explained as they walked around the building, "and was rebuilt in the 1670s. It has some fine windows inside. I recommend a visit tomorrow to view them whilst I am at my business."

"Good afternoon, Colonel Fitzwilliam." A voice sounded from a doorway.

Jane looked up to see the parson, who had noticed them and who clearly knew the colonel by name. Introductions were made and the proposed outing mentioned. The parson beamed. "Friends of the colonel, you say? Charming. Delightful. Yes, indeed, do come tomorrow, Miss Bennet and Mr Bingley. Lovely windows, lovely. I shall expect your visit."

This familiar welcome was repeated as they walked along the high street, with townsfolk calling out their greetings and inquiring after his health, to which he responded with his accustomed good-natured friendliness and regards to the other's kinfolk.

The more the colonel grinned, the more Mr Bingley grimaced. The momentary camaraderie they had enjoyed when first they set out had evaporated. By the time they returned to the inn to wash and rest before dinner, the younger man was in a rather foul mood, quite unlike the happy creature Jane had known on their stroll the previous day. He excused himself the moment they entered the building and stomped off to his room, leaving Jane and the colonel in the small vestibule by the stairs.

"Oh dear. I fear I have gone a bit too far." The colonel's words were contrite, but his eyes sparkled, and Jane wondered what, exactly, he meant by that, what his playful expression suggested.

He seemed almost gleeful, and yet his words intimated regret. It made little sense. But she, too, was tired and eager for a rest before dinner, and could not exert herself adequately to think about it at the moment. She mumbled something inarticulate, excused herself and made for the room the innkeeper now offered to show her.

They met for dinner half an hour later. For the first time, Major Hawarden joined them, and Jane was able to get a sense of the man. He was tall, about thirty, and with a serious manner and few unnecessary words. His presence, however, seemed to have a salutary effect on the small party of travellers.

Colonel Fitzwilliam seemed a different person now. He refrained from his excessive attentions to Jane and his gentle provocation, and Mr Bingley seemed, if not entirely content, then in better spirits than earlier. It must, Jane considered, have been as much the exhaustion of the journey as anything else; in the little time they had spent together, their new neighbour seemed naturally of a cheerful disposition and uninclined to excesses of unhappy emotions. Yes, it must be the tedium of travel. And yet... something nagged her, and she began to put some thoughts together, which she dared not contemplate too much at the moment.

The food that was set before them was excellent, which Jane's father remarked upon, for it was more common than not to manage with poor quality meals whilst travelling.

"They know me and my family here," was all the colonel replied, "and almost certainly put some effort into the meal."

Not for the first time did Jane wonder just what sort of position the Fitzwilliam family had, that an inn some twenty miles from their hunting lodge would cook a special meal for him. It seemed impolite to ask, but in time, perhaps, she would learn the answer.

Mr Bennet did have a serious question, which he asked as they were taking their tea after the fine meal was cleared away. The brew was hot and fragrant, unlike the watery concoction Jane had expected, and the lemon tarts were, as promised, quite fine. She was contemplating a second of these when her father raised his concerns.

"I understand that this man who is chasing your friend might be in the vicinity."

The colonel nodded. "Wickham. Yes, that is true. I fear he is close. Too close."

"Are we not, then, putting ourselves into some danger in approaching the area?"

Mr Bingley leaned forward, forearms resting upon the table, eyes as large as the saucers before them. "I must protest this plan, then. I would not have Miss Bennet placed in any peril." Across from him, Jane's father concurred with a single, slow nod.

How vexing to be spoken about as if she were an ornament on a wall, or not even present. Jane raised her voice. "Do not forget, gentlemen, that I insisted upon joining you. Lizzy is my sister and I would do anything to help. She will want me to be there, and I will not be put off."

"But Miss Bennet..." Mr Bingley protested. "Surely you do not mean it. Can you not remain here? I am certain there is a respectable lady in the area who would offer you accommodation until we return with your sister."

She levelled a glare at him from beneath lowered lids.

"Miss Bennet has other ideas," the colonel opined. Mr Bingley swallowed.

"Well, there you have it, young man," her father quipped. "My daughter is not to be gainsaid. But are you certain, Jane? This might not be entirely safe."

Now the colonel cleared his voice and spoke on. "Major Hawarden and I have been putting some thought into this. I believe we can achieve the lodge with minimal danger. Wickham will be expecting Darcy, and if he has some brains in his head, me as well. But he will not be expecting Mr Bingley's carriage, and certainly not a country squire and his daughter inside it. I had considered riding beside the coachman, but now I have a better idea. I shall procure some livery from an acquaintance in the neighbourhood and shall ride on the rumble like a servant. No one will imagine it is I, and when we pass through the village, the three of you can alight and all will see that I am not there. When I speak to the colonel of the local militia tomorrow, I shall request a handful of good men who, along with Hawarden, will dress as outriders beside us for the final approach. We will be well protected. Wickham is a coward at heart, and will not come near a guarded carriage in broad daylight, especially if he has no reason to believe you involved in this matter. If you are asked, you are my guests, whom I invited some months ago."

"And if he recognises you?" Mr Bingley asked.

"Then, if he has any wits about him, he will flee for his life. My cousin Darcy is a peaceful man who wishes to see justice done at the end of the pen. I am a military man. My sword takes over where the pen leaves off."

There was little to say in contradiction to this statement, and the scheme was agreed to by all, after which they soon retired for the night.

IT WAS by the last rays of the setting sun that Darcy finally drove the cart into the stable yard he sought in Llandrillo. They were only ten miles by road from their destination, but he did not wish to approach the lodge by night. The paths they must take were tricky and uneven, and it was long enough since he had taken them that he did not wish to submit Elizabeth to the vagaries of his recollection in the pitch of night.

Furthermore, those were not paths for a horse and cart, no matter how small or agile, and he must stable Dobbin somewhere. He knew the people here; they would take good care of the beast. It was also a town where his name was known, if not his face. If necessary, he would be able to procure supplies with an appeal to present the bill to the Fitzwilliam family's hunting lodge. Still, he fingered the few remaining coins in his pocket and hoped he had enough, so he would not need to mention his name. The fewer people who knew he was here, the better.

He went first to the stables to arrange matters with regard to the horse and wagon, and then he and Elizabeth stowed their few supplies in their bags and headed for the inn. They would be brother and sister here, his final coins paying for the two rooms and a bit of food for the next morning.

But he had not walked more than two feet into the establishment when some voices from the public caught his attention. These were English voices, not Welsh as he had expected, and what he heard sent bolts of alarm through him.

"...watching all the roads. 'E said we'll get more if we prove 'e's dead. The bugger wants 'is head, believe it!"

Ice encased him, and his feet turned to lead. Beside him, Elizabeth stopped perfectly still, not even breathing, as the next man asked a question.

"And the girl? What of her?"

"That one, we bring to 'is nibs, for 'is amusement! That's what 'e said. Can't think but that 'e'll off 'er after, but that's 'is business, not ours."

"And you know what he looks like? That one will want the right man."

"Never saw 'im. But they all look the same, don't they? We'll hear 'im before we see 'im, more'n likely. Them toffs with their fancy talk, heh? Oy, barkeep, another beer!"

Something brushed his hand and he jerked back in alarm. He almost sagged in relief when he saw it was only Elizabeth, reaching out in concern.

"We must leave now..." he began, but at that moment a matron, likely the innkeeper's wife, entered the space from a side door and asked if they needed a room.

Darcy opened his mouth to speak again, then froze. Just as he had been drawn to the uncultured English words in the tavern, so those men would likely hear his polished tones, exactly the ones they were seeking. It would spell his doom as surely as walking up to them with a noose around his neck and stating his name. And so, he did the only thing he could think of.

He replied to the lady in Welsh.

He did not speak the language with any sort of fluency, having learned bits here and there from some of the staff at Coed-y-Glyn and the surrounding areas on his tramps with his cousin. The short conversation he had endured with the Welsh farmer in the barn had all but exhausted his meagre knowledge of the language. But it was enough, now, to conduct the business he needed with this woman, and he just prayed that she did not switch to English. Could he put on a convincing enough accent to avoid the attention of Wickham's stooges? He drew a deep breath and hoped beyond hope.

For once, fortune was on his side, and he managed to request some bread and cheese without tripping over his tongue. "*Gawn ni fara a chaws os gwelwch yn dda.*"

"Will you not stay the night? Or stay to eat?" the proprietress asked in Welsh.

He released his tense breath. Elizabeth stood beside him, jaw tight. Heaven forbid the woman tried to speak to Elizabeth.

"No, *diolch*, we have some distance to travel still tonight. We cannot linger."

This brief conversation, he was sure, would fade from her memory almost at once, more so than had they entered and then left at once. Two wandering strangers looking for a bit of food was nothing unusual. She would almost certainly not mention it at all.

Still, they had to flee, and soon.

The woman returned with a package in a few moments, in exchange for which Darcy handed her the appropriate amount of coin, and then they were out once more in the night air.

"What do we do now?" Elizabeth whispered, although they were far from the men's earshot. "I hardly believed it until I heard them speak. I know we saw Mr Wickham at the inn that first day, but I almost wished to think it some sort of game. But it most assuredly is not, is it?"

He grabbed her hand. "No. It is no game. Here, this lane leads from the town to the woods. Once we are among the trees, we will be safer. It is a shorter distance than by the lanes, but it is not an easy walk. I believe some of the hills have shallow depressions, not quite caves, but somewhere that will provide shelter of sorts. It will not be a comfortable night, I am afraid."

He walked quickly as he spoke and was gratified that she was able to match his long stride without complaint.

"An uncomfortable night with you is far preferable to anything those men could promise." Her voice was grim.

They walked for about an hour, at first skirting the line of trees that stood near the town, then plunging into them. The land rose on either side, foretelling of the mountains that rose to the west, the little stream they followed leading them on a somewhat level path through the woods, but one strewn with rocks and tree roots that made the route challenging. There was almost no light left now, and even if he had a torch or lamp, Darcy would not dare to use it. The moon was a sliver in the sky and provided no illumination through the trees. They would have to stop soon.

There! He knew these paths. There was the tree he and Richard had marked as youths, the unusual shape calling to mind the prow of a ship. If memory served, it was just through there, and over that low rise...

They found it at last, more a fold in the side of a hill than anything that could be called a cave, but it would have to do. They were protected from the back and sides, and the clump of trees through which they had to slither provided some barrier from the winds to the front. More importantly, unless one knew where to look, they were safe from casual eyes.

Elizabeth spoke before he could think of what to say.

"It will do. Here is a patch of moss that is almost soft, right against the hillside, for us to sleep on. It is good fortune, Will. We have our blankets, and it is not raining." He could not see her expression, but she sounded resolute. "We will be well."

What a remarkable young woman she was. Once more, she met adversity with a determination of spirit and calm sense. She was a lady, gently born and accustomed to the finer things, but here she was, having traipsed through rough woods after dark and looking at a bed of rock under the cold night sky not with wails and protestations, but with acceptance and the intention to make the best of it. "We will be well."

Darcy pulled the blanket from his pack and arranged it on the moss and against the rocky wall before he and Elizabeth sank to the ground. She was correct. The moss made it, if not comfortable, at least tolerable. Then he helped her arrange her own blanket across them to help ward off the chill. His face brushed hers as he did so, her skin soft under his growing whiskers, and he hoped he hadn't scratched her. Her response, however, was not one of complaint, but a soft sigh as she nestled closer to him and laid her head on his shoulder. She ought to hate him, he mused, but she clearly did not, and he thanked the heavens for that small mercy. He extended an arm to wrap about her shoulders, and with the blankets around them, out of the wind and pressed side to side, they were tolerably warm.

"Are you comfortable?" He hardly heard his own voice in the deepening darkness. He dared not speak louder, loath to disturb the silence of the woods. A movement on his shoulder was her reply, yes. There was no need for words for a moment, between these two desperate souls hoping to keep the chaos at bay for one last night.

Darcy tried to imagine his friend Bingley's sisters in such a situation, miles from home, out in the forest with no real shelter, and sleeping in the same clothing they had worn for a week. No! He could not picture it at all. Even a straw-filled mattress under a rough wooden roof would be too far below them to contemplate. His admiration for Elizabeth grew, and he realised that his goal now was not to convince her to marry him—for this she must—but to somehow learn to love him. The love of such a strong lady would be a prize well worth winning.

He felt her shift against him to make herself more comfortable, if such was possible, and he did likewise. But before they slept, he must speak.

"Elizabeth..." His quiet voice sounded strange to his ears.

"Yes, Will..." Was that resignation in her voice? She must know what he had to say. Should he refrain from his offer? But that would not do. He had an obligation.

How was he to begin? What sort of speech ought he to make? This was hardly how he had envisioned this momentous event in his life, when he offered himself and his future to the lady he hoped to make his wife. More pragmatic than romantic, he nonetheless had imagined a suitable scene for such a proposal. Perhaps in a manicured garden by silvery moonlight, as the orchestra played for the dance in the ballroom, or in the shade of a beautiful bower near the manor house. Or in the lady's family's parlour, having requested permission to speak to her alone, the event to be celebrated immediately thereafter with sherry and sweets.

Nor was she the lady he had imagined himself proposing to. She was not the daughter of a baron or earl that he had imagined, not some elegant lady one step removed from the nobility as was he, but rather, the second daughter of a minor landholder of no consequence and little wealth, who climbed trees and slept on the ground with no complaints.

With every preconception denied to him, he decided to forgo protestations of passion or poetic words and speak plainly. She would, he hoped, appreciate this.

He took a deep breath. "You must be aware that after all this time we have spent alone, we will be expected to marry."

Silence. Then a small noise that sounded like "*yes*."

Was this encouragement? It was not enthusiastic, but neither had she had not told him to stop speaking. He decided to press on.

"I would be most pleased if you would do me the honour of becoming my wife."

There. He had said it. What should he expect now? A rush of gratitude? A sensible discussion of terms?

It certainly was not the quiet word that issued from Elizabeth's lips.

"No."

FOR THE first time in nearly a week, Jane did not approach the day with that same leaden sense of dread. They were to remain in Oswestry for the day; she did not need to fold herself into the carriage and face a day of cramped discomfort and the increasing animosity between Mr Bingley and Colonel Fitzwilliam. She could take her breakfast at leisure, return to the church to enjoy the windows, and wander through some of the interesting shops they had walked past the previous evening. The skies were heavy, but there was no rain yet, and her umbrella would serve well if it grew wet. This was no holiday, but the thought of buying something for her mother and younger sisters felt almost normal and it lightened her spirits somewhat.

She dressed in suitable attire for such a day's activity and descended the stairs to the private parlour where they had dined the night before, there to break her fast. Her father, Major Hawarden, and Colonel Fitzwilliam were already present, heads close together over what looked like a detailed map, their empty teacups suggesting that they had been discussing something for a while.

"Jane, my dear," her father greeted her. "I thought we would be quite out of sorts not to spend another day in Mr Bingley's fine carriage, and thus I have arranged for the driver to lead us in circles around the town for six or seven hours, before returning us here to the inn. Sip your tea quickly, my dear, for time is a-wasting."

She shook her head at his yarn and kissed his cheek.

"We had best call him inside, then, Papa, for I have other thoughts. There is a milliner I wish to visit, and the bookshop had an interesting display in the window."

"You make your own plans, my dear. I have some business to attend to with the colonel here. If he is asking his fellow officer for the loan of some men, I must accompany him, for Elizabeth is my daughter, and I would know the people charged with retrieving her."

"Perhaps your friend Bingley will keep you company, Miss Bennet." Colonel Fitzwilliam gestured to the teapot, and at Jane's nod, poured her a cup. "Sugar? Toast? Some eggs?" He handed her a plate of food. "I was up early, and spoke to the parson's wife, who has offered her company for the day, whilst your excellent father and I are at our business. She and Mr Bingley will, I am certain, keep you entertained and safe whilst you explore this town."

The thoughts that had teased the edges of Jane's mind last night surfaced again. What was the colonel about, first vying with Mr

Bingley for her approbation, and now all but thrusting her into that other gentleman's arms for the day? What had he been playing at? More ideas tumbled unordered through her brain until she began to think she had some small grasp of things.

How odd. How decidedly odd!

Nevertheless, thus it was arranged.

Jane was not entirely certain how she felt. It would be a great relief not to have this peculiar silent duel being fought between the two men, but instead of spending the day with her father, or alone with the company of one of the inn's maids, she was to pass the time with a stranger and one of the men who was puzzling her so.

She allowed her thoughts to turn to Mr Bingley. She had been intrigued by him from the first, with his understanding eyes and eager willingness to help. Furthermore, she could not deny that he was handsome, as every rich young man should be if he can at all help it. His mood had soured when he thought the colonel was seeking Jane's affections over his own, but he had been nothing but solicitous and polite to both her and her father. And she had enjoyed the short time they had spent together in Wolverhampton, laughing over those dreadful hats. Perhaps a day in his company, without the unhappy influence of the colonel, would show her more of the man he was in ordinary circumstances.

Thus, she smiled and said it would be lovely.

And she hoped with all her heart that it would, indeed, be so.

# Chapter 15
# A Fraught Discussion

"No?" Darcy shook his head, trying to make sense of what Elizabeth had just said. He had offered her marriage, a secure future, excellent connections for herself and her family. "You are refusing me?"

He felt her shift next to him in the darkness, and in a moment he felt her head come to rest on his shoulder. "I am not rejecting you. But I am not accepting you." He was about to protest that these were the same, but she hurried on. "I like you. I like you a great deal. But a marriage, in my world, at least, should arise from love and not obligation. I have not been raised with the expectation of selling myself to the highest bidder.

"My mother, at one time, opined how fine it would be if one of us were to marry our cousin, Mr Collins. He," she explained, "is the man who will inherit Longbourn after our father passes on. We have never met him, and I have no reason to suppose him a bad sort of a man, but the very thought of it was abhorrent to me. To marry without love—that is the worst sort of torture."

A small piece of his heart broke at these words. She did not love him. He had no reason to imagine that she did, but he had hoped beyond reason that there might be some affection in her heart. But regardless of her feelings, other issues still loomed large.

"I am afraid we have no choice. Your name will be ruined. Your reputation, and that of your sisters, will be destroyed. None of them will be able to marry well if we do not wed. I could not live with myself if I knew I had forever shattered their hopes. And when your cousin does inherit your estate, what then? Where will you go, if you have not wealthy husbands?" The idea of five unmarried women, trying to survive on scraps and handouts, chilled him more than the cold rock at his back.

The pressure of her head on his shoulder shifted and she nestled into him, a strangely intimate gesture from somebody refusing his offer of marriage.

"I have considered this," she whispered at last, her voice scarcely a breath in the darkness. "We must say... you must say that I have died. You can tell them that Mr Wickham caused my death, if you wish. It will mark him more of a villain, and me a martyr. My sisters, then, will be sought after *because* of their association with me rather than reviled. There will be no stain on them."

"Elizabeth! You cannot be serious. What will you do?"

"I had hoped," she breathed, "to find a position at the hunting lodge. I can cook, or I can teach the village children their alphabets and how to play the pianoforte very ill. I can take a new name and nobody need know I am still alive." She gave a sniffle. "I..."

Oh heavens! She was crying. He was terrible at consoling women when they cried. His sister had told him so many times. He shifted inside the cocoon of his blanket, and raised his arm a bit, so Elizabeth could move away if she wished. Instead, she nestled in even closer to his side and when his arm pulled her in further still, she buried her face against his neck.

"Do not cry, Lizzy. Would it be so very terrible, being married to me?"

If anything, she started to cry even harder. Without words to soothe her, he just held her close and let her weep out her tears until the sobs abated and she could speak again.

"No, not so terrible, Will," she said at last, the words punctuated by the last of her sobs. "Not terrible at all. But all my dreams were for something so very different. I cannot live as nothing but a duty to be fulfilled. I wish to be loved."

What was he to do? Was this the time to confess his growing feelings for her? To make such a declaration would seem ingenuous, especially in light of their most unusual situation and the very short duration of their acquaintance. But neither could he leave her thinking there was no affection on his part.

"I feel no pain in making my offer, Elizabeth, no unwelcome obligation. It is necessary, yes, but that does not make it onerous. I have come to like you a great deal, and will do everything in my power to make you happy."

"Will, I..." She fell silent and just lay against him for a while.

"Hush. I will not force you to do anything you do not wish. Just know that I... I have come to care for you."

*I love you,* he wanted to say, but the words would not come. They would only send her away.

In answer to his gesture, she pressed herself closer to him still and lay against his chest until her breathing suggested she had drifted into sleep. But Darcy stayed awake for a very long time, half-reclined against the rocky walls of this not-quite-cave, wondering how Elizabeth could reject him but still be comfortable enough with him that she sought his presence and touch this much.

JANE AND her companions rose early in the morning and enjoyed a good breakfast before starting on the final leg of the journey. It was about twenty miles to their destination, so the colonel told them, less than half of their accustomed daily distance. With fortune, and a change of horses at Llangollen, they would arrive long before noon.

The colonel had somehow procured a set of livery, which he wore with a swagger that belied his putative status as a servant. But Jane had to admit that if one were looking for a wealthy military officer, the green-garbed man in the white wig, clinging to the back of the carriage, would draw no attention. Beside Major Hawarden, two more large men on larger horses now rode alongside the carriage, and there was little doubt that the pistols they carried were ready to fire. Contrarily, their ominous presence led Jane to feel less, rather than more, safe, but she had to trust the colonel's best judgement, and tried to ignore the import of their armed guard.

As arranged, they stopped in the market town close to Coed-y-Glyn for a short time, ostensibly to ask directions and procure a few final supplies; in reality, to parade about and look like a party of three newcomers making good on an invitation to visit for a time. Mr Bingley played his part well, asking about the hunting and looking quite excited about it all, whilst Jane and her father made some comments about waiting for the rest of their party to arrive in a few days. If anybody noticed the silent servant upon the box, or knew the identity of one of the outriders, not a word was said.

At last, they set off for their destination. The entrance to the estate was just a mile down the road, but the road to the house wound for four or so miles through the woods. They rode in silence for much of the time, although Mr Bingley seemed much relieved at having no competition for Jane's attention.

He had been, as Jane had expected, delightful company the previous day. They had enjoyed the church and its fine windows, taken tea with the parson and his wife, strolled along the streets and admired the shops, and enjoyed hearing each other's opinions.

They agreed on many things; their thoughts on music, poetry, and the merits of scientific endeavour were all quite in accord, although Jane had to admit to herself that her thoughts on science were more noted by their lack of existence. Nevertheless, coming from a family who made their fortune in industry, Mr Bingley had a firm grasp of some of the more recent contributions to engineering, which subject enthralled Jane more than she imagined she ever would.

The day had passed too quickly, and she was almost sad not to have more time for unguarded conversation with her new neighbour.

Her father's low cough brought Jane's attention back to the present, and the lane down which they now travelled.

The heavy growth of trees on either side of the path provided no suggestion of what was to come. They followed a stream that flowed between the steep hillsides, turning this way and that as the lane coiled its way into the heart of the park, dark and mysterious, with occasional glimmers of the brook's sparkling water through the leaves.

Then, at last, they broke through the trees and into a clearing, and the hunting lodge was visible at last.

"Good God!" Mr Bingley exclaimed, his face going slack and draining of colour.

"Hunting box, indeed," Papa tutted. "That is not quite what I would call it."

Jane stared out the window, not quite believing what she saw. Her mouth hung open and she closed it carefully.

This was not the modest lodge she had expected, nor a humble cobblestone cottage with an outbuilding or two for the horses and perhaps a smaller structure to the side for some of the staff. She had been concerned there might not be space for her to have a room separate from the men. Her fears were unwarranted.

Instead of the squat and rustic structure she had imagined, here before her stood a building that could only be called a palace.

It rose up, all grey stone and tall chimneys, in the Tudor style, with a great square turret at one end that might once have been part of an ancient castle and a more modern looking addition at the other. It faced onto a large courtyard at the front, enclosed on three sides by beautifully kept shrubs and hedges, and beyond the main body of the house, Jane could see what looked like fine stables and low buildings that might be storehouses or possibly servants' quarters. It put Longbourn to shame in its size and grandeur.

In a moment, the horses came to a stop directly by the majestic wooden front door, and the colonel himself leapt from his perch and handed them out of the carriage.

"Welcome," he intoned, "to Coed-y-Glyn."

Seemingly from nowhere, a small army of servants appeared by the door to see them inside.

"*Croeso,* Colonel," Jane heard from a smart-looking lady who could only be the housekeeper. Her accent held a hint of the sing-song music of the Welsh language. "Welcome to you and your guests. All is prepared. I have put Mr Bennet in the India Room, with Miss Bennet beside him in the China Room. When Miss Elizabeth is retrieved, she shall have the adjoining Rose Room. Mr Bingley is down in the hall, in the River Room."

"*Diolch,*" replied their host. "Very good." He introduced his guests to Mrs Lloyd, who was exactly what Jane had surmised, and then stood back with his arm extended, inviting them to enter the family's great house.

It was as grand inside as out and appointed beautifully. The marble floors gleamed, and the furnishings that Jane could see were elegant and in the finest of taste. She allowed Mrs Lloyd to lead her and the others up a wide staircase at one end of the main hall, and then down a long passage.

"This is the guest wing," the housekeeper informed them. "The family's wing is on the other side of the portrait gallery." She gestured in the opposite direction, where a large glass cupola spanned the area open to the floor below. Running along the back of this was a wall covered with more paintings than Jane could think to count. Another hall led off the far side.

"This is a very fine house. The family must be quite old and important." Mr Bennet nodded his appreciation as his eyes, too, scanned the wall of portraits. "One does not collect so fine a set of ancestors without some diligence."

"Important, indeed!" Mrs Lloyd crowed. "Do you not know? Did the colonel not tell you? He does enjoy a prank, that one."

Jane cocked her head in curiosity. "No. We know he is cousin to Mr Darcy. Is there something else we ought to know?"

The housekeeper laughed, a rich sound that fit her pleasant appearance. "The colonel is the second son of an earl. This lodge is one of several estates belonging to Lord Matlock."

Beside her, Jane watched as Mr Bingley turned as pale as his shirt and swayed on his feet.

IT SEEMED mere moments after Darcy's eyes finally closed that the sky began to lighten. Elizabeth was still asleep, if restlessly so, and he could not bear to wake her before it was necessary. She was wrapped tightly in the blanket they shared, her head resting on his arm, as his rested on the crunched up satchel they used to carry the blankets and last bits of food. During the night, they had somehow shifted to lie down on the moss, curled against each other between the trees and the hard rise of the hillside. Darcy's back was pressed against the rocky wall, and his free arm wrapped protectively about the young woman who nestled against him, her back snug against his chest.

Oh, in more comfortable, less perilous circumstances, this would be his idea of heaven. Right now, it was torture.

Elizabeth sighed in her sleep and shifted against him. Her hair, wild and untamed, tickled his lips; the sweet scent of her, even through the grime of a week's rough travel, taunted him. He sensed, more than felt, the thrum of her heartbeat as she wriggled closer to him, perhaps in search of security, or perhaps just against the chill of the morning. He wished he knew. They had huddled together before for warmth, and he had fought his instincts before, but this time something was different. Against the barely felt tattoo that invaded his soul, the rest of the world faded to oblivion. Gone were the trees and the rocky cliff face, gone were the distant hoots of owls and the rustle of rodents in the darkness. It was only her. She curled in closer and his arm pulled her tighter in to his protective embrace. She moved her head again, and he could resist no more. His face dipped and his lips grazed the top of her head where her chestnut hair danced across his cheeks. What was he thinking?

But reason had long since deserted him, and when she responded with a sigh, he kissed her head once more. She gave another sigh, a sleepy sound of deep content, that did nothing for his own equilibrium. Then she wriggled against him again. All was lost. Fire rushed through his veins, red and gold and flashing, and all his reserve and regulation all but vanished and his hands longed to rove over the lovely soft body pressed far too enticingly against his own. Only the hard stone pressing into his back and the rough woollen blanket that scratched at his hands let the distant chant of sanity break through: *You are a gentleman, gentleman, gentleman...* He struggled back into some semblance of self-control, but he could no longer deny that he liked this unusual young lady far too well for his own good.

He must have drifted back to sleep, for the sun was higher when Elizabeth rolled out of his loose embrace. She said not a word about his display of affection, and he hoped she had truly been asleep, or imagined it was only a dream.

They struggled up from their uncomfortable den and prepared for the final leg of their journey. It was only five more miles, a distance Elizabeth claimed to walk in a morning before breakfast, but this was a trudge through rough and rocky wood, not a gentle path between farmers' fields. There were streams to cross and ridges and steep inclines to negotiate, and the faint track wound snakelike through the trees. It would take several hours to complete the distance.

They made their way carefully and slowly. As well as the difficult terrain, Darcy was also concerned about unwanted eyes tracking their progress.

"We are coming to the lodge through the estate's forests, from the back," he explained as he helped her over a large boulder that impeded their path. "You will see when we arrive; it is, I believe, the safest access to the house, if not the easiest. Here, let me assist you across this rivulet."

It was six full hours later that they finally neared the house itself. They had stopped more than once to rest and eat what little they had left from their supplies, and had to retrace their steps two or three times when the path that Darcy had thought was correct turned out to lead nowhere, or ended at a rock face on a hillside. Their feet were wet and muddy from fording streams and clambering over rocks, and their clothing was, if anything, in even worse repair. Filthy from the mud and dust and several days' wear, and now ripped and covered with burs and leaves from the foliage through which they passed, they must look perfectly frightful. Darcy hoped they would not be turned away at the door.

"Aha!" Elizabeth exclaimed at last as the lodge came into view. "I understand your path. I had not expected this arm of the woods to extend almost to the outbuildings. Are those the stables?"

She was correct. In an effort to keep the rear part of the property as close to the natural as was possible, the woods encroached a good distance into what would, in many other such places, be parkland. There was plenty of that on the far side of the house, to be certain, but from this direction there were only a hundred or so yards between the last trees and the gate through the surrounding wall that adjoined the stables.

"Are you ready?" Darcy asked. His eyes scanned the surrounding area for anything unusual. He saw nothing: no strange men, no unexpected flashes of colour in the woods, no glints on the roofs that might betray a spyglass. "Do you see that doorway? Can you run?"

She nodded. They had, in concert, agreed to leave their bags just inside the perimeter of the woods, to be retrieved later if necessary, and preferably by one of the lodge's manservants. They could now make their final dash unencumbered.

"Now!"

They slipped from behind that last tree and tore, as fast as they could, across the stretch of field, finally achieving the welcoming door, set as it was into the tall wall that surrounded the courtyard. It was, to the surprise of neither of them, locked. But the door itself was set into the thick wall, allowing them a couple of feet under the protection of the arch above them.

They were not entirely safe yet, but they were close. Unless somebody approached them from the field directly behind them, they would not be visible. Darcy raised his roughened hand and began to bang on the door. "Help! Please! Let us in!"

In a few moments, there came the sound of people moving on the other side, and then the welcome grind of the key in the lock. The door cracked open, and a very large man, taller even than Darcy himself, glared down at them.

"*Pwy dych chi*? What you be wanting?"

*"Ffrind dw i."* Darcy replied. He did not know this man and his name would almost certainly mean nothing. But there were others who did know him. "We need your help. This is my uncle's estate. Mrs Lloyd knows me. Is she near?"

The giant glared at him once more. Of course, he looked nothing at all like the nephew of an earl at this moment, filthy and unshaven, clothed as a field labourer. He pulled himself to his full height and tried to look imperious, hoping his demeanour alone would help to convince this man that he was someone important.

"You be the colonel's cousin?" The suspicious eyes narrowed. "You don't be looking like a gentleman. What be your name?"

"I, good fellow, am Fitzwilliam Darcy of Pemberley in Derbyshire, son of Lady Anne, the present earl's late sister, and cousin to Colonel Richard Fitzwilliam of His Majesty's Army." He glanced to his side. "And this is Miss Elizabeth Bennet, of Longbourn in Hertfordshire. May we please come in?"

"Very well. You be sounding the part." The giant stepped aside and let them enter the courtyard before locking the door behind them. "Stay right here." He yelled for a groom to seek out Mrs Lloyd in the house, and remained, keeping guard over them lest they not be who they claimed.

At another time, Darcy would have been more than offended to be treated thus. Now, he was thankful that some pains were being taken to keep the property secure. Furthermore, he was so relieved to be safe, at last, and with the prospect of a hot meal and a bath, that he would have forgiven the rough giant almost anything short of being flayed alive.

"We are safe now," he whispered to Elizabeth. Her response did not come in words, but in action, as she leaned against his side and allowed him to wrap an arm about her waist, pulling her close. He was her comfort and security. Now if only he could somehow convince her to let him become her husband. Perhaps Mrs Lloyd would have some advice for him, or some words to offer Elizabeth.

Any thoughts, however, of allowing this remarkable young woman the gift of a choice came to an abrupt end when, instead of Mrs Lloyd, a greying man of moderate stature and the dress of a country gentleman came hurrying across the courtyard.

"Lizzy!" he called out as soon as he set eyes on her and, quite unexpectedly, began to run towards them. "My darling girl, Lizzy!"

She stiffened in Darcy's arms.

"Papa!"

FROM THE moment she saw her father striding across the enclosure, Elizabeth knew her fate was sealed. There would be no opportunity now to feign a tragic death and live out her life in obscurity, leaving her sisters without stain. There was no chance of pretending she had not been with Will this last week, or that they had been keeping a most proper distance between them.

No, here she stood, looking like a castaway with her hair in disarray, her clothing soiled and torn, and wrapped up in the circle of Will's strong arms. There could be no explanation, no escape. For her sisters' sake, she would have to marry him.

She ought to be furious or horrified, but she could not find the anger she sought. Instead, a small thrill worked its way up her spine. She was... relieved!

But there was no time to think about this or talk to him now. In a moment, she was ripped from Will's embrace and pulled into her father's.

"Lizzy, my girl, you do not know how worried we have been! Are you well? I am so very pleased to see you. Are you injured? Your mother will never let you hear the end of this. Come, my girl, give me a hug."

She returned her father's embrace with one of her own, equally shocked and delighted to see him. Only now did she realise that, had she carried through on her scheme, she never would have seen him again. She froze at the thought, but then let herself revel in this familial affection once more.

"I am well, Papa. A bit dirty and tired, perhaps, but quite unharmed. Will..."

"And you, sir, must be the scoundrel who abducted my child." Her father stepped back and faced Will, looking up at him above the rims of his spectacles. "What have you to say for yourself, sir?"

Will had the grace to turn red. "I must confess to this crime, for which I offer my deepest apologies, sir. I had no thoughts of embroiling Miss Bennet in my plight, but I cannot be sorry now, for otherwise I would not have had the chance to know her. Fitzwilliam Darcy, at your service." He stood straight, gave a brief bow, and then extended his hand.

"I ought to call you out. But you have brought her here safely, and in good spirits, and so I shall let you live another day."

"It is appreciated. Your carriage and horses are quite safe as well, and will be returned to you as soon as I am free of this man pursuing me."

"Yes, yes," Mr Bennet waved him off. "More of that later. Come inside, Lizzy. Your sister is quite anxious to see you."

"Jane? Jane is here? I must see her at once. Will, you must meet her."

He reached out for her hand before she could move too far away. "I would be honoured, but—" He looked down at himself and groaned. "I should like to look more presentable first. I am hardly fit for polite company."

"No more than am I." She caught a glimpse of the two of them reflected in a window and laughed. "I am surprised our large friend there did not send us both packing. We are quite the sight!"

"A sight for sore eyes," came a voice from the door to the house. "Will! You are alive!" The man rushed forward to pull Will into a fierce but brief embrace. "And this must be Miss Bennet. Colonel Fitzwilliam, at your service, Madam. Come inside. I have already called for baths to be drawn, and clothing to be found. Your rooms are ready. We can discuss matters later. Come along, come along."

His tone was that of a man accustomed to being obeyed, and with the promise of a bath and fresh clothing, Elizabeth was happy to do as he commanded. She followed first him, and then a fine-looking woman, up a long flight of stairs from the back door, and down a hallway to a room that, after these last few nights on hay, rough cots, and plain rock, looked fit for a princess. Somebody had already filled the copper tub, and a maid stood by, ready to assist.

"You'll be burning these, then, miss?" she asked, looking at the remains of Elizabeth's rustic dress.

"No. I think I should like to keep them as a memento of a rather unusual week, if you please."

The girl wrinkled her brow at that, but merely replied, "Very well, Miss," and set about helping Elizabeth into the steaming, fragrant water.

Oh, what bliss this was, to lie here, warm and clean, smelling the scent of lemon and lavender instead of the stench of horse dung and unwashed bodies. She did nothing at all for a very long time, other than luxuriate in the water, allowing the aches and tension of the last week to ease from her bones.

She must have drifted off, for the next thing she knew, the young maid was rousing her with a soft touch on her arm.

"Begging your pardon, Miss, but I was told not to let you sleep in the tub. I've called for more hot water, if you wish to wash your hair, and some of milady's lemon soap, if you wish."

"Yes, yes, of course." Elizabeth forced her eyes open. She would sleep very well tonight, but now she wished to wash, dress, and find her sister.

It was a while later that she finally descended the main staircase to find the small sitting room where the others had gathered for tea. Her hair was clean and dry and pinned up with some competence by the maid, whose name was Gwen, and her skin was clean once more and now softened with a delicate rose-scented lotion. Her clothing, however, was less expected. Mrs Lloyd had been unable to find anything suitable in the house, and Jane's garments were all of a very different size, she being both taller and more slender in build than Elizabeth. The only garment of a suitable size and that was appropriate for any sort of company was a dress from some two decades before, with a low, fitted waist, and a very full skirt. She had forgone the embarrassment of the paniers and petticoats that went with the frock, but still she felt like an exhibit at a museum, or a creature at a masquerade ball.

Let the others laugh. She was clean and warm, and quite in need of some tea.

A servant pointed the way, but she needed no guidance. The aroma she craved drew her in the right direction, and soon she was at the door to a sitting room of surprising size and elegance for a mere "hunting lodge." It was decorated in the finest of taste, with the pale greens and creams of the walls and upholstery mirroring the sylvan view from the large windows that opened onto the park at the side of the house.

The gathered party rose as she entered. Beside her father, Jane, and Will, there were three men—Colonel Fitzwilliam, and two whose names she did not know—all of whom looked delighted at her arrival.

But first, there was Jane, who rushed up the second she crossed the threshold.

"Lizzy! Oh, Lizzy, you poor dear! What an ordeal you must have been through. You had us all so worried. I am so very happy to see you." Uncharacteristically, Jane's voice was tight with emotion, and she caught her sister in a fierce embrace before kissing her cheek. "I am so pleased to see you." She stepped back to assess her sister now. "You look well, and that dress is a delight! Wherever did Mrs Lloyd find it? That style suits you. You must tell us everything!"

Before she could respond, Will was at her side. "Elizabeth." He caught her hand and pressed a kiss to the back, leaving her more flustered than the two nights she had spent in his arms. He, too, had washed and exchanged his ruined farm worker's garb for something more suited to his station. The clothing must have belonged to his cousin, for the coat was too loose about the shoulders and the trousers came further up his shins than fashion dictated, but he looked every inch as regal as a lord. He had shaved as well, and for the first time since the evening at Milden Hall, Elizabeth saw his face unshadowed by any growth of beard. My heavens, but he was a handsome man!

"May I make proper introductions?" he asked, his voice low and velvet in the calm of the sitting room. "My cousin, of course, whom you have seen briefly..."

He presented her formally to the man she had already learned was Richard Fitzwilliam. He was the second son of the earl of Matlock, and the lodge, or palace, or whatever this grand house was, belonged to his father. The colonel bowed deeply, welcomed her once more to Coed-y-Glyn, and said every proper word with such sincerity and genuine pleasure at her attendance that she was quite ready to believe him the most gentlemanlike man in the world.

Then she met the two strangers. The younger man turned out to be their new neighbour in Meryton, Mr Bingley. Yes, of course, she recalled now. Netherfield Park had been let at last, and this was the new tenant. Such matters had quite slipped her mind during the week of her and Will's flight.

The other, closer to the colonel's age, she believed, was introduced as Major Hawarden, the colonel's assistant and friend. He shook her hand like an old acquaintance, but then retreated to the corner where he had been sitting when she walked in with scarcely another word.

It was Mr Bingley, Jane now gushed, who had supplied the carriage and horses that brought them here.

"But how are you connected?" Elizabeth asked. "I understand Mr Darcy and Colonel Fitzwilliam knowing each other for they are cousins, and you and Papa knowing our neighbour, but what of their acquaintance?"

Will cupped her elbow and led her to a chair. "I shall tell all soon enough, but you surely would like some refreshments."

And indeed, this was so. For only a few feet away was a tray laden with a mouth-watering array of teacups and plates of food. Her stomach growled and she hoped nobody had heard. She had, after all, eaten almost nothing since a very early breakfast before they left their rocky refuge, having only the remaining scraps of old bread and cheese to sustain them on their final scramble through the thick woods.

Jane rushed off at once to prepare her a plate, and soon Elizabeth was enjoying hot, sweet tea and a selection of delicate pastries, as Will explained his friendship with Charles Bingley.

She finished her cup as Will finished his story. "Then you and Mr Bingley were friends already, and Mr Bingley had met your cousin in London, and brought him to Hertfordshire to help find me. What a strange and welcome set of coincidences. I cannot thank either of you enough."

Both men beamed at her.

"My greatest pleasure," Mr Bingley asserted, as the colonel crooned, "Anything for a lady." My, what a charming manner he had.

The men's eyes met, and a look passed between them that Elizabeth did not quite understand. There was more happening here than what she saw on the civilised surface. Perhaps Jane would know.

There was one more person in the room, almost hidden from view in his wingback chair, but whose impatient throat-clearing indicated a wish to speak.

"Mr Bennet?" Will nodded towards the gentleman who, until now, had sat silently with his tea and buttered fruit bread.

"Indeed. I believe, Mr Darcy, you and I have some matters to discuss. I am pleased enough for the time being, seeing my daughter unharmed and in good spirits, that I shall not demand it at once, but by tomorrow, sir, we must have words."

"I am yours to command," Will replied. He had taken the seat beside Elizabeth and now reached for her hand. He gave her a weak smile, which she attempted to echo. Her future, it seemed, was no longer *hers* to command.

# Chapter 16

# Conversations

The conversation over dinner veered from the continued threat posed by George Wickham, and encompassed, instead, the journey the two parties had undertaken. Jane described the carriage ride to Northampton, Wolverhampton, and then Oswestry, giving an account of the inns and the scenery along the way.

For one less familiar with Jane's particular manners and reserve, it would seem an open and complete accounting of that party's experiences, a traveller's tale fit for any audience. But Elizabeth knew her sister intimately, and understood the cast to her eye, the way she pinched her lips and let her fingers toy with the fork in her hand or the stem of the wineglass before her. There was more that Jane had to say, but not here. This tale would be for Elizabeth's ears only.

She caught her sister's glance and offered a subtle nod, which was answered with a momentary smile. An entire conversation was carried out in those miniscule gestures. They would talk in one of their rooms later.

Quite oblivious to this interaction between the sisters, Will took up the thread of their own, much less comfortable, travels. He explained their choice to journey down through Abergavenny and only then, having achieved the quiet lanes that few knew existed, back north threading as close to the mountains as the tracks allowed, and stopping at small towns and villages for supplies. Elizabeth noticed he said nothing about the nature of their accommodations other than that they were rustic. He certainly gave no indication that they had even been in the same room at night, and breathed not a word about the ruined church or the night in the crease in the hillside that was not quite a cave.

The others seemed to accept this intimation of propriety without question. There were no accusations, no expressions of dismay or alarm, only the joy of everybody being well and safe and under the same roof.

The accounting would come later.

Likewise, there was no prolonged tea or a suggestion of cards after dinner. This was not a house party, after all, and Elizabeth was exhausted. That bed in her room was the most beautiful thing she had ever seen, and she wished to acquaint herself intimately with it forthwith. She excused herself from the gathering and prepared to make her way back up the old staircase to seek her room.

"I will come as well and help you, Lizzy." Jane rose and dipped a curtsey to the men before following Elizabeth out of the room.

Elizabeth forced a smile onto her face. She both longed to acquaint her dear sister with everything that had happened, more than the tidy version that Will had told, whilst at the same time, wishing to hold on to those experiences and keep them personal and private for a while longer. Those nights lying with Will, feeling his warm body against hers, and the comforting circle of his arms warding off all danger, these were gems to be jealously guarded, as if sharing them would somehow diminish them.

Dared she talk about the hunting shack? The not-quite-cave? What would Jane say? And Jane, she understood, had something she wished to tell Elizabeth. Perhaps, tonight, she could allow Jane to speak, and hold her own tongue for later.

The bedroom seemed miles away, not merely up a few stairs, and Elizabeth felt her energy fail her with every step, until at last, they entered her chamber. That large and soft bed beckoned, but Elizabeth suspected it would be some hours before she could, at last, succumb to its embrace. Sisterly duties must come first.

"Now, Lizzy, tell me everything," Jane insisted as she closed the bedroom door behind her. "Not only the parts that Mr Darcy wanted Papa to hear. He is very handsome."

Elizabeth eyed the bed with longing but resigned herself to conversation. "Help me with this gown, Jane. I am not quite certain how Gwen did it up. There are straight pins somewhere, I think, and I very much wish to throw myself into that soft chair. Very well. What do you wish to know?"

Jane set to work removing the pins and laces from the old dress, commenting here and there about some features of the twenty-year-old style. For a while she concentrated on her task, but once the bodice was unpinned and Elizabeth could step out of the heavy skirts, she asked again about Will. "Was he… was he a gentleman? He seems so very proper, but Lizzy! He stole the carriage, and with you in it! I thought I would never see you again." Jane caught Elizabeth in another fierce hug, crushing her close, and Elizabeth gladly returned the embrace. For a time, she had despaired of ever seeing her dear Jane again as well.

After a moment of reassuring each other, Elizabeth stepped back and began to fold the voluminous garment. She laid it upon a chair, along with the bodice, and stretched. "It feels strange to have clothing so fitted to my waist. It is far tighter than our stays." She gestured to the undergarments she had borrowed as well, which she began to unlace, leaving her clad only in a clean white shift.

"You are avoiding my question, Lizzy." Jane eyed her like a school master examining a naughty student.

"Will… Mr Darcy…"

"Will?"

"When I first confronted him, I thought him a labourer or something, certainly not a gentleman. His clothing looked like something he stole from a rubbish pile, and he was covered in filth. He introduced himself as Will Darcy, and I addressed him by name. Once his status was made clear, it seemed disingenuous to revert to something more formal."

Jane's reply was a knowing smile, her delicate brows high on her forehead.

"He has been a perfect gentleman, Jane! His sense of propriety would satisfy even the vicar. Even when we—" She stopped, but had already said too much.

"Lizzy?" Jane pulled her hand until they both sat on the bed, side by side. "What happened?"

"Nothing, really. But we did not always have the luxury of fine inns or private accommodations. And..." She would not divulge everything, but this seemed comprehensible, if not laudable. "Last night, we had to flee the town where we stabled the horse and cart, and found ourselves in the woods as it grew dark. It was cold, and the small cave we found provided little protection from the weather."

"You did not!"

"It was perfectly innocent, but yes, I admit to us huddling together to keep warm. It was dark and cold in there, for we dared not light a fire, with only enough of a projection to shield us from the worst of the wind. There was not even a place to lie down properly. We leant against the rocky wall and tried to sleep. I know how it must sound. Oh, do you detest me, Jane?"

At once, her sister swept her into another fierce hug.

"Detest you? Not at all. I cannot think anything ill of it, and if you did sleep in such proximity, I am certain it was entirely necessary. But you do know, you must marry. There is no hiding this, no matter how proper his behaviour."

Elizabeth nodded. She still had not found the words, even to tell herself, how she felt.

"Do you like him, Lizzy? If you do not, I will plead with Papa on your behalf. I cannot have you married to a man you cannot like."

"I must, Jane. You have to see that. If we do not marry, then you, and Mary, and Kitty, and Lydia, will all be stained by my disgrace." Oh, heavens! Why did her voice sound so thick? Was she crying? The warm tear that threaded its way down her cheek confirmed her fear.

"I would rather die an old maid than have you tied to somebody against your will. And our sisters..."

"Will never have the opportunity to make this decision. I cannot do that to you. I had thought, for a time, of having Will proclaim me dead. I was going to apply to Mrs Lloyd to stay here and work for my keep. You would not be tainted by my misfortunes. But when we arrived, and Papa saw us, well, Will's arm was around my waist, and there was no pretending we had been ten feet apart the entire time. Our father is a most indulgent parent, but too many people were witness, and he could not hide it forever. I understand that. I have accepted my fate."

Jane's embrace tightened for a moment. "But tell me, can you like him? Is he a good sort of man?"

"Oh yes. He is the very best sort of man I have ever known. I do like him. I think... I think I love him."

And, unaccountably, she dissolved into a flood of tears.

Jane found a handkerchief from somewhere and gave it to Elizabeth to dry her face. "Do not cry, Lizzy. It cannot be so dreadful if you like him."

"How can I be happy, when he is marrying me only out of duty? I want to be loved, but I also want him to be happy. In marrying me, he will be burdened with a wife he did not want."

"Can you be certain of that? He seemed most attentive earlier. I cannot imagine he does not care at all."

"I have to believe he thinks of me only as a friend."

"Marriages have been built on less, and friendship is the surest foundation for love."

Elizabeth gave her eyes a final pat with the handkerchief and tried to smile. "I can only wish it so. Now," she forced her voice to be bright, "what of our charming host and the handsome Mr Bingley? I noticed some glances there as well. There must be a tale."

The mouth so often turned up in a sweet smile now tightened. "They are both admirable gentlemen," she began.

"But?"

"But... Oh, I do not know what to do." She stood up from the bed and walked to the window to stare out into the darkness. "They are like schoolboys, one taunting the other, and the other responding poorly. They both seem to want the same toy, and I am afraid that the toy is me."

"Say it is not so! The colonel, acting like a schoolboy? Is he the taunter? What has he done?"

The curtains rustled as Jane pulled them closed and spun around to face her sister. "I believe that Mr Bingley is not impartial to me. He has been most attentive, and when we received your letter, he offered his carriage without a moment's hesitation. I thought, at first, that he was merely acting in a neighbourly manner, that he would do the same for anybody.

"He rode all the way to London to seek out Colonel Fitzwilliam, hoping to ask his advice on where Mr Darcy might have gone. The colonel returned to Longbourn with Mr Bingley, and has been ever helpful and gracious."

"I see. He seems a most amiable gentleman."

"That he is. But every time Colonel Fitzwilliam pays me a compliment or says something that might gain my favour, Mr Bingley grows quite agitated. I would almost imagine Mr Bingley to be jealous!" Her hands twisted the handkerchief she had lent to Elizabeth.

Elizabeth had to stifle a chuckle.

"You are a very beautiful woman, Jane. It ought to come as no surprise that you are the object of their attention."

"You sound like Mama. 'You cannot be so lovely without a reason,' she always tells me. But I cannot like it. It is flattering to have captured one man's eye, but to be a cause of the discord between two? No, I cannot like that at all. I am most uncomfortable."

Elizabeth patted the bed beside her. "Come and sit. Now, of the two, which do you like the best? You cannot be certain of the intentions of either, but have you a preference? I have only now met them, and both seem like fine men."

Settling beside her again, Jane stared at the wall for a moment before replying. "They are, I believe. Our acquaintance has been short, and hardly ordinary. I met Mr Bingley the day you... you disappeared, and the colonel two days later, and we have had a singular common purpose since then.

"I can only believe the colonel to be acting in the best interests of his cousin. He is polite and friendly, and very kind. But I do not think his attentions are particular. I quite suspect he pays me such honours merely to watch Mr Bingley's reaction, which is not quite gentlemanlike. Is it?"

Elizabeth hardly had a wealth of experience with the man from which to draw her own conclusions, but Colonel Fitzwilliam did not seem a cruel sort. He would not have taken leave from his regiment and carried three strangers across the country to this excellent house had his intentions been borne of caprice or malice.

"Perhaps this gentle teasing is merely his way. Mr Bingley is the one who chooses how to respond."

The tension broke when Jane began to laugh. "Oh, how the shoe is on the other foot now, Lizzy! I am usually the one cautioning you to look for the good in people and to excuse their seeming faults. Yes, you must be right. The colonel has been nothing but good and generous."

"And Mr Bingley? He does like you, it seems. Do you like him?"

"Yes. I believe I do. Besides the use of his carriage, he has insisted upon supplying the coin at each inn and rest stop. And he is rather handsome, for those who care about such things. I would enjoy the chance to know him better."

"And that, from my sister, is high praise indeed!" Elizabeth gave Jane a quick one-armed hug, but could not stop the yawn that now overtook her.

"Forgive me, Jane. This has been a long day... a long week. I am looking forward to sleeping in a comfortable bed with soft sheets and a pillow!"

"But," Jane smirked as she stood and walked towards the door, "No Will Darcy."

DARCY swallowed a yawn and covered his lapse by bringing his glass of port to his lips. He wished for nothing so much as a long sleep in a warm bed. Well... perhaps he might wish for one more thing, but he was too much of a gentleman to admit to the thought, much less to put it into words.

After the two Bennet sisters had retired for the night, the men sat a while longer. Richard brought out a decanter and glasses and poured a finger for each of them. The conversation was general, more about the hunting lodge, the estate, and the neighbourhood than about anything substantive. After a while, Mr Bennet rose to bid his good-nights, his eyes informing Will that they would speak on the morrow. Then Bingley, too, declared a wish to retire. It seemed he was not entirely comfortable with Richard, for what reason Will could not entirely comprehend. After a few minutes' further conversation, Hawarden rose to retire for the night.

Now Darcy was alone with his cousin, and as much as he longed for sleep, he also had questions.

"How did you come to join the Bennets? I had not imagined that when Elizabeth sent her letter, they would know enough to connect me with you. I did not even know she had given my name."

"They would have found me somehow. A letter to anyone with a knowledge of London society would have supplied the link. But it was your friend Bingley who came searching. We had met previously, of course, and he remembered where to find me."

Darcy gave a slow blink. "You did not need to join them."

"You are my favourite cousin and my best friend, Will. If you were in danger, I had to help in any way I could."

"I return the compliment, Richard. I could not imagine being closer to a brother. But you could have given the direction and taken a fast horse, arrived here days ago."

Richard shrugged. "Perhaps. But I wished to see what these Bennets were like. When I heard that Miss Elizabeth was in the carriage, and had some knowledge of her age and unmarried status, I understood at once what must eventually happen. I wanted to ensure that these were the sort of family with whom you could tolerate being associated."

"And had they not been a suitable connection? Had they been hopeless, or of poor character? What then?"

"Then I would have done everything under my power to convince Squire Bennet that there was no need for you to marry Miss Elizabeth, that there was a maid along as chaperone the entire trip—and yes, I would have produced such a woman to attest to this. That solution is no longer possible, but if you do not wish to wed the lady, I will think of something."

Darcy swallowed.

"What is it, Cousin? Do you not like her? You seemed most solicitous of her comfort earlier, and she seems a fine sort of person, and more than tolerably handsome."

"She is remarkable. I like her a great deal, more, perhaps, than I ought."

"But you do not seem happy. Is it the family? I confess I have known Bennet for only a few days, but he seems harmless enough. The mother, so I have been told, is subject to fits of nerves, and the younger sisters are perhaps a bit silly—"

Darcy threw his head back on the chair and let out a groan. "Do not remind me of silly sisters. If mine had acted with more propriety, I would not be in this awful mess. As for a matron with nerves, I would prefer a well-meaning and doting mother like that to an officious harridan like our Aunt Catherine. She is still after me to offer for our cousin Anne and will not hear my refusals."

"Yes. Indeed! I see that. What, then, is your worry? Miss Elizabeth is pretty, charming, and as you say, remarkable. And you like her too. What stops you from beaming from ear to ear?"

Darcy glared at him. "I do not beam. I occasionally permit myself a small grin."

Richard rolled his eyes.

"We have to marry; this I understand. I wish it, but I do not think she feels the same way. She likes me well enough, but she wants to marry for love. What lady does not?" Richard nodded, so he continued. "I understand that to mean she desires to love the man she weds, and if that man were me, she would be less apprehensive. She even proposed a scheme to feign death to avoid this union." His sigh all but shook the walls.

Richard rose and poured another amount of port into his glass. "You do not think she cares for you." It was a statement.

Darcy shook his head and let it fall forwards in his distress.

Out of the corner of his eye, he noticed his cousin set down his glass and pull his chair very close to Will's own.

"Talk to her honestly, Will. I cannot believe her entirely indifferent to you. Time has given me a great deal of experience discerning where attraction and affection lie, and the way she glances at you, and how her eyes follow you around the room, make me think her heart is more committed than you imagine."

"I am afraid to ask. If I do and she states she will never love me, it would quite destroy me. Oh," he slammed his glass onto the table with more force than he expected. "Listen to me, mooning about like a love-struck calf. I have known her for a week. How did she ever become so important to me? Richard, she shot a rabbit for me!"

"She what?"

By the time Darcy had finished the story of the tree and the rabbit, Richard was laughing and Darcy was feeling much more the thing.

Then Richard's face grew serious again. "There is one more thing you should know, Will." He leaned forward, forearms on his thighs. "We stayed two nights in Oswestry, as we have recounted. I did have some matters to discuss with the colonel in charge of the French prisoners on parole there, but there is something more. That second morning, very early, Mr Bennet and I took two fast horses up to Wrexham to speak to the Archdeacon there. It is only fifteen miles."

A strange sensation rose from Darcy's feet. This could only mean one thing.

"I have bought you a licence. It would be best for everybody if you were to marry before returning to England."

Darcy sat perfectly still, quite unable to move for a moment. He had known what he must do. But the immediacy of it was a shock, nonetheless. That tingle in his feet, now shooting up into his spine—was it dread? Or excitement?

He was going to marry Elizabeth! As the idea settled itself onto him and made a nest for itself in his mind, the tingle resolved itself into one of qualified joy. He loved her, or near enough. If she proved to be half the woman she had shown on this strange journey they had just taken, she would suit him perfectly. Oh, there would be whispers in society about her lower status and lack of exalted relations, but he cared little for what the muttering matrons thought. She would stand up to them and prove herself every ounce worthy of the Darcy name. Anybody who could shimmy up a tree and shoot a darting rabbit was more than capable of facing society. She was that impressive a young lady. If he did not love her entirely now, it would not be long until his whole heart was committed.

Was Richard correct? Did she, indeed, hold some sort of real affection for him? He needed to talk to her, and soon, before the necessary events of the following day overtook them. Before her father informed her as to her destiny. And before they had to deal with the shadow of George Wickham, which even now cast a pall on his happiness.

He had to speak to her, and find out what he could possibly do to let her be as pleased as was he.

SOMEWHERE in the house, a large standing clock chimed three o'clock in the morning, and Darcy was wide awake. He had gone straight to his usual room after that conversation with his cousin, and had sunk into a deep and dreamless sleep. The mattress was soft and did not poke him in strange places or cause him to itch, and the sheets were like butter, light and supple on his tired limbs. He hardly felt the pillow, for his eyes closed almost as soon as his head touched it.

But now he was awake, and irredeemably so. Perhaps he was accustomed to interrupted nights, or perhaps it was the unfamiliarity of the bed. It mattered not. His eyes were open and would not close. He rose and walked to the window, pulling the draperies open just enough to peer out into the darkness. This part of the house, the family's wing, was in the more recent addition to the building, and rather than being in a line with the old Tudor structure, it stood perpendicular to it, forming two sides of an enclosure of the gardens behind the house. He had, therefore, a fine view of the back of the main part of the house, and of each window that looked out over that beautiful garden, backed as it was by the woods in the near distance, and the mountains behind.

It also gave him a fine view of one window that was not dark. A thin line of orange light cracked from between the curtains in one bedchamber. Somebody was awake. He counted the windows from the end and tried to recall what Richard had told him. Bingley... Mr Bennet... Jane... Hawarden was in the house as well, but he had his usual rooms in the far wing. It was not he, but one of the travellers. Now, who had which room?

Yes! He remembered now. Elizabeth was in the Rose Room. It had seemed so fitting at the time, for she brought images of that beautiful flower to mind. He envisioned her sitting on a delicate garden bench, surrounded by rose bushes, or lying on a white bed, her hair loose on the pillow behind her, rose petals strewn all about...

He chastised himself for such errant thoughts, but did not expunge it from his mind. In truth, he did not think he could.

Then he counted the rooms again.

The hallways of Coed-y-Glyn were empty and silent. The family not being in residence, there were no footmen waiting in niches or sconces lit for late-night revellers. There was nobody to see as Will crept in his stocking feet down the passage, across the portrait gallery, and down into the guest wing. There was nobody to hear the occasional creak of the wooden floor or the soft swish of the silk banyan he had borrowed from Richard. The lamp in his hand flickered, the flame a wisp in the black night, its aura swallowed by the darkness. But it was enough to light his way.

Had the household been awake and the common sounds of footsteps and murmured conversation been present, his scratch at the door would have disappeared into nothingness. Now, the sound all but echoed from the ancient ceilings. There was a sense of sudden stillness from the other side, the world holding its breath for that one instant, and then the shuffle of slippered feet on soft carpet.

The door cracked open. "Will." She had not even glanced to see who it was, but just seemed to know. "You should not be here."

"I know. But I need to talk to you. May I come in?"

Her face, half hidden by the wooden door, went immobile. Then her eyes blinked once and she dipped her chin. "Very well."

He slid in and closed the door behind him, careful to make no noise.

"What if we are found out?"

He huffed out a short laugh. "It can hardly change our fate now. No—" he stopped as her face went hard and white. "I mis-spoke. We must wed regardless. Being found together will not change anything, and I would rather spend the time with you, talking, than being alone. Will you hear me?"

Another slow nod.

"I am not dreading this, Elizabeth. It is, perhaps, a decision I might have wished to make for myself, but I am not displeased with it. No, not displeased at all. We... we rub along well. Do you think you can be happy as my wife?"

He moved towards the bed with its rumpled sheets and blankets, and reached for her hand, urging her to sit beside him. Her eyes betrayed caution, not fear, and a great deal of uncertainty.

He felt the mattress move as she settled beside him, rather closer than he had hoped for. "I shall be content. I know full well the honour you do me. I shall do everything to be a good wife to you." The trepidation in her regard, if anything, increased.

"No, content will not do! I want you to be happy, as happy as you can be with me. I shall never hurt you, you must know that. I will demand nothing of you, if you do not wish it."

She seemed to understand his meaning, and the worry in her eyes eased. And Will's heart clenched. It was true, then. She cared for him as a friend, but no more. Very well. He would take her friendship if that was all she could offer him. It was far preferable to not having her in his life at all.

He took a deep breath. "There is something more. Your father will tell you of it tomorrow, but I wished you to hear it from me."

The anxious pinch reappeared between her delicate brows.

"Richard and your father made a second journey on their way here, up to Wrexham. There is an archdeacon there, and he was able to provide them with a common licence for us to marry. I do not know your father's thoughts, but Richard suggests we would be best to wed soon at the village church before we leave here. Certainly, before we return to our homes. Our home. For Pemberley will be yours as well."

A spark of curiosity lit her eyes and it kindled his own fire, the flame of deep love he held for his ancestral home. At her encouraging smile, he spoke with growing animation of his estate.

"You will love it, Elizabeth! The house is quite grand, but the grounds and the park, ah, those are its true beauty. There is a river that runs through the immediate park, swelled into a lake near the house, and wonderful gardens. There are paths through the woods, and a folly on a small hillock on the far side of the lake where my sister and I enjoy taking a picnic. At times, we wander there early in the morning or at dusk, just to spend time and watch the birds. Do you draw? I ought to have asked before now? It is a lovely site to set up an easel. Or, if you prefer, I can have a servant set up a spinet there in the warmer months, or a loom, or a sitting room with a library.

"You will have anything you desire. If I can afford it, it will be yours. My deepest desire is for you to be happy. Can you be happy? Will you try?"

Her eyes were wide and a bit damp. "You are a good man, Will Darcy. I am still growing accustomed to our circumstance. I have known you a week, and in a few days we will be married. But I will be happy. I am not made for melancholy."

He put an arm around her shoulders and she cuddled into his side. He cherished the feel of her, warm and soft against him, the slight pressure of her arm against his chest, her head coming to rest on his shoulder. He only hoped she would learn to feel likewise about him.

They sat there for a while, resting against each other, comfortable with the silence. Then Elizabeth yawned, a subtle and gentle sound, but a yawn nonetheless. And her yawn engendered a yawn in Will, which he could not stifle.

"I am, perhaps, a little tired," Elizabeth whispered. "I might lie down. It is strange, but I could not sleep without you. Will you lie down with me, just for a moment?"

Darcy's eyes were suddenly leaden. "Yes. Just a moment."

Without thinking, he lay down and pulled Elizabeth to him, and they fell asleep together on the top of the bed, and stayed there until the sun threaded its bright fingers through the chink in the curtains.

# Chapter 17
# The Lay of the Land

"What have you heard?"

Darcy eyed his cousin over the lip of his coffee cup. Many mornings he preferred tea, but today he needed the bitter jolt of strong coffee. He had woken with the sun and realised his predicament, half in shame and half in delight. Sleeping with Elizabeth in his arms felt so very right, he could hardly recall his life without her. She, too, seemed happy and at peace with her company, and as he stirred, she nestled up against him and let out a soft sound of contentment. He sent up a quick prayer that once they were married, she would allow him more than this chaste embrace through layers of clothing.

But now, he had to return to his own chambers, and soon. The household would be stirring, and although they would be wed very soon, it would not do to be caught in her room.

And only in his nightclothes.

Heaven forbid!

He ensured his banyan was securely tied, gave Elizabeth a gentle kiss on her cheek, which evoked another happy sigh, and cracked the bedroom door. The corridor was empty, and he returned to his own chamber without being seen. He hoped.

Nobody said a word or gave him assessing glances as he descended, fully dressed in his borrowed clothing, to the breakfast room some time later. Richard was already there with an empty cup at one side, a plate with a half-eaten pile of kedgeree on the other, and a detailed map of the region spread out on the table before him. Matthew Hawarden sat across from Richard, his eyes also on the map. The major nodded to Darcy and Darcy nodded back. Their accustomed greeting, friendly but not exactly voluble. They would both be better company after they had dealt with Wickham.

Richard glanced up as he took a sip from his cup. "What have I heard? From the village? Very little. I cannot imagine that my presence here is unknown, but neither have I been there myself. I did ask one of the more reliable grooms to stop by his usual pub and keep his ears open. I hope to hear from him today."

Darcy gulped back his coffee and went to pour himself another cup. This time he added some *bara brith* to a plate, and a small helping of eggs. "And my arrival? What of Elizabeth?"

Richard's shoulders rose and he pinched his lips. "As I said, no news yet. Mrs Lloyd has also heard nothing from her daughter who lives there, so I believe your presence is still unknown. Nevertheless, this cannot remain quiet for long. We must be ready." He waved his hand over the map before him.

"Always the soldier, planning his tactics," Darcy quipped. But he felt the blade of fear taunt him behind his teasing words.

Richard's expression remained clouded. "If I were Wickham, where would I go? What would I do? I cannot think him foolish enough to try to storm this bastion. It would be better for us if he did. We are well armed, for it is a hunting lodge after all, and the servants here are all capable with weapons. And Hawarden here is a skilled soldier; my staff trust him. This place is as secure as a castle. But it is more likely Wickham will try something from the village. Now, where? What sort of place would he seek?"

"Better the question," Darcy replied, "is what he plans to do. Will he be content to have me live in fear? I cannot imagine it, not after what he has done. We heard some men in the public in Llandrillo, as they were talking. If they are Wickham's men, and I must think they are, he wants my head—quite literally—sent to him as proof of my demise. He wants Elizabeth as well, for what nefarious purposes I cannot bear to think.

"Promise me this, Richard." He fixed his stare on his cousin and did not release it until the soldier met his gaze. "If matters become dire, Elizabeth's life and welfare must take precedence over mine. Keep her safe. Please."

Richard's mouth opened and Darcy expected some teasing quip, but then he snapped it closed and gave a sharp nod instead. "Understood."

The three men pored over the map for a time, looking for locations both within and around the village where their nemesis might lurk. The village—little more than a few houses, a tiny church, a mill, a blacksmith, and a tavern—did not have an inn worthy of the name. There might be a room to let above the tavern, if a man were to sweet-talk the proprietor with a suitable coin. They would have to inquire there. The smithy also provided a possible place he might seek accommodations. The mill, less so, since there was no loft that Richard knew of. But the storage sheds were a possibility.

"The village is small enough that he would be noticed at once," Darcy commented, scanning the plan with the buildings all sketched as neat little squares. "The town?"

"Too far, I should think." The closest market town, where the family did any necessary shopping and where Mrs Lloyd bought many of the supplies for the estate, was nearly five miles distant, too far to keep a close watch over the comings and goings at Coed-y-Glyn.

"What about the farms in the vicinity? Are there any around here who might give him shelter?"

Richard stroked his chin. "It is possible. We try to be good neighbours, and do not own any property other than the house and surrounding lands to hunt. None of the farmers are our tenants. Still, we are English, and therefore a natural enemy to some. I know of no particular rancour, but we are, quite frankly, foreigners here."

"Who would know where to ask?" Darcy peered at the map as if it would magically display the exact location where Wickham lay in wait. If he were even in the country. He might very well have gone on to Pemberley or the house in London to wait there.

"I shall put Mrs Lloyd on it. She knows the area and the people. She speaks the language. Her curiosity, phrased in Welsh, will be far better received than my demands in English."

This discussion was now halted by the sound of other voices, and in a moment Mr Bennet and Bingley entered the room, followed a few minutes later by Jane and Elizabeth.

Darcy's eyes were drawn at once to the latter. Although he had slept much of the night beside her on her bed, he could not get enough of her. He drank in the sight of her bright eyes and soft pink cheeks, her lips the colour of roses, calling for his kiss. He fought the urge to walk up to her and sweep her into an embrace, to feel her in his arms again.

Something of his desires must have betrayed itself, for she coloured a touch when she looked at him, and her lips parted. He was all but undone.

"Lizzy, you look well this morning. Are you rested?" Mr Bennet's voice interrupted his improper thoughts.

"Good morning, Papa. I slept exceedingly well." Her eyes flickered in Darcy's direction and he sent her a secret grin.

"Does she not look fine? What a wonder Mrs Lloyd was, to find this frock for her so soon." Jane gestured to Elizabeth's gown, a light blue garment that Georgiana would probably describe in some fanciful terms. To Darcy's eyes, it was a perfectly ordinary day frock, quite unremarkable... until he recalled that she, like himself, had arrived here with nothing but the clothing they wore.

Elizabeth spun around in a slow circle. The garment, perhaps, did not fit as well as something from her own wardrobe would undoubtedly do, but it was more than serviceable. "Mrs Lloyd sent a note to the market town a few miles away when we arrived yesterday, and this was delivered, with two others, in reply. I believe it belongs to the daughter of a friend of hers, who has lent it to me. I did like that old gown I wore last night, but this is much more comfortable, and I feel less like one of those portraits upon the wall." Her eyes sparkled and she made another revolution to show off the dress.

Now that Darcy was able to tear his eyes from her lovely face, he noticed that her hair, too, was dressed in the modern style. He had rather liked it before, half-pulled from its pins and streaming down her back, but she looked more than fine with it up in a pile upon her head. Did Jane do it, or was one of the maids adept with ladies' hair?

Her eyes caught his again and she let them linger for a moment as she flushed a pale pink once more.

"Good morning, Miss Elizabeth." He could not hide his smile. "Please, allow me." He stepped aside to pull out the chair next to him and noticed that Bingley did likewise for Jane. "What would you like? Command me, and it shall be yours."

Her laugh was the sound of angels' bells. "I shall command an army later, but for now, a cup of tea will suit, thank you."

He brought her the tea, prepared as she requested, and a piece of *bara brith* on a plate as well. Then, with yet another cup of coffee, he sat back to observe the room, ensuring from time to time that she had everything she wished.

Mr Bennet's expression was unreadable. He could not have failed to notice Darcy's attentions to Elizabeth, and his glance darted their way often, but the man's views on the matter were veiled. Was he pleased to see his future son-in-law dance attendance upon his daughter? Was he angry that this was necessary? Anxious that the marriage occur forthwith? Neither his eyes nor words conveyed his thoughts.

Bingley was another story, for his eyes spoke volumes. Darcy had not had the opportunity for private conversation with his friend since his arrival here the previous day, and found the currents circulating between Bingley, Richard, and Jane unsettling. He was the first to confess his shortcomings when it came to understanding unspoken sentiments and subtle intonations, but even he could see that Bingley was rather taken with the eldest Miss Bennet and was not at all happy with Richard's perceived competition.

This was not a surprise. Darcy could hardly recall a dinner, dance, or other social engagement where his friend had not discovered the most beautiful girl in the room, and then promptly fallen in love with her. And Jane Bennet was most definitely beautiful. She was tall and slender, with translucent skin and a classical symmetry to her lovely features that would put Aphrodite to shame. But her beauty, much though Darcy might admire it, did not touch his heart. Likewise, her manner was everything cool and elegant, everything that would see her lauded in the finest company. She smiled sweetly and said everything proper, but he detected no passion behind the look and the words, no force of personality to grab at the soul.

Let others moon before such classical perfection. For him, he preferred a sparkle, a touch of impertinence, that would challenge him and keep his interest. Alabaster ladies with their perfect posture and immaculate manners paled now before the image of an outspoken firebrand who climbed trees and aimed true with a bow and arrow. His eyes drifted to Elizabeth, who sipped at her tea beside him, and his heart overflowed. Yes. It was true. He loved her.

He brought his attention back to his friend. Was Bingley about to fall in love with Jane Bennet? Or, to be cynical, was Bingley about to form an infatuation with Jane Bennet, to be forgotten the moment the next pretty face appeared? Miss Bennet did seem a charming young woman, if cool, and her father was a landed gentleman. For Bingley, one generation removed from trade and not yet in possession of an estate, it would not be a bad match. Although, from what he believed, the Bennet daughters had little wealth and would need to marry well once their cousin inherited Longbourn.

He must watch Jane Bennet, in case her smiles at Bingley were merely aimed to fix him, to secure her own fortune, without any real affection on her part.

And then there was Richard. Whatever was his cousin playing at? For every simpering smile Bingley cast Jane's way, Richard gave a mighty grin. If Bingley offered to bring her a cup of tea, Richard offered the entire pot. And every time Richard offered a kind word of compliment to Jane, Bingley turned red and fumed.

This was quite unlike his cousin. Richard was good humoured and as garrulous as Will was taciturn, but never had Darcy seen him goad anybody thus before. Could his cousin really have his eye turned by Jane's beauty? It hardly seemed likely. Still, the man was expected to marry one day, and although Jane did not have the fortune Richard needed, she would be a pleasant wife, and one who would look well on his arm, as unfair as it would be to the lady.

These next few days might prove quite interesting. Should he survive them.

THE WEATHER was fair, and Jane expressed an interest in exploring the gardens. Elizabeth was less eager to be outside again, having spent a great deal too much time in the open air over the last week. And, if she were honest with herself, the spectre of George Wickham, lying in wait behind every rock and tree, was more than sufficient incentive to keep her safe within the building's walls. Mr Bingley, however, rushed to offer Jane his company, and for once, the colonel did not insert himself into their arrangements. Instead, he offered a gentle warning.

"I would beg you, Bingley and Miss Bennet, to remain within the formal gardens and in full view of the house. I shall set a couple of servants at the gates as well, to ensure your safety, and have Hawarden keep an eye open."

Mr Bingley swallowed. "Do you believe us in danger? Could Mr Wickham be this close?"

The colonel raised one shoulder. Although the man was dressed in the familiar clothing of a country gentleman, Elizabeth could all but see the flash of an officer's epaulette in the efficiency of this gesture. "I do not believe there to be any particular peril in it, but I would prefer to be cautious."

Jane thanked him in a weak voice and excused herself to dress for the outdoors, offering to meet Mr Bingley at the doors to the gardens in fifteen minutes. Elizabeth's father seemed pleased enough with the plans.

"If they are within view of the house and of two stout manservants, I cannot believe they need a chaperone. Very well, Jane, enjoy the flowers."

Elizabeth sipped the last of her tea and looked about the room. She had not seen very much of the house, and asked if there was a parlour where she might sit and read, or perhaps write to her mother and her friend Charlotte.

"If you will permit me, Elizabeth, I would be pleased to show you the house, if my cousin does not object." Will was on his feet, one arm out in invitation.

She could not hide her smile. Why, after having been abducted by the man and then forced to spend every minute with him for nigh on a week, was she so eager for his company? She ought to hate him, not love him. But love him, her heart insisted, she did. And now, relieved for a time from the pressures of rough travel, she looked forward to conversing on matters simple and ordinary, like the furnishings of a hunting lodge.

She rose and took the elbow he offered, and allowed him to lead her from the breakfast room.

Will showed her the great hall and explained its history, then led her to the back parlour with its vista onto the gardens where Jane and Mr Bingley would take their walk, and then proceeded to the formal dining rooms.

"The family usually dine in the breakfast room, but when my uncle hosts a hunting party and there are more than a few guests, they use this space." It was a tall chamber, in the newer part of the house, with large windows hidden behind heavy draperies, and a massive table down the length of it that might easily seat thirty with comfort.

From here, he led her to the kitchens, "should you desire to ask Cook for something," and down a long hallway leading towards the courtyard where they had entered yesterday. "If you wish to engage in some sport, there are croquet sets in here, and some badminton racquets." He showed her a door, opening it wide to display the supplies within. "We also have some targets and bows and arrows in the weapons room. The ladies, at times, enjoy demonstrating their prowess during house parties. None has ever matched you in skill." He led her into a further room off the long hall and pointed to another door leading from it. "The firearms are in there, but it is kept locked."

Lizzy's eyes returned to the archery equipment, and she let her fingers trace the graceful curve of the small bow that hung on a hook on the wall. Then she eyed the painted target that leaned against a wall beside a sturdy easel. Yes, some archery might be a fine diversion should they need to stay here for a while.

She voiced her approval of all she had seen, and at last, followed Will to the room she had asked about at first, the library.

This was not a large space, the house being a country retreat for hunting and other pastoral pursuits, but the collection of books on the shelves was more than she had expected. The shelves lined the walls, rather than protruding from them, leaving the centre of the room open. A large desk sat in the pool of light from the window, and two armchairs crowded the fireplace.

"There is paper and ink in the drawers," Will explained. "Shall I leave you, or..."

He stood to the side of the desk, tall and handsome and only somewhat awkward, hands palm-up in supplication. He did not look like a man who wished to leave, and she did not wish him to do so. Could he learn to love her? He certainly seemed to like her. It was enough to spark hope in her heart.

"I shall be quiet as I write, but that does not mean I am unhappy for company if you can abide my silence. There seems to be plenty worth reading in here."

"My uncle enjoys his books." Will walked to a shelf and pulled out a volume. "I have started this one several times and never finished it. Perhaps I can proceed to the next chapter whilst you write." His warm smile bathed her with a sense of comfort, and she nodded with satisfaction.

How pleasant it was to be in company with him, even whilst not speaking. The silence was that of understanding, a shared refuge from the world, full of peace. Her smile lit softly upon her face as she retrieved the instruments she needed from the desk drawer, fixed her pen, and began her missive to her dear friend back at Longbourn.

# Chapter 18
# Council of War

When they returned to the small sitting room sometime later, Elizabeth's father was sitting beside Colonel Fitzwilliam and the major, staring at the map that had earlier been in the breakfast room.

"Good, you are back," the colonel uttered by way of a greeting. "I have spoken to Mrs Lloyd, and she has news." He pointed to an area a small distance from the squares that Elizabeth took to be the village. "A stranger has been lurking about, his description matching George Wickham. We fully believe him to be in the vicinity."

Ice shot up Elizabeth's spine. It had been easy to put the danger out of her mind. Here, in this comfortable and protected house, with soft beds and good food, the worry of the last week had melted like ice in the summer sun. The presence of Jane and her father, too, lent that sense of security and familiarity that made the looming spectre of Wickham's plans feel like something from a bad novel.

How easy it would be to imagine the past several days a dream, to return to the mundane concerns of whether to wear her green frock or the blue, or if the ground was too soft to walk in her new boots. How enticing to believe herself quite safe here within these walls, with no perils awaiting on the lanes toward the village or the roads into town.

But reality was elsewise. Now every intimation of the real danger they faced rushed in, threatening to sweep her off her feet and drown her. She caught her foot on the edge of the carpet and stumbled, only to be caught by Will's strong hands. He kept his hand around her waist now, pulling her close to him, a gesture of intimacy that could not be lost on the others in the room.

"Here?" he asked. "Where?" His voice was urgent.

The colonel leaned back on the sofa, eyes still fixed on the map before him.

"That, we do not know. He is not in the village, although he has been there asking questions. The villagers have been asked to say little, but who knows if they will obey or if a word might slip out inadvertently." The colonel then looked at Elizabeth directly, his eye tracing the dress she wore. "Further, Mrs Lloyd's request for some frocks is surely no secret. Such matters do not occur every day, and it would not take a genius to discern that there is a lady here who arrived without her wardrobe. He knows you are here. We have to assume that much. Now we must determine what to do."

Will's hand dropped from Elizabeth's waist, but fumbled for her fingers to keep the contact. He moved towards the sofa across the low table from the two seated men, pulling her with him. They sat down together, a small council of war convening to discuss strategy.

"I insist upon keeping my daughters safe," her father spoke up. "Is this house secure?"

"It is," came the reply, "but we cannot keep them locked up here as prisoners forever. It might be gilded, but it is still a cage. We need to find this rat and deal with him."

"My concern," Will interjected, "is what he has planned. Can he really think he will emerge triumphant in this? Even should he succeed in finding and killing me, what then? Does he expect to leave the area in a blaze of glory, free to live his life? He must know that if I am harmed, his life will not be worth the dust on the bottom of his shoes. And knowing that, he is almost certainly desperate. Who knows what he might do?"

"Angry men are not always wise, son." Papa shook his head. Elizabeth startled at her father's choice of words, but the conversation around her continued.

The colonel sighed his agreement. "He has lost hold of sanity. His irrational need for revenge seems to have overwhelmed all other considerations. You must take the greatest of care. Hawarden has made some suggestions, which are excellent, and I have requested from the regiment at Oswestry whatever assistance they can offer us. If necessary, we can smuggle you out, disguised as one of the soldiers. But we must find Wickham. That is imperative."

"What do we do?" The words escaped before Elizabeth could stop them.

"You, my dear, do nothing," her father replied with a stern gaze. "You remain here and do not set foot out of these grounds. I may confine you to the house, if Colonel Fitzwilliam thinks it better."

"Keep close to the house, Miss Elizabeth," the officer said in a softer voice. "I shall set guards all about the gardens. As for you, Will," he continued, "you are also to stay low. No, none of that bluster. I know it will rankle to be chained up like an errant pup, but we need to draw Wickham out, and if you will not go to him, he must come here. And here is where we will catch him."

"And so, I just wait for the viper to come to the nest?" Will was still holding Elizabeth's hand, and she felt his grip tighten.

"No. We will smoke him out. As well as the soldiers I hope will be coming, I have requested, through Mrs Lloyd, for a small regiment of local men to be formed. She knows those whose sentiments towards our family are friendly, and who will help us with open hearts. They will come from the village, as well as the market town, and will meet here this evening to set a plan to hunt for our quarry.

"If Wickham is near," he articulated, eyes steely, "we will find him. And soon."

Elizabeth's breath caught in her throat. Wickham's approach meant danger for Will, and at once, the threat of losing him, even before she had him, dawned upon her. Her fingers gripped Will's as he held her hand, and he answered likewise.

"Lizzy," her father's voice penetrated the black spectre about her. "I had hoped for a moment alone with you, but it seems action must proceed more quickly than I had anticipated. You surely understand that you and Mr Darcy must marry." His mild eyes remained fixed upon her until she nodded. "I know he might not have been your choice, but I imagine he is a good enough sort of man."

Beside her, Will sputtered and then clamped his teeth together with an audible snap.

"Despite having absconded with you in a most impolite manner, he has brought you safely to this house, and at some cost to himself, and for that, I supposed, we must forgive him. He will, in time, become somebody you can like."

*I do not like him, I love him!* she wished to cry out, but that would not do, not here with the colonel staring at her in his inscrutable way. Instead, she nodded again and shifted ever so slightly closer to Will's side. "I believe we can expect happiness." Such mild words, so weak and damning, but the only ones suitable for the ears of others.

"Very good, my girl. Mr Darcy, we must talk terms, but the good colonel here says we can expect the town parson here in the morning, that the chapel in the village is still a consecrated church." Colonel Fitzwilliam nodded. "You shall marry tomorrow."

"What? Tomorrow? How can that be? This is not Scotland, sir," she exclaimed. Tomorrow was so close, and rather than trepidation, her concern was that they had not time to call the banns. How had it come to this, that she was worried that a wedding might not take place?

But her father could not hear her thoughts.

"We made a trip, the colonel and I, whilst he was engaged with his business at Oswestry, and made our request to the archdeacon."

"An old family friend," the colonel supplied.

"Colonel Fitzwilliam vouched for you, Mr Darcy, and I for you, Lizzy. We have a licence. It will all be perfectly correct. It appears, my girl, that tomorrow you will be a bride."

The rush of dread she expected at these words never arrived. Instead, she caught a glimpse of Will's serene smile as he sat next to her, and he squeezed her hand once more, a gentle and assuring gesture. Her father's eyes alighted on their joined hands and his brows rose toward his receding hairline.

"Mr Darcy, shall we? Colonel, is there a library or study we may use?"

Will stood, urging Elizabeth to rise beside him. "I am more than pleased to offer a generous settlement, but this is Elizabeth's future we are to discuss. I insist she join us."

The brows rose again. "It is most unusual, sir."

"Perhaps, Mr Bennet, but Elizabeth is a most unusual young lady, and I would have her no other way." He turned soft eyes to her. "You will join us?"

"Thank you." This gesture, as much as anything else he had done, convinced her that he was the best sort of man in the world. If only he could grow to love her.

JANE AMBLED along the paths that threaded through manicured hedges and decorative shrubbery, feigning deep interest in the varieties of roses that grew in this part of Wales. She looked at the grass, at the flower beds, at the stones along the side of the small pond that formed the centre of this garden—everywhere but at the man walking beside her. Why now, after having been in company with him for so long, could she think of not a single thing to say? And Mr Bingley, likewise, had been uncharacteristically silent.

They had spent that pleasant afternoon in Wolverhampton, strolling down the high street, and then the entire day at Oswestry, with the parson or his wife as company, but now things felt different, somehow. What was it? The answer taunted Jane, but like a flitting butterfly, danced around her but constantly evaded her grasp.

How odd, to finally have the time and opportunity for real conversation, and not have the words. It was almost as if her father or the colonel's looming presence, whether real or imagined, had been the key to their previous solidarity. Two souls, at odds with—

She took in a short gasp. Of course!

"A penny for your thoughts, Miss Bennet?"

Mr Bingley's voice brought her out of her ponderings.

It was too soon, perhaps, to say out loud what she had just realised. It had been deliberate! The colonel, she now understood, had been taunting Mr Bingley on purpose. His goal had never been to secure her affections at all, for now that they were here and with other matters to deal with, he had all but forgotten about her.

How ungentlemanlike.

How very strange.

But why? Had the colonel been baiting Mr Bingley deliberately? Could it have been at her father's request? What a ridiculous notion! But still... Surely her father was not trying to test their new neighbour's mettle. Not even he would resort to such a thing. It was most perplexing.

She could hardly discuss this thought with the young man walking beside her. She would have to ponder it later. Instead, she turned to her companion and smiled in that way that Lizzy always told her looked too practised, despite her assurances that it was sincere.

"Have I said something to disturb you?" Mr Bingley asked. "You seem somewhat out of sorts today. Or have I done anything foolish? I do hope I have not, although I fear that it is my lot. My sisters are always chiding me for not behaving as they believe a gentleman ought. They say I am not serious enough, not sufficiently discerning."

Jane stared harder at the ground. How was she to respond to this? It was an intimacy she had not expected, far beyond their cautious conversation over hats and ribbons. Could Mr Bingley also wish to talk about the colonel's strange behaviour? She screwed her forehead, trying to think of a response, but Mr Bingley continued before she could find the words she wanted.

"Even my friend Darcy complains that I am too gullible, too eager to be pleased by everything. But I do not consider that too serious a fault. Is it?"

So plaintive was his voice that Jane had no option but to look up at his face. His expression was confused, almost hurt, and she was struck by the urge to comfort him.

"No, I do not believe it a failing at all. To call somebody gullible is merely an acknowledgment of a generous nature, which seeks the best in everybody. And why should one not be pleased with the world, unless there is some reason to find it otherwise? A happy attitude can only bring one satisfaction, and what more can one wish than to be at peace with oneself?"

"Oh! Do you really believe so?" His shoulders straightened at her words and his large eyes shone. "How extraordinary! My sisters always feel they are missing something, and no matter how much they have, it is never enough for them. I would not wish—"

"No! I cannot imagine a life marred by constant envy or unhappiness." Jane pinched her lips. "Do you mean your friend Darcy is that way inclined as well, always seeing ills that are not there? It seems he is to marry my sister, and I would not have her be unhappy all her life. It is not too late to stop the wedding."

Mr Bingley paused in his steps. They were now about as far from the house as the perimeter of the garden would allow, just steps from the tall iron fence that enclosed the area. The forest encroached upon the gardens here, much like the area near the outbuildings where Lizzy and Mr Darcy had entered the day before, if not quite so close. The gate in the fence was closed now, but the pathway on the other side meandered through some low and sparse bushes to where the stream poked its watery way out of the wood for a moment, before darting back into the deep shade. A stone bench backed against the fence near the gate, and that is where Mr Bingley gestured, inviting Jane to take a rest.

They sat quietly, and for a moment all Jane could hear was the breeze ruffling the leaves and the calls of distant birds. It was rather pleasant.

"Darcy is most unlike my sisters," Mr Bingley said after a pause. "They were raised to look higher than their station, I believe, and so will never be pleased with what they are allotted in life. Darcy is quite the opposite. He has nowhere to climb, and has no such aspirations. His faults, if he is permitted any, are of pride, and in expecting the world to live up to the same lofty standards he sets himself."

Jane could not suppress a giggle. "He did not look so very lofty yesterday when he arrived, all filthy and unshaven, in ripped clothing not fit for a vagabond."

"Indeed not." Mr Bingley smiled at her and then began to laugh as well. "Perhaps the experience will have been edifying."

The leaves rustled again...

But no! That wasn't the breeze.

"Sir!" Jane's voice caught in her throat. "Do you hear that?"

Mr Bingley was already on his feet, staring out over the fields towards the trees.

"Get down, Miss Bennet!" He all but pushed her to the ground before the stone bench.

"Oi, there! You in the woods... show yourself!" he yelled, his voice far louder than Jane had expected.

She dared a glance upwards. Something was definitely glinting in the trees. A spyglass? A pistol? The sun was reflecting off some object that most assuredly was not a bird.

"What is it, Mr Bingley?"

"I cannot… I do not know… You there, show yourself!"

But he was answered only by the sounds of somebody retreating quickly through the thick woods.

"He is gone."

Jane's pulse thrummed in her throat. "What was it? Was that really somebody watching us from the woods? Or was he trying to get into the gardens?"

Already, Mr Bingley's cries had summoned a small army of large footmen, whose presence would have sent any miscreant scrambling for safety.

"Never fear, Miss Bennet. Nobody will trouble you while I am here." His chest puffed out, although his eyes, to Jane's glance, looked as troubled as hers.

They walked back to the house, Jane clinging a bit more tightly to his arm than civility required. She was unsure if he would present nearly as much of a challenge to an attacker as would Colonel Fitzwilliam, but she did feel better in Mr Bingley's presence. And that, perhaps, was the answer she needed to her own unasked question.

# Chapter 19
# Taken

Darcy let his head fall back into the pillow on his soft bed as his thoughts arranged themselves in his mind.

That had not gone badly at all. Instead of Elizabeth's father raking him over the coals and demanding everything under the sun for her in the marriage settlement, he had been polite—friendly, even—and more than pleased with what Darcy had offered. To be fair, Darcy had been more than generous. He could do nothing less for the woman he loved—yes, despite having known her for only a week, he knew she was the one for him—and for the woman who would, he dearly hoped, be the mother of his children. She deserved nothing less than what he had offered.

How could he have fallen in love so completely, and in so short a time? It was all but impossible. In the normal course of events, he would hardly have learned her name in the few days they had known each other. But, of course, he had been in her company, day and night, for a week. They had spent more time together in this short span than in a year of formal courtship, he reckoned, and without the strangling effects of social niceties and disapproving companions. He knew Elizabeth better after their week of frantic travel than he would have after months of exchanging comments about the weather in some over-furnished salon.

He had seen her at her worst, and he could imagine nothing better.

Tomorrow… Tomorrow they would be married. It seemed quite unreal, like something from a dream, or tale about another. Would he awaken in a moment and discover this was all nothing but a moment's delusion, that Elizabeth was a figment of his imagination and nothing else? His heart shuddered at the idea. But no, it was real. Elizabeth might be the stuff that dreams are made of, but Wickham was not. Nor, Darcy realised as he felt for the spot on his ribs, still tender from where Elizabeth had attacked him with her umbrella on their very first meeting, was his bruise.

It was true. He was betrothed, and by eleven o'clock tomorrow morning, would be a married man. Married to Elizabeth. His heart soared at the thought.

But a darker voice whispered as well, one that he could not ignore. He had been generous in his settlement for Elizabeth because he loved her and wanted her to be happy and secure, but he also needed to know that if Wickham did find him, she would be well provided for as his widow. How could he even contemplate leaving Elizabeth his widow before having her as his wife? He swallowed at the lump that lodged in his throat and tried to let his eyes close against that possibility.

He pressed his head into the pillow once more and let himself yawn. It was unlike him to need a rest when the day was only half over, but the previous week's flight had quite sapped him of energy, and he had not slept well the previous night. Not until he found Elizabeth and wrapped himself in her presence. Now that image supplanted his dread: Elizabeth by candlelight, in his arms. She, too, had declared she would rest in the afternoon, and Darcy tried not to imagine her as she unlaced the borrowed dress and pulled her long chestnut tresses from their pins before taking to her bed.

Soft skin, made golden by the sun, sparkling eyes, rose-pink petal lips, dark fanning lashes... He sucked in a stern breath, a warning to himself to regulate his thoughts. How would he ever manage to control himself if she requested a marriage in name only?

His arms ached for her.

"...FARMHOUSE in the shadow of the forest."

Hawarden's voice filtered through the doorway as Darcy made his way into the parlour after abandoning his rest. The echoing murmur suggested two other men, or more, were with him. Three sets of eyes looked up as he stepped into the room.

"Ah, you have decided to join us," Richard exclaimed. "We were telling Mr Bennet of the message we received only minutes ago. Well, are you interested in the news or not?"

Darcy nodded. "Indeed, I am. What have you heard?"

"We have word of Wickham. The men I called in, the ones from the town, have run a couple of his henchmen to ground and have them secured. Two unsavoury-looking oafs, from what I'm told. Would you know them by sight?"

"No. I did not see them, only heard their voices in the public. But they sounded like a couple of London toughs, quite out of place here in these mountains. Elizabeth heard them as well."

"That sounds like them," Richard acknowledged. "They are not saying much yet, but they will. When the alternative to spilling all they know is the noose, their tongues will loosen quickly enough."

"I will be pleased when they've had their say. What of this farmhouse I heard you mention?"

Hawarden replied.

"Thompson, one of the local men, heard them talk of a farmhouse before they were captured, likely where Wickham is holed up."

"Yes, it appears he is in the neighbourhood," Richard continued, "and no, we do not yet know exactly which farmhouse he has found, but it gives us direction."

"I propose to ride out shortly to search for the exact location. One can never know too much about one's enemy." Hawarden's eyes were hard. It seemed the major had as little love for Wickham as did Richard.

"We'll find him, Will, and soon. You can marry your lady with that weight off your back."

Bennet exhaled at these words, his shoulders relaxing as he did so. Darcy imagined his stance echoed the older man's.

"I am relieved. Thank you both, and thank your men. What steps are being taken?"

Richard gestured to the map that still lay on the table. "These are the locations we are searching. You can see where the woods encroach on the fields, here," he pointed, "here, and by the bend in the river. Clifford Thompson and Owen Beddoe are going with Hawarden. They know the area well, and I trust them. Both former military men, now farmers. They respect the rank, even though we are English. I have, by your leave, invited them and their wives to join us at a wedding breakfast tomorrow."

Darcy broke into a grin. "Of course. They are welcome and I will be pleased to know them."

For the first time in nearly two weeks, Darcy finally felt free of Wickham's looming shadow. He felt lighter, somehow, more so than he had in years; the candles burned brighter, and the wine that Richard procured from the cellar was richer than any he recalled tasting for a long time.

"You look happy," Richard observed later as he helped Darcy into the coat they had found in the attic. It was, perhaps, several years out of fashion, but it fit better than the ones Darcy had borrowed. "Good gracious, that cravat looks odd with this cut of waistcoat. Better a frilled jabot than a neckcloth with it. No, no, it will have to do. I doubt Miss Elizabeth cares much whether your clothing is of the latest cut and style. She liked you enough dressed in rags and smelling of horse dung, and I imagine her clothing will be likewise imperfect."

Darcy scowled at his cousin. "Do not malign the lady." His brow cleared. "To me, she is the epitome of perfection. To dress her in silks and pearls would merely be to gild the lily."

Richard rolled his eyes and gave a final tug at Will's cravat. "You really are completely taken with her. Will Darcy in love. I never thought I would live to see the day. Mother will be surprised! I fancy, though, while your lady is more than tolerable to look upon, she is nothing to her sister."

At Darcy's snort, Richard threw up his hands. "You must admit it. The oldest Miss Bennet is beautiful, a work of art, really."

"Richard!" Darcy growled. "This is no game. You begin to sound like Bingley, always falling in love with whatever angel he happens to cast his eyes on. But, cousin, you must leave your poking and prodding. Do not raise expectations that cannot be met. Jane Bennet is a beauty; any man with eyes can see that. But she is not to be toyed with. Stand back."

"What?" Richard mimicked a hurt expression. "You believe that the beauteous Jane Bennet thinks my attentions are in earnest? No, not for a moment! I am merely playing with the pup, taunting him a bit. Miss Bennet is, if anything, exasperated by me."

"Then why do it? You know you cannot seriously woo her, and you do not know that she sees through your game."

"Boredom, cousin, nothing but boredom. You know my ways. Mother had such perfect manners drilled into me at so young an age, it flows naturally from me. It is hardly my fault if people cannot resist my effortless charm. You laugh!"

"I am exasperated. Must you encourage the ladies so?"

Richard had the grace to look chastised, if only for a moment.

"It is a habit I have, perhaps, developed over time, to deflect suspicion. It is unconsciously done. But you surely know I had no intentions of playing this game. I wished only to be friendly and of use, and to assist a family who were as concerned for Elizabeth as I was for you. If your friend Bingley took such exception to my every solicitude, well, what choice had I but to play with him?"

"Badly done, cousin."

Richard tutted. "Turn around. Good. That coat lies well on your shoulders, and the breeches are a better fit than those trousers I lent you yesterday. No, chastise me no more. I shall explain all to your friend later. Miss Bennet is in no danger from me, and Bingley has a clear field, if he wishes to hunt in that quarter. Now, shall we see if the others have come down yet?"

THEY WERE a merry party that evening.

Elizabeth was already in the parlour when the men arrived. To match Darcy's brightened spirits, she, too, looked different. Lighter, somehow, buoyant. Once more, she wore one of the ill-fitting frocks that Mrs Lloyd had procured for her from the town, and her hair was done simply, if neatly, but somehow, she glowed. She was not formed for melancholy and had given Darcy more than his share of smiles during their forced flight, but her laughter now came more freely, her eyes shone more brightly. She, too, was now free from the threat that had hung over them both.

She broke into a great smile as she noticed Darcy and walked over to greet him at once. He said nothing, but took her hand to kiss, and then just grinned in return.

An addition to their gathering was Mr Heatherington, the rector from the nearby town, who was to perform the ceremony the following morning. He had driven in to Coed-y-Glyn with his wife, an elegant lady of subtle wit, and their presence, in addition to Bingley's accustomed vivacity, Jane Bennet's pleasant manners, and Mr Bennet's sardonic observations, was only beneficial to the general conviviality of the evening. Even Major Hawarden was enough at ease to offer a wry comment here or an astute observation there.

The dinner itself was no elaborate affair. Mrs Lloyd had been given almost no notice with which to order food and have Cook prepare an elegant table, but she had managed, nonetheless, to arrange for tasty fare, and plenty of it. Instead of endless wine, they sampled good local ale, and in place of ragouts and French sauces, they dined on hearty bread, fresh meat, and tender vegetables. After the dried crusts and hard cheese he and Elizabeth had gnawed upon during their flight, it was the nectar of the gods to Darcy. He believed he would never again take the delicacies of his accustomed diet for granted.

Likewise, the conversation was unpretentious and nourishing. How many times had Darcy been forced to sit through a stultifying dinner, listening to some bore drone on about his pocket lint collection, or complain about the poor quality of staff these days? Too well-bred to object and with no option of other company, he had come to equate fine dinners with a sort of endless torture. Tonight, however, was nothing of that sort.

Mr Heatherington was a scholar of sorts, who at once found in Mr Bennet a kindred spirit, and their discourse over some of the less commonly studied Greek myths was surprisingly fascinating. His wife felt no hesitation in adding her voice to the conversation, providing some enlightening observations, which Elizabeth took up in her turn.

She was clever and unexpectedly well-informed. She offered her opinions with a firmness of sentiment, but was not so set in her decisions that she would not change her mind when presented with a strong argument. What a gem she was. Darcy could have spent the night just listening to her talk. The conversation bubbled like the fresh waters of a country brook, easy and bright, in no hurry but neither stagnant nor slow, the perfect accompaniment to a most pleasant meal. Even Richard, at times the joker or mischievous instigator of trouble, was on his best behaviour, leaving Bingley to dance attendance on Jane Bennet.

With so small and informal a gathering, they decided to forgo the customary separation of sexes; Darcy had no desire to be anywhere other than in Elizabeth's company, after all. And tomorrow... tomorrow she would be his wife.

"We have a small spinet in the morning room." Richard's voice broke into Darcy's reverie. "Do any of the ladies play? Or the gentlemen, for that matter? Mother insisted I learn the pianoforte, although I never had the patience to practice my scales."

Mrs Heatherington offered her talents for a sweet sonata by Mr Clementi, and Major Hawarden surprised the gathering with his rich tenor voice, with which he presented a humorous—and rather shocking—rendition of a country ballad about a young maid and her swain.

"You play so well, Lizzy," Jane declared once the major had taken his bow. "Will you not play for us? We are not so many that we can dance, but a lively air is always suitable."

"Perhaps," Elizabeth replied, "you will sing with me instead. What of that air from the dance in London, before..." She broke off and for a moment, her face went blank. Almost at once, however, she recovered herself. "Before our adventure. Yes, that is how I shall always think of it from now. An adventure."

She began to hum a tune, which Darcy half-recognised.

"Is that a new composition? I do not believe I know it, and yet it sounds somewhat familiar."

"It is called 'The Arrow's Flight', and it was played at the ball we attended. Here, Jane, sing the words with me."

> *"Cupid's bow is magic-touched,*
> *His arrow's flight is true.*
> *For when his arrow takes its flight,*
> *My eyes are fix'd on you."*

Jane sang and Elizabeth laughed. "Silly words, indeed, but a lovely melody."

She went to the keyboard and sounded out the tune, improvising a simple harmony to her sister's vocal line. It was no masterful performance, but it was enjoyable, and the melody was quite lovely.

*His arrow's flight is true...* The words danced in Darcy's brain for the rest of the evening.

If this was the ambiance with which he was to begin his life as a married man, Will Darcy was most content. This was the perfect ending to a rather hellish week. Now, with Elizabeth ready to become his bride and Wickham all but done for, nothing could go wrong.

IT CAME, therefore, as a most dreadful shock when, as the party were gathering for tea the following morning, the alarm was raised.

Jane Bennet had been abducted by George Wickham!

# Chapter 20
# Wedding in Haste

The first intimation Elizabeth had that something was amiss was when one of the servants brought her morning cup of chocolate.

The previous night, she and Jane had retired at last from the salon and had a long and comfortable talk in Elizabeth's room. This had been a custom of theirs since childhood, and it would be their last for a while, for Elizabeth would not be returning to Longbourn as the second Miss Bennet of the house, but as Mrs Darcy, which station held very different expectations. They had daydreamed and wondered about the future, which was closer at hand than either sister could have imagined.

"Are you quite certain about this, Lizzy?" Jane had asked, her lovely profile a silhouette against the growing darkness. "I know it would be difficult to explain matters, but I could not have you marry a man you do not like. You have known him for so little time; you have hardly had time to determine his character."

But Elizabeth had laughed. "On the contrary! I have been in his company almost without a break for many, many days, and often in the most trying of circumstances. He has not always been the most pleasant of companions, but not once has he lost his temper or behaved in any way poorly. He never once spoke harshly to our poor horse, or whipped him, and that speaks more loudly than any words. He has been a gentleman, without fail. I have no reservations at all. I only hope he grows to care for me as dearly as I have come to care for him."

All Jane could do was offer a tut. "I do not believe you will have long to wait for that. He seems quite besotted. Now, what are you to wear tomorrow? I shall come up with a tray and then help you dress. You will be such a beautiful bride!"

They examined the borrowed gowns Elizabeth had been offered and selected the best of them for her to wear. Jane, who had a talent for such things, suggested some ideas to dress it up as much as possible to make it a suitable frock for such an auspicious occasion.

"Be certain not to go down for breakfast! We must be mindful of the tradition for the groom not to see his bride before the wedding. I shall come to you, and we can remain here until the men have departed for the church."

But it was not Jane who walked through the door the following morning.

"Where is my sister?" Elizabeth felt a stab of ice up her spine.

"I rightly don't know, Miss," the young girl replied. "She went down to the village early this morning to see to some flowers in the church, and she's not returned. Rhys and Evan are out looking for her." Her lyrical accent was at odds with the strain in her voice.

"Looking for her? But the village is not far, no more than a mile down the lane, from what Colonel Fitzwilliam tells me."

"So it is, Miss. We don't know where she might be. Shall I stay...?"

Elizabeth tried to smooth the crease forming between her eyes. "No, thank you. I shall manage for now. When my sister returns, please ask her to come to me right away."

"Yes, Miss." The young maid bobbed her head and slipped back through the door.

An hour later, Jane still had not returned, but Mr Bingley had.

Elizabeth heard the commotion from the entrance hall even up in her room, and could no longer sit there alone, waiting. She had to know what had happened. Tradition or no tradition, she was determined to go down.

She had not made it to the top of the stairs when it became clear that something was very, very wrong. She followed the sounds of distress to the parlour, where Mr Bingley lay upon one of the long sofas there. Gone was the jovial and merry man Elizabeth had come to know; in his place was a miserable, pitiful creature, utterly distraught and quite incomprehensible. A white cloth lay across his forehead, with what looked like a hunk of ice fixed atop that with another strip of fabric.

Will and the colonel stood looming over him, their backs to Elizabeth. Her father was collapsed in a chair near the window, as white as a sheet.

"Take a breath, man," the colonel commanded the stricken creature on the sofa, "and tell me once more what happened. Every detail is important."

Mr Bingley started a sequence of sounds, and only slowly was he able to make any that coalesced into words.

"We were out... we went out... Went to the church. Miss Bennet wanted to see to flowers. For the wedding. Wedding flowers..." And so it went, in fits and starts, until the whole sad tale was related.

Jane, it appeared, had risen early and had decided to walk down to the village, only a short distance away, to decorate the small chapel there with flowers. Bingley, not normally fond of mornings, had nevertheless also been up with the sun and had offered his company on the walk in lieu of one of the footmen.

"I told you not to go anywhere without one of my men," the colonel growled, and Mr Bingley whimpered like a stricken pup.

"It seemed safe. It is no more than a mile, and along the park's lane. You said there were guards at the gate. It seemed so safe!"

They had walked to the church without incident, and had looked inside, where there were, indeed, suitable flowers for a wedding, thanks to Mrs Lloyd.

"And then... I heard... I thought I heard my name, or perhaps not, for the memory is not quite clear. But as we left, I remember hearing something and I turned around, and there he was, large, with something in his hand." Mr Bingley groaned and went silent for a moment. Even from her position at the top of the stairs, Elizabeth could see he had gone quite white.

Eventually, he rallied and choked out the next words. "I tried to fight, tried to stop him. I had to protect Jane. Miss Bennet. I swung and... Oh, my hand does ache. But he was not alone, and I could not prevail against two. The next I knew, I was lying on something hard and being carried back here."

The colonel straightened up and, turning around, seemed to notice Elizabeth for the first time as she stood in the doorway.

"A sad tale, Miss Bennet. You heard that? I was afraid so. I can supply you with the report from my watchman. He observed Mr Bingley and Miss Bennet walk into the village and took it upon himself to follow them. He was too far behind to act, but he saw it all. Two men approached the church and set upon them. Our friend Bingley, here, put up quite a fight and managed to fell one of the assailants, but the other grabbed Miss Bennet and threw her into a cart, which he then drove off at great speed, with no regard for his friend, and before James could reach them."

"Oh no!" The air swam around Elizabeth, threatening to send her off balance, and only by grabbing the door frame did she keep her legs steady. "Then all is lost."

"Indeed, it is not. James was able to secure the second man before he could move again, and we have him here, under lock and key." Any suggestion of the mischievous gentleman from the day before had vanished. This man who now wore the colonel's appearance was all officer, serious and really rather frightening.

"I have seen this cur," Will confirmed. "He was Wickham's associate, the one, I believe, who tried to kill me at the coaching inn."

"The man told us everything, as I suspected he would. This sort knows no loyalty, and knowing that his words save would his neck, he did not waste a moment in telling everything he knows. Our young pup Bingley delivered him into our hands, and he will lead us to your sister."

"But what of Jane?" Elizabeth cried. Her heart was racing, and she did not know if her hands were dry or covered in perspiration. "What will happen to poor Jane?"

"He will not harm her, my dear," Elizabeth's father breathed from his chair. "We have to believe that. She is no good to him if he harms her."

"I believe your father is correct," Will said. "It is me he wants. Your sister is merely a bargaining tool to bring me to him. And," he added with a great sigh, "it appears that this is exactly what shall happen."

No! It could not be. "You are not going to offer yourself up to him, are you?" She could scarcely form the words.

"It appears I must."

"It is not entirely so dire, Miss Bennet," Colonel Fitzwilliam now said. "Presented with the news that we had Wickham's henchman, those two toughs we captured yesterday decided their silence wasn't worth their necks, and within moments, they were also singing like canaries. It took far less time than even I expected. That sort have no principals; they are out only for themselves, and happily gave up their master.

"We have enough on Wickham now to send him to the gibbet. We also know where he is holed up. Hawarden has found the place and has given his report. Wickham is alone. We have his last henchman. He will not escape. I have sent word to the men I called upon yesterday, and they are forming a platoon as we speak. Hawarden will lead them."

"But where…?" Like Mr Bingley, Elizabeth found she could form words only with the greatest effort.

"There is an old house, now abandoned, at the very edge of the woods past the village, no more than two miles further down the road. It is in poor repair, but it will provide shelter for one in need. It is no difficult matter to hear of it; everybody knows it is there." He glanced down at the map that still lay open, and Elizabeth dragged herself across the carpeted floor to stare at it.

Will laid a gentle finger on the site of the old house. The road curved in a compacted U, with the result that the village and house were quite close if one cut through the arm of the forest. The colonel noticed the object of her focus.

"Yes, if one could lay a path through there, it would be little more than a ten-minute walk, but it is rocky and steep, and the stream makes passage impossible for a dray or anything on wheels. A man with sturdy boots can do it easily enough if he does not mind wet feet and a bit of mud on his hands. We do not know if Wickham realises quite how close he is to the village, for he seems to have absconded with someone's horse and cart." Colonel Fitzwilliam raised his head to look into her eyes. "Jane is going to be well. And so is Will. Your husband."

"There can, of course, be no wedding today." The words were almost as difficult to say as were the ones about Jane. "We can... afterwards..." Thoughts would not form.

But Will turned to her and put two fingers under her chin, tilting her head up so she gazed directly into his dark eyes. "If you agree, Elizabeth, I still wish to marry you today. If... If I..." He gulped before continuing. "If something should happen, my greatest wish is that you be provided for. You will have an independence and your reputation intact. Allow me this."

Oh, how could he be so calm in the face of this horrible thing? How could he confront his own mortality—for, despite the colonel's assurance that matters were under control, Wickham was out for blood and there was a very real chance that Will would not return—with concern only for her own future and security? He spoke with such cool reserve that for a moment, Elizabeth stood in shocked amazement. Her own heart was beating a rapid tattoo, and the room all but swayed around her. How she kept to her feet, she could not say.

But then she saw the twitch at the corner of Will's eye, the faint sheen of sweat across his lovely forehead, the turn of his mouth. He was terrified, but he was doing this for her. He was willing to sacrifice himself to save Jane. She could not imagine a better man.

"Say you will do it. If this is to be my last day in this world," he breathed the words so low that she almost did not hear them, "I could think of nothing I would like more than to know you are my wife."

A lump formed in her throat, and she swallowed around it.

"Yes," she nodded. "Yes, I will marry you this morning."

From that moment, everything moved in a rush. It felt as if time had been suspended, coiled back upon itself and held taut, until some mystical hand released its burden and let the minutes spring free, with everything now happening in double time to make up for those moments of suspension. Elizabeth was caught up in the momentum, carried along like a leaf in a rushing stream.

"We must hurry," voices called from everywhere and nowhere. "There is no time to lose. We must catch him while his guard is down."

"Come quickly, Miss Bennet," the colonel urged, as Will dashed about in search of... what exactly, Elizabeth could not guess. "The carriage is waiting."

She stood rigid, trying to resist the gale about her, thinking furiously.

"Yes," she said at last. "But I have one thing I need to do before we leave."

Within short minutes, Elizabeth was bundled into a carriage, which sped off towards the village which she had not yet seen. She wore a simple morning frock, its skirts too wide for fashion and the hem too short, and in place of the elaborate antique garment he had tried on the previous evening, Will had found an old coat that had seen better days some years before. Her hatpin, with which she had tried to fight him off only a week before, he now wore in his plain neckcloth like a diamond cravat pin. She glanced at him in question, and he smiled and took her hand. "It will give me strength," he whispered, "and the inspiration of a woman who would not be cowed," and said nothing more.

All too soon, they had arrived at the church. She and Will walked in together, all traditions and expectations be damned, ignoring Mrs Lloyd's raised eyebrows. Mr Heatherington hurried through the bare necessities of the standard service, and almost before she had caught her breath, Elizabeth was Mrs Darcy.

# Chapter 21
# Facing the Enemy

It ought, by all rights, to have been the happiest day of Darcy's life. He was a married man, and while only two weeks ago, he would not have deigned to offer more than a nod to Elizabeth Bennet, he now understood what a gem he would have given up. He was a changed person, and hopefully, a better one for it. She was his. Mrs Darcy. The world should have been glowing with sunshine and music, trumpets and angels singing from each cloud.

Instead, he was terrified.

Rather than drinking a toast with his cousin and friend, enjoying a celebratory wedding breakfast, and riding off with

Elizabeth to begin their lives together, he was preparing to face the man who had been a thorn in his side for too many years to count, and who now was quite literally out for his blood. Any dreams of a wonderful wedding night with the woman he loved were put aside. He would be lucky to survive the morning.

But terrified or not, Darcy knew he could betray not the slightest weakness. Wickham might succeed in ending his life, but he would not give the blackguard the satisfaction of seeing him cower. He would face his enemy with stoicism. That alone would be a victory, no matter how hollow.

Richard's mixed regiment of farmers and soldiers met them outside the church. Twenty men were assembled there with Major Hawarden at the front, all armed with muskets or rifles, some in regimentals and others in the everyday garb of the common man, all ready to take on their foe. They had assembled a procession of carts and wagons for their purpose, and within moments of Darcy and Elizabeth leaving the chapel, he found himself on horseback beside his cousin, in preparation to lead their band of makeshift warriors.

He had not even had the chance to kiss his bride.

They moved quickly now, as fast as the horses could draw the carts that followed them. Down the long, snakelike road they travelled, around curves that almost turned back on themselves, through stretches of wood, and past small farms, until they reached the lane leading to the house where Wickham had Jane held captive.

"Are you ready?" Richard asked. There was no need for more. Words were quite inadequate for a moment such as this. All Darcy could do was nod.

He guided his horse onto the lane, and the carts behind him followed. Almost at once, the path widened into a clearing, past which the house, crumbling and decrepit, could be seen down a narrow trail that led through a fallow field.

Darcy gazed into the distance, past the old house. It had been less than half an hour since they left the village. A lifetime and a moment. His entire existence seemed to be focused on this one point. This was the fulcrum upon which his future depended.

Without a word, he pulled the reins and nodded to his cousin.

"We stop here," Richard commanded as he turned around towards his troops. "Are you set, Matthew?"

Hawarden nodded, silent and stern.

"Men?" Richard called louder.

"Aye," came the response, and the miniature army alit from their wagons to approach the house.

The noise they made was remarkable, sounding for everything like a motley crew of untrained rustics. They yelled and hooted, some singing and others issuing bizarre whoops and yodels. It was a most unusual scene, and a far cry from the silent approach Darcy would have anticipated from seasoned officers like his cousin and his assistant.

As expected, within seconds, the door to the house swung open and a shape emerged. It looked, at first, like a strange creature with two heads and an unnatural number of legs, but quickly resolved into a sight that left Will horrified. The front of the shape was Jane

Bennet, her hands bound before her, a knife held to her throat. The knife was held by George Wickham, standing behind her, with black thunder written on his once-handsome features. This was a man who had nothing left to lose, and who would stop at nothing.

At once, Darcy's fears for himself dissolved into a fear for Jane. He had to get her out of Wickham's lethal embrace, and he had to do it now.

He took a deep breath and stepped forward, face-to-face at last with his enemy.

"Well, well, well," Wickham taunted from behind the trembling woman. "Whatever brings you here, Darcy? I wondered when I'd see you. Have trouble finding me, did you? I didn't think it would take this long."

Darcy gathered his wits.

"Let her go. What sort of depraved ghoul holds an innocent woman hostage like this? I expected better, even of you." His voice carried through the din still emanating from the rag-tag army behind him. "Let her go now!"

"You're a fool, Darcy. You should have known there'd be no escape. You asked for this. Now watch her die!"

Wickham began to wave his knife, and Jane began to crumple. Only his other hand, snaking around her and pinning her to him, kept her upright.

"Let her go. She's not involved in this. It is me you want, not her."

"Offering yourself as a sacrifice to secure this piece of skirt's safety? How noble of you. Maybe I don't want to let her go. Maybe I'm more interested in what she can offer me. She's far more enticing than you are."

"Enough, Wickham!" Richard bellowed and made a sideways gesture with one arm. Behind him, the men stopped making their noise. "Let Miss Bennet go free. We can talk like sensible men."

Wickham laughed, a chilling sound in the bright morning sunlight. "It's too late for sense. I want what I want, and if I'm not given it, I'll just take it."

"Be reasonable, George. I am offering myself to you. That is your goal, is it not? You wanted revenge? Well, take your revenge. Myself for the lady. You must know that if you harm her, you will not survive a minute." Behind him, Will could hear the assembled regiment shift, raising their weapons at some command he had not seen.

Wickham's eyes narrowed. He scanned the men once more and then directed a malevolent glare at Will.

"Very well. That is, after all, why we are all here. I am not so very unreasonable. You for the chit. But I have my demands."

Somewhere in the ranks, a man started singing. That was Hawarden's voice, steady and strong. It began as a low thread, almost a hum, and grew louder and louder as the others joined him, until the entire assembled crew were singing in full voice. It was not a battle anthem or a hymn, but, incongruously, a dance tune. The men were a strange sort of army, but they could sing very well. It appeared there was more than just rumour to the tradition of fine Welsh voices. Wickham's scowl turned to a frown of confusion.

"What nonsense is this? Are we to have a party before I kill you? Is someone ready to serve tea and cakes? Shall we waltz?" Wickham stepped forward, pushing Jane before him, the knife beginning to wave through the air before pointing, once more, at her ivory throat.

The singing grew louder still, and some of the men began banging their weapons together, creating even more noise and confusion. In the midst of the din, Jane began to scream, and it seemed, for a moment, that all chaos was about to break loose.

"Be quiet!" Wickham screamed. "You do this exactly according to my orders, or the chit dies. Understood?"

The noise quietened down.

"First," Wickham yelled, "I want Darcy. There will be no argument. I want him, and the fastest cart you have. Is there a curricle or a gig? What sort of back-woods place is this? That one, in the back." He gestured with his head, keeping the knife at Jane's throat. "Get it ready for me. Not too close. Good."

At Richard's nod, two men began to do exactly that.

"Now," Wickham continued, "This is what's going to happen. The first thing that everyone will do is put down your weapons. There, on the other side of those bushes, in the field. Unload them all. I want all your hands empty."

"Very well, men." Richard agreed, and the men did as requested.

"No surprises!" Wickham yelled.

"As you see, George, every man here is unarmed."

Out of the corner of his eye, Darcy saw the men hold their arms before them, hands clear and empty; most of his attention, however, was still on the sight before him.

"Good. Now, step back, away from the weapons. Further. Another step." Wickham's voice was slightly less wary. "Next, you will bring the cart here, into the clearing. Then secure Darcy's hands. Nice and tight. When he's close enough, and you've all stepped away, I'll let the girl go."

Darcy swallowed and gave a nod that he hoped was more confident than he felt. His heart was racing, and the world seemed to waver before him.

"Why go through this pretence, George?" Richard called out. "You know you will not make it a dozen yards before you are stopped. Just let Miss Bennet free and give yourself up. I might arrange for a lenient judge."

"Never!" Wickham shouted back. "Darcy will be my ticket out. I might decide to let him live, after I've had my fun with him. But if you raise one hand against me, I'll kill him. Is that the cart? Fine. Now bind his hands. Let me see."

"Are you certain?" Richard whispered in Darcy's ear. "We can try..."

"No. He will harm her, just to spite me. This is the only way. I am ready."

He held his hands out before him, waiting for someone to find and bring a rope.

Was this what a calf felt like, being bound and trussed before the slaughter? Darcy thought he might never eat meat again. He was to be offered as a sacrifice, and unlike the biblical Isaac at the thorn bush, there would be no convenient ram to take his place. Wickham would see justice; of that, there was no doubt. But would he, Darcy, live to see it? The rope was rough against his wrists, not as tight as it might be, but no easy matter to twist free from.

"Now to the cart. Bring another rope. Good. Get in, but keep his hands bound, and tie his feet down. I won't have him running once I've let the girl go."

This was it. Darcy began the march to the scaffold, head held high. He would not let Wickham see him so much as blink. He scrambled into the cart, which was several yards from the doorway, positioning himself as far away from his odious foe as possible.

"I am waiting, George," Richard stated in a calm voice. "Let Miss Bennet go. I shall step back five paces."

In a moment, it was done. Wickham dropped his blade and pushed Jane away from him. She staggered and looked about to swoon, but she righted herself and ran. Richard stepped forward and caught her in his arms, holding her against him. Darcy could see her sobbing into his chest.

"Where is Lizzy? My father?" They were close enough that Darcy could hear their conversation.

"Your father is waiting around the corner in a carriage," Richard murmured to her. "Mr Bingley was injured and rests at the lodge, and Elizabeth is quite safe. She reminds you of the song you were singing."

"The song?" Will heard confusion in Jane's voice. Then, with some clarity, she repeated, "Yes, the song."

"Sing it to me," Darcy called out. "Miss Bennet, sing me that melody we heard last night. It will bolster my spirits and remind me of happier times. You are free, and I shall rejoice in that. Sing me that melody."

"Have you gone mad? You are all mad!" Wickham shouted. "You want a song? You may sing all you wish once we are gone from here, but only a funeral march will do for Darcy. Now, let us be gone. I shall untie your hands and you will drive the carriage. My pistol will keep you on the right road, I dare say." He pulled a large weapon from some pocket. "These things are quite inaccurate, but at the distance of a few inches, I doubt that will be a problem. You will take me where I wish to go, and these good men will let us through."

It was pandemonium. Jane was sobbing, Hawarden was singing, the makeshift army was humming and clapping their hands, Richard was shouting, and Wickham began his approach. He began to raise his hand holding the pistol to aim at Darcy and—

A whistle, a scream, and the sound of an explosion rent the air. And then, suddenly, all was silent.

# Chapter 22
# Resolution

As quickly as the entire company fell silent, so did the uproar begin once more. Elizabeth dropped from the tree where she had been hiding, her pulse fluttering like a captured bird. She had hardly dared draw breath from the moment she clambered into the branches, waiting, praying, for the perfect moment to act. Now it was over, but what, exactly, had transpired? There was so much sudden commotion, so much sound and movement, that she hardly knew where to look. Her eyes flickered here and there as scenes from the drama unfolded before her.

At first, the world seemed to have dissolved into chaos, an unimaginable cacophony of sights and sounds, a maelstrom of activity; in retrospect, she recalled everything as a series of crystallised vignettes, to be examined and reflected upon in turn.

In the first image, she saw Wickham, or rather, the spot where he had stood. That space where the man had been a moment before was now empty; Richard and a few of his men rushed forward in a blur of red and brown, their moving forms obscuring everything from her sight.

A separate image, although it occurred at the same exact moment, was of the horse which was harnessed to the cart, taking alarm at the sound of the explosion from the pistol as it discharged and rearing, dangerously, hooves slashing at everything in its path, its panicked cries splitting the air. Through the black haze that threatened to overwhelm her, Elizabeth saw Will, hand and feet still bound, trapped in the cart, at the mercy of the panicking beast.

A third vignette was Jane, collapsed in Richard's arms, as Mr Bingley came staggering into the clearing, the bandage still wrapped around his head, one eye obscured by a dark bruise, an expression of utmost defeat etched upon his face.

And finally, there was the plume of smoke and dust, rising from the earth only a few feet from the cart's back wheel, and the shouts and calls of what seemed like a hundred men.

For a moment, Elizabeth stood paralysed in place, so tugged between this tumult of simultaneous tableaux that she knew not where to turn, where to look. She could not make sense of them, could not decipher what her eyes were seeing. It was an incomprehensible pandemonium. And then, suddenly unable to remain still another moment, she lunged forward towards the scene of chaos. She had to know...

Will! What had happened to Will?

*Please, let him be alive... let him be alive...* These words, a desperate prayer, were all that kept her moving as she stumbled the last few feet to the clearing before the house through the frenzy of sights and sounds that swirled around her.

At last, the vignettes formed and reformed, until finally, she could make sense of the scene before her.

Wickham lay on the ground, a pool of blood spreading around him. Oh heavens! Was he dead? No. He groaned, and then yelled out an obscenity as someone turned him over and hoisted him to his feet before looping a rope around his hands. The man stepped back, and Elizabeth could see a shaft protruding from the side of Wickham's leg. That was what had felled him. He was not going quietly, but he was clearly defeated.

"We have him secure!" someone called out, and the men cheered.

Another group of men had dashed towards the cart, where they were succeeding in their efforts to calm the rearing horse. The cart itself was still upright, and there was no prostrate body on the ground beside it, or—thank Heavens—before it, crushed beneath its wheels.

Elizabeth stepped around the smoking hole in the ground, where the pistol had discharged, and was able to approach the cart sufficiently to see the one thing that she had wished most dearly in the world to see: Will Darcy, tossed onto his side on the bench, looking quite the worse for wear, but most definitely alive. As she stood gaping, Richard ran up to his cousin and sliced at the restraining ropes with a knife, and Will, free from his bonds, half-staggered and half-fell from the now-still cart.

He drew in a ragged breath that Elizabeth could hear, even at this distance, and all eyes turned towards him.

But another motion drew her notice, and she caught her breath. Somehow, Wickham had loosed his hands from the coil of rope and the moment his guard's eyes were turned, started lurching towards the cart, and towards Darcy, the arrow still protruding from his ruined leg. Suddenly there was a knife in his hand, pulled from some unseen pocket or sheath, and a snarl on his lips.

"Wickham!" she yelled as loudly as she could, hoping against hope the men would be able to stop him.

Her cry had some effect, for it startled him enough to break his stride. At that moment, Will lunged as well, something thin and metallic in his hand. Wickham gave one last bellow and dropped to the ground again. Elizabeth's hatpin, which Will had worn in his neckcloth as a talisman or amulet for good luck, was now lodged in Wickham's hand.

Richard's men were upon the miscreant in an instant, and this time, she was certain, he would have no escape. They were safe at last.

"Will!" Elizabeth called out, almost before she could form a thought. She did not notice her feet moving; all she knew was that she was suddenly before him, ready to throw herself into his arms.

"Have a care, madam!" somebody shouted, and she stopped, all confusion. Then realisation struck, and she let drop the object she still held tight in her hands, that which she had quite forgotten she still grasped.

"Elizabeth! Oh, my dearest Elizabeth!" Will caught her in his embrace and they clung to each other, quite unwilling to be separated, the bow which she had used to shoot Wickham abandoned and quite forgotten on the hard ground beside them.

BREATH by breath, order was returned to the clearing. A doctor had been found, probably called in from the town before the motley regiment descended on Wickham's bolthole, and he made himself busy tending to the wounded man. He had taken a quick look at Will and pronounced him perfectly fit beyond the chafed skin on his wrists and some bruising where he had been rattled about by the bolting horse. As for Wickham, he tutted that the miscreant would likely never walk normally again, but that a limp would be the least of his problems. Desertion, abduction, robbery, and attempted murder were no easy charges to shake off.

Elizabeth was only relieved that she had not been the one to end his life. Her aim had been true and she had incapacitated him quite thoroughly, but she had not killed him. She did not know how she could live with herself had she done so. Far better to leave matters of judgement and punishment to others. She was only relieved that she and Will were finally safe from his machinations.

Jane had quickly been handed over to one of the burlier men, who hoisted her up in his arms like a sack of flour and set off for the carriage where her father waited around the corner. Richard had commanded them to remain there until he was at liberty to see them back to Coed-y-Glyn. Poor Jane had looked quite stricken with shock, but was bodily uninjured. Bingley, who still staggered around the periphery of the assemblage, seemed in far worse shape, and by the way his knees buckled, Elizabeth suspected that he would be returned to the lodge prostrate in the back of a wagon.

The horse, now perfectly calm, had been unhitched from the cart and had been led over to a small stream, where he was partaking of the bubbling water. How long all this had taken, Elizabeth could not begin to say. Time had taken on unworldly properties, every second being stretched into infinity or contracted into nothingness, until the slow progression of the shadows across the fields seemed to lose all meaning.

All she cared about was that she was in Will's arms, both of them safe at last.

As the whirlwind had unfolded around them, she and Will had limped off towards a fallen log at the edge of the lane—Richard had warned them not to leave the vicinity yet—and there they had all but collapsed together. The sun shone bright, but Elizabeth was shaking.

"You are cold, my love." Will's voice was honey, balm for a wounded heart. He ignored the shake of her head and took off his coat, wrapping it around her shoulders before he pulled her towards him once more. Oh, how she needed this embrace.

"I thought I should never feel your arms around me again," she whispered. "I was so very scared. But here, it is I who should be comforting you. You were the one in danger. I was so worried, so terribly frightened." She pressed herself into his side, letting her arm free of the borrowed coat to snake around his waist and then let her head fall onto his chest. This was a most indecorous show, but let the men chastise them all they wished. He was her husband, and all Elizabeth cared about at this moment was not letting this precious man go.

His heart drummed under her ear, that too-rapid but reassuring tattoo, tethering him to the earth and her to him. It was not only his heart pounding; he was shaking as well, she now realised. His whole body was trembling, and he said not a word. He had given her his coat, when he needed it more than she did. But she could not let go of him, even for a moment. She caught the faint whiff of his eau de cologne, applied this morning before the world almost came to an end, overlaid with the earthier odour of perspiration and fear. She would cherish that scent; it was perfume to her. His breaths, still heavy from his recent encounter with the madman, were music to her, and she hugged him even tighter.

For a moment, he just let her hold him.

"It must have been dreadful," she said at last.

He nodded and gave a great shiver. "I did not expect to be bound hand and foot and lashed to a cart." Will let out a great rush of air. "When the horse bolted after the pistol went off, I was certain I had breathed my last. Thank heavens someone was wise enough to hitch the slowest horse to the fastest-looking cart. A more spirited beast would have meant the end of me."

"I would have felled the horse too." She tilted her head to stare into the most precious pair of eyes in the world. Had he said he cared for her? He had called her 'my love.' She would let him know, as soon as they were alone, that his feelings were quite reciprocated. Her lips twitched into a smile, and she noticed his gaze flicker to them. His head began to bend to meet hers and—

"I had no notion you were so fine a shot, Elizabeth." Richard's voice sounded from nearby, jolting them both back to their circumstances. Elizabeth sucked in a breath and spun her head to see the colonel leaning against a tree. He looked amused. Will would surely hear his cousin's thoughts later.

"A lady does not like to boast, but I am skilled with bow and arrow."

"Darcy told me you had taken a rabbit, but I never imagined you could take down a larger predator as well. I must learn to be more cautious of harmless-looking young ladies. But enough of your archery achievements. The singing! I thought you were quite mad when you suggested it. But once again, I am pleased to be mistaken."

"I know it sounded outrageous; I hoped, indeed, that Wickham found it so. It proved to be an excellent distraction."

The colonel offered her a rather formal salute. "Excellent tactics, General Bennet... or, should I now say, General Darcy. Having the men sing quite confounded our prey."

"And the noise and distraction," Will added, his voice still a bit rough, "provided enough of a cover that Wickham did not notice her as she approached the tree, nor did he hear her as she climbed it. Or, for that matter, when she let the arrow fly."

"Indeed, it was slow work," Elizabeth confessed, "finding my branch with the bow and arrow, and I feared I would make a sound at every moment. Jane helped as well." She had to acknowledge her sister's role. "Her sobs and screams also caught Wickham's attention, so he did not hear me. I did not know if she would understand the message."

"*The Arrow's Flight*. That was the song. You sang it together only last night. I believe she understood very quickly what you intended. Thank heavens everything worked out as planned."

"And from a tree, at that!" called one of the men who was standing nearby and overhearing. "Good work, Mrs Darcy. I'd be proud to have you on my side in any battle."

"Thank you, Owen." Elizabeth had earlier asked his name. "But I hope that all my pursuits with bow and arrow from now on will be at an archery range. No, my mother lamented all my years growing up that I would never make a fine lady if I insisted on scampering from branch to branch."

"I am forever thankful that you ignored her." Will pulled her closer to his side. "You have saved my life twice now."

"Twice?" Richard furrowed his brow.

"Ah, this lady you see here is a dab hand with a heavy tavern serving tray! Let me tell you..."

THE SUN was beginning its journey back to the horizon when affairs at the old abandoned house were finally settled. Wickham, wounded but alive, was in chains to be sent for justice, and the makeshift army had been disbanded, with a word that Mr Darcy would be good for whatever coin they chose to spend at the tavern in the village.

"It is in lieu of my wedding breakfast," Darcy announced, "which is now cold and unfit for consumption. But the ale and pies, I am certain, will be good recompense."

"What of your own repast, cousin?" Richard had asked. "You must be faint on your feet. The carriage with Miss Bennet and her father has left for the lodge, but there might be room on the cart with Mr Bingley. What possessed the man to come here, when he can hardly sit up, I will never know. Not even the lovely Miss Bennet is worth breaking one's head for."

"We can ponder over Bingley later," Darcy replied. "For now, I wish only to be with my bride. Elizabeth? Do you wish to ride? Or..." Darcy gestured towards the wood at the back of the house.

"The village is a short walk, if one does not mind a scramble over some rocks and a narrow stream. The road has to bend, of course, but anyone with two healthy legs can make the trip easily. After today's troubles, I confess I would be pleased for the exercise. If my husband agrees, of course." Elizabeth gazed up at him, lips curved into an inviting smile.

"I would like nothing better."

"That is how Wickham had no notion that I was close. He only saw the road ahead and did not realise how near this arm of the wood is to the village. I was here, waiting, almost before your procession arrived, and I believe we will be back there before they descend in their happy masses to the tavern."

"Are you fit to walk, Darcy?" Richard asked. You took quite a jolt.

Darcy grasped Elizabeth's hand. "With this lady at my side, I have never been better."

How different was this walk through the rocky woods from that they had achieved only days before. Relieved of their hunter and the terror his pursuit had caused them, the dark and perilous track through the forest became a picturesque stroll; the rocks and roots that had loomed, threatening, were now interesting diversions along their path, and an excuse for Elizabeth to cling to Darcy's arm.

She needed no assistance on the walk; she was perfectly able to make the journey, as she had done earlier, and armed with a bow and a quiver of arrows at that. Nor did she need any such excuse to hold tight to him, for they were now wed, man and wife. But she seemed to like the contact and he was in no mind at all to complain.

"This slope is a bit steep, sir." Elizabeth turned to him with an arch grin. "I do believe I need your assistance in managing it."

"Shall I carry you, my lady, in my strong arms?"

"Like that rather large farmer did with poor Jane earlier?" She let out a peal of tinkling laughter. "No, indeed. For there, Jane looked quite mortified, whereas I should not be upset at all. I might, however, feel the need for extra security of my person, and might wish to wrap my own arms about your shoulders."

"Like this?"

Darcy answered her laughter and swept her into his arms.

"And like this!" She twisted so she was facing him, her hands locked behind his neck. Oh, the tempting minx!

"Did you mean what you said?" Her question came from nowhere.

"What did I say? I recall saying a great many things, most of which were born of terror."

"You called me your love." She stopped wriggling in his arms and her eyes grew serious.

"Ah. Indeed, I did. That was born not of terror at all, but of a momentary lapse in my self-regulation. Was it..." he took a deep breath, "was it unwelcome?"

She did not seem disturbed by the words, but Darcy knew he was not the best talent at understanding the words that people did not say.

Elizabeth's lovely face grew even more serious for a moment, and he felt his heart might stop beating. He had confessed his love for her, but did she feel anything similar for him? She liked him enough, this he knew, and she had married him only this morning. How strange to be talking of love only now.

Then she blinked, letting the fringe of lashes fan across her pink cheeks, and her rose-hued mouth softened into a gentle smile.

"It was the most welcome thing I have ever heard. How strange, for all that we have known each other for less than two weeks, but I cannot think of ever loving anybody else."

"Then, Mrs Darcy, it is a fine thing that we are wed!"

He set her down on her feet and gazed at her. This was where she belonged, surrounded by trees and moss, the sky her canopy. She would look very well on his arm in a ballroom or at dinner in some fine house, but this was how he would always think of her: her hair blown by the wind, her cheeks reddened by the sun, her eyes aglow.

She was staring at him as well. What was going through her remarkable mind? What does one say to the lady who has saved your life not once, not twice, but thrice? Surely thrice, for without her, his life would surely be an endless succession of nothings that would drain his soul.

She raised her hand to touch his cheek. Was it smooth enough? He had shaved this morning, but was it too rough now for her precious fingers? He pulled in a breath. But she did not recoil. "Are you worried, Will? After all we have been through, are you worried now?"

She cupped his cheek in her palm and pushed herself up on her toes. She was not particularly short for a woman, but he was tall and needed to dip his head to meet her. His eyes closed as he felt their lips meet, once, softly.

"I love you back," she said, and the world was a perfect place.

# Chapter 23
# Home

Elizabeth and Will took a great deal more time returning to the lodge than distance would suggest. Their path first took them past the village, long before the wagons and carts arrived along the laneway that curved around the rocky hillsides. But this was no time for a pint of ale at the tavern. They looked at each other with smiling eyes, and in unstated agreement, disappeared back into the forest whence they had come.

When, at long last, they did stumble, laughing, to the great front door of Coed-y-Glyn, Elizabeth had been quite thoroughly kissed, and had begun to expand her knowledge of matters between men and women. She was certain she would very much enjoy the rest of her education.

"Aha! The lovers have returned at last." Richard's voice emerged from the back parlour, followed in short order by the man himself. "We thought you had decided to walk back to England. Wherever have you been? No, no, do not answer that. It is nothing fit for my delicate ears. I suppose I ought to ask Mrs Lloyd for some tea and cakes. You will not have had your breakfast, and it is nigh on three o'clock! Mrs Lloyd," he called, "tea and cakes for the newlywed pair!"

He bestowed them with a cheeky grin and gathered Elizabeth into a brotherly hug. All traces of the soldier, serious and commanding, had vanished with the morning dew, to be replaced once more by the playful gentleman Elizabeth had first met.

"Tease me at your peril, cousin," Will growled, but his smile belied his words. "We have merely been taking the air in peace, a pleasant diversion after so many days looking over our shoulders or trapped within these fine walls."

"Indeed. I see by Mrs Darcy's high colour that your walk must have been invigorating. You must forgive me, Elizabeth. I am most pleased to call you cousin. Ah, and here is Bingley as well, awake and with us again at last. Well met, sir. Do you need assistance? You look rather like you have been through the wars."

Indeed, Mr Bingley appeared behind them, shuffling along from the direction of his chamber. He looked rather hard done-by; his eye was now an alarming mixture of blue and purple which would surely darken over the next few days, and he walked as if he were a hundred years old. He still wore the bandage around his head, although there was no trace of ice.

"No, indeed. I need no help from you," he replied in as cold a manner as Elizabeth had ever heard from him. "Blast, but my head throbs."

Will scowled at his cousin, but Richard was already leading them through the doorway into the large room. Jane was sitting on a low sofa, her fingers fussing at some piece of needlework Elizabeth did not recognise, her father at her side with a book in his hands. At their entry, she looked up and broke into a great smile as she met her sister's eyes.

"Lizzy!" she cried out, and leapt up to embrace her sister.

"Oh, Jane! My poor Jane! I am pleased to see you so well recovered from your ordeal. You look a great deal better than when we parted ways this morning."

"I am much recovered. I am quite back to myself." Jane now looked beyond Elizabeth to where Mr Bingley stood stiffly by the door, rather supported by Major Hawarden, who accompanied him. She greeted both men and bobbed a curtsey. Elizabeth thought she was about to say more, but Jane's eyes widened and she closed her mouth without a sound.

The major's glance was, once more, inscrutable, but Bingley looked completely miserable.

"Miss Bennet," the young man winced. "I believe... I believe I am to wish you joy."

"Sir?" Jane's lovely brow wrinkled in confusion.

"You and the colonel. I know what I saw. Or, I think I do. It is all a bit muddled. I am not quite certain how I got there, or how I got back, but I saw you... I saw you in his arms. He has been pressing his attentions on you this entire time, and I know when I am defeated. I shall return to Hertfordshire at once. Oh, that I had never left London!" He threw himself onto a chair in a black cloud of despondency, and then winced at the motion.

Richard looked like the puppet master who had set up the melodrama, ready to burst with suppressed laughter.

"I do not perfectly understand you, Mr Bingley," Jane replied. She had regained her outward composure, but Elizabeth knew her well enough to know she was most distressed. "We have known each other but a week; how can you imagine me to be engaged to the colonel?"

"Your sister and my friend are wed, and they have known each other for only a day or two longer."

"It is hardly the same—" Jane began, but she was interrupted by the colonel's laugh.

"Cousin," Will sighed. "It is time to end this game of yours. Enough of this nonsense. Bingley, whatever makes you think Miss Bennet is marrying my reprobate of a cousin?"

"He was embracing her. Or kissing her. Or… I am not entirely certain what, but it was more than just friendly. I bow before the better man."

At that moment, Mrs Lloyd entered with the tea trolley. Richard thanked her and sent her away with a gesture before moving to the centre of the room. He stood tall, an orator about to pronounce words of wisdom. And, perhaps, chastisement.

"In a moment, we shall toast the couple with tea, and perhaps brandy or wine for those who wish. But my cousin has it right. No more games. Bingley, whatever you think you saw, you were entirely mistaken. Miss Bennet had, only seconds before, been released by Wickham, who had been holding her at knifepoint. She was terrified and distraught, and I was there to offer immediate security. I also had something I needed to say to her, which saved our friend Darcy here. My affection for Miss Bennet is entirely platonic, for she is my new cousin's sister. I have no romantic intentions towards her whatsoever. I might be one for a bit of teasing, but I am not a man to toy with a lady's affections. My own heart has long been engaged elsewhere."

"What?" Bingley cried out before wincing again. Then, "Why did you make such a show of vying for her? That was most cruel. What if the lady had developed affections for you?"

"Ah, but you did not, did you Miss Bennet?"

Jane's eyes flickered down to her hands that lay demurely in her lap.

"I thought not," the colonel replied. "It was never my aim, and I had no thought of stirring your envy. My cousin has taken me to task for this already. I have often been accused of excessive gallantry, a habit I developed as a young man for... various reasons. It has become so natural, I do not think of it. Nor is it insincere; my aim is to please. That my intentions are, at times, taken amiss is unintentional."

He turned towards Mr Bingley, still ash-faced and squinting, a rag doll collapsed into his chair.

"I do apologise to you, sir. But when you bristled so at my every genuine entreaty as to Miss Bennet's wellbeing, how could I do anything but rise to the occasion? You offered me sport during a most tedious journey, and I, the scoundrel that I am, accepted. Mother warned me about this. Had you been more temperate in your responses, I should not have had so much incentive to play the cad. Forgive me, Miss Bennet."

Jane glared at him, an expression most unusual for Elizabeth's serene sister.

"That was poorly played, sir. My heart was not touched by your attentions, but you had no way to know that. Another might be truly injured by such actions. And I had wondered as to your motivation, for I knew it was a game of sorts."

"Let us say, Madam, that it is a habit I have developed as a form of armour to protect myself. Will that suffice? Will that be enough to claim your forgiveness?"

Jane's fixed stare did not waver. "I shall consider it."

"Who, may I ask," Elizabeth's father spoke up for the first time, "is this paragon for whom you would forsake even my beautiful Jane?"

His quip broke the tension in the room, and even Mr Bingley smiled.

Richard uttered a wry laugh. "Somebody of whom my family would disapprove in the most vehement of manners, leaving me—us—with nothing to live on besides my meagre soldier's portion. I beg you not to speak of it."

"She must be quite a woman," Elizabeth said. Will just shook his head with a deep sigh before exchanging an odd look with Richard.

"Then... then you are not engaged?" Mr Bingley's eyes all but bulged from his head. Or, rather, his good eye did. His purple eye remained mostly closed.

"We are not." Jane's voice was firm, but almost at once her entire demeanour softened. "You, Mr Bingley, were the hero. I saw you, in the church, fighting so valiantly against a much larger foe, one accustomed to brawling and heavy with his fists. But you fought so courageously, and you felled him." She rose and moved towards him, hands held out before her.

Mr Bingley opened his mouth to say something, but Jane spoke on.

"Even before I learned that thanks to you, he was captured and offered information that saved us all," she said, "I thought you were the bravest and most valiant man that ever I had met. You are my white knight."

Mr Bingley's face turned a shade of red that strove to match the violet of his bruised eye. "Oh, dearest Jane!" he burst out before clamping his jaw shut.

"Is there something you wish to discuss with me, young man?" Mr Bennet asked his new neighbour, a twist of a chuckle on his lips.

THE AFTERNOON was drawing to a close. Elizabeth's father had taken himself off to the library to write home with the news of the day, and Jane and Mr Bingley were walking through the gardens. Or, rather, Jane was walking. Poor Mr Bingley was shuffling beside her, a painful sight to see even through the windows that opened upon the scene.

Only Elizabeth, Will, and the two officers remained in the room. Major Hawarden seemed as easy in this reduced company as ever Elizabeth had seen him, and she wondered, not for the first time, if he was uncomfortable amongst those with whom he was not well acquainted. Much like her Will, she imagined. He, too, improved greatly with more familiarity.

The colonel, likewise, was well at his ease. It seemed that after his apology and rather incomplete explanation to Mr Bingley, he was able to let go of some artifice that had, until now, clouded his manner. Nobody else seemed dissatisfied with the colonel's excuse of a previous attachment, but Elizabeth could not quiet the questions that flooded her thoughts.

At last, she could temper her curiosity no more and had to ask.

"Colonel, if I may, I should like to know more of this paragon who has kept your heart from being touched by my sister's beauty." Her words were teasing, but she knew the colonel understood her meaning. "What sort of person is this, whom you would keep such a secret from all who know you, that you must flirt with unsuspecting women as a disguise?"

"And you know," Will joked, "disguise of any sort is an abhorrence to me. Although, here I must state I understand your choice."

Elizabeth eyed her husband sidelong. He knew!

"What sort of lady is she, sir? An actress? A foreigner? Surely not somebody French!"

A strange air settled in the room, and Elizabeth was puzzled by a series of glances between Will, the colonel, and even Major Hawarden. Of course, the major must be in on the secret. He seemed more than intimate with Colonel Fitzwilliam, and would know all there was to know about the man. But...

"Shall I, Will?" Colonel Fitzwilliam asked his cousin.

"Matthew?" He turned the question to his assistant.

Or was he? A glimmer began to form in Elizabeth's mind.

"This paragon, my dear Elizabeth, is such that no woman can turn my head."

"But shall I ever meet her? We are cousins now, and I would be pleased to welcome anyone beloved by you into my circle. Will I ever know this person?"

The colonel cleared his throat. "You already do."

Elizabeth blinked at him. Beside her, Will's face was a mask. Across the room...

"It is no woman, after all." It came out as a statement, not a question. "Am I to believe...? I shall not think poorly of anybody who can love under such strictures that make an announcement all but impossible. Indeed, while the notion is rather strange to me, it is not unknown. If you love this person, then I shall love him too."

Major Hawarden's stern face broke into a large grin, revealing a rather handsome man beneath the stiff exterior.

"Mrs Darcy, please call me Matthew."

WILL TURNED the key in the lock and held open the door to allow Elizabeth to enter. "We do not need to return with your sister and father," he suggested as he then locked the door behind him and set the key down on a small table. "We managed the journey here very well by ourselves, and I daresay we can equally manage the one back. This time I can promise a comfortable carriage and good inns, rather than ruined churches and cave walls. Well, do you like it?"

He gestured around the room. It was not large; in fact, it was absolutely cosy. The small wooden table and chairs, two large, overstuffed armchairs, and a rather ugly sofa that looked like it had been there for fifty years, all but filled the room. A fire crackled in the grate, its flames warding off the evening chill, and the scent of rich red wine and spiced biscuits perfumed the air. Through a set of draperies uglier still than the sofa, and quite mismatched from them, the vista quite outshone anything a house decorator could manage.

"When one sees that panorama, one does not notice the furniture at all," Elizabeth joked, echoing his thoughts. "It is beautiful."

"Then it meets with your approval?"

"Indeed, how could it not? How strange, that after being forced into each other's sole company for a week and more, all I crave now is to be alone with you. It was generous of Richard to offer us this space."

"Generous, and wise. I rather demanded it from him, in the most ungentlemanlike terms." Will laughed, and Elizabeth's answering tones, rich and warm, filled the space with joy.

This small cottage, part of the estate, was where Will and Richard and their other cousins had come as children to escape the demands of their parents. Far enough from the main house to be quite removed from it, but close enough to have everything necessary readily at hand, it was exactly what Will had wanted for this night, the first of his married life. Mrs Lloyd had supplied the place on extremely short notice with warm food and drink, and the linens in the equally cosy bedroom had been freshened and aired. He felt like a child again, carefree and at peace with the world.

Elizabeth had ceased a slow turn as she took in the ambiance, and now stood in the centre of the tiny space, gazing at him.

"Are you happy?" he asked.

"Mmmm." It was not a word, but it was the answer to his question.

"May I pour you some wine, Mrs Darcy?"

"It is rather unfair, do you not think, that I should be known to all as a married woman by the alteration in my name, but yours remains quite unchanged? We must think of something to make it known that you, too, are now married."

"I believe the smile on my face will be sufficient to announce that to the world. It is, I am led to believe, an uncommon expression for me."

Elizabeth laughed again. "If I am the cause of that smile, I shall be most delighted."

The sun was setting in a blaze of red and orange glory. "Come, sit by me, my love. This sofa is not beautiful, yet it is comfortable. I can think of nothing I would like more right now than to have you at my side."

"Nothing?" One eyebrow floated upwards, an expression he found quite intoxicating. "I am disappointed in you. But I shall gladly sit beside you for now."

Minx.

She curled into his side with her head resting on his shoulder.

"This is rather more pleasant than that cave in the woods," she murmured after a minute.

"Or the wagon in the old ruined church, or the loft above the stables."

"And yet, all of those places are quite special to me now, for they brought me to you."

He nuzzled her hair with his nose, and pressed a chaste kiss to the top of her head.

"Mr Darcy!" Elizabeth gasped, quite incensed. "Did you dare to kiss my head?" Then she broke into another peal of laughter. "Let us see what else you can do. You are quite the seasoned criminal, sir. First you steal my father's carriage, then you steal me, and now you have quite stolen my heart."

"Ah, but that, my love, is entirely fair, since in return, you have quite stolen mine."

# The End

# Notes

## Oswestry, Shropshire

Every so often, while down the rabbit hole of historical research, I come across something that grabs my attention and will not let go. Sometimes it's a discovery or invention; sometimes it's a poem or a painting. And sometimes it's a place.

In the course of planning *Pride and Pursuit,* I needed to plot out my characters' routes quite carefully. They had to go through the right places, and take the appropriate amount of time to get from one to the other. In a world before automobiles and macadamised road surfaces, travel was much slower and smaller centres of more importance. You simply could not hop in the car in York, spend the afternoon sightseeing in Chester, and find your hotel room in Conwy that night. Travelers needed more frequent stops, for themselves and for their horses, and at much closer locations that we think of.

Lizzy and Darcy took one route, up through the centre of Wales, stunning country that it is; Jane and her party took another, with no need to feint south before going north again. The colonel led them directly to his family's property, and this route, too, needed to make sense.

All of which brings me to Oswestry. It seemed, at first, like nothing more than a good place to stop for the night, a good enough distance from their previous lodging, but still far enough from Coed-y-Glyn to make the break necessary; it was also a large enough centre that it would have the sort of establishment that could treat the Fitzwilliam family in the manner they desired.

And so, I began a bit of digging. What was there? What sorts of accommodation for travellers might there have been? What points of interest? Well, what a gem this place turned out to be. The more I read, the more I was intrigued, until I knew I needed to give my weary wanderers more than a single night there.

Oswestry's past comprises both the historical record and the rich tapestry of myth and legend. The great Iron Age hill fort on the edge of the town is said to be the birthplace of Queen Ganhumara, whom legend later renamed as Guinevere, King Arthur's queen. The Arthurian connections do not stop there. King Arthur's last descendent, Cynddylan, was said to have fought with King Penda of Mercia to defeat King Oswald there at the Battle of Maserfield in 642CE.

Oswald, a Christian, was dismembered during the battle, and the story tells of a raven who picked up one of his arms and carried it to an ash tree, which subsequently became a site of miracles. This became known as "Oswald's Tree," which, the story goes, is the origin of the name Oswestry. Similarly, a spring with curative properties was said to have burbled up on the spot where the saint-king's arm fell to the ground and became known as "Oswald's Spring."

Over the following centuries, the town found itself alternately Welsh or English hands, depending on where the border lay that year. It was almost destroyed by Welsh rebel leader Owain Glyndŵr in 1400, and the castle was reduced to rocks during the English Civil War.

There are records of Christian worship on the site of the present Church of Saint Oswald for over 1000 years. A tithe document in Shrewsbury Abbey from 1086 records the church and monastery, as it was then, as being dedicated to St. Oswald. William Morgan, whose translation of the Bible into Welsh has been credited by many as saving the Welsh language, was appointed Vicar of Oswestry in 1599. The church seems to have survived the turbulent Middle Ages mostly intact, but it suffered extensive damage by the Parliamentarians during the Civil War the 1640s. Reconstruction was not completed until the 1670s.

There was substantial restoration of the church in the 1870s, resulting in the jewel that stands today, but it was a lovely spot in the early 1800s as well, as some sketches from that era show.

I quite envy the Bennets and Mr Bingley as they spent their day wandering through the town; I have plans to follow in their footsteps before too long, to see for myself what my imagination has filled in so enticingly.

# About the Author

Riana Everly was born in South Africa but has called Canada home since she was eight years old. She has a Master's degree in Medieval Studies and is trained as a classical musician, specialising in Baroque and early Classical music. She first encountered Jane Austen when her father handed her a copy of *Emma* at age 11, and has never looked back.

Riana now lives in Toronto with her family. When she is not writing, she can often be found playing string quartets with friends, biking around the beautiful province of Ontario with her husband, trying to improve her photography, thinking about what to make for dinner, and, of course, reading!

If you enjoyed this novel, please consider posting a review at your favourite bookseller's website.

Riana Everly loves connecting with readers on Facebook at facebook.com/RianaEverly/.

Also, be sure to check out her website at rianaeverly.com for sneak peeks at coming works and links to works in progress.

Also, be sure to check out her website at rianaeverly.com for sneak peeks at coming works and links to works in progress!

# More from Riana Everly

Teaching Eliza: Pride and Prejudice meets Pygmalion

The Assistant: Before Pride and Prejudice

Through a Different Lens: A Pride and Prejudice Variation

The Bennet Affair: A Pride and Prejudice Variation

Much Ado in Meryton: Pride and Prejudice meets Shakespeare

Preludes: A Modern Persuasion Improvisation

***The Miss Mary Investigates* series**

Death of a Clergyman: A Pride and Prejudice Mystery

Death in Highbury: An Emma Mystery

Death of a Dandy: A Mansfield Park Mystery

Death in Sensible Circumstances: A Sense and Sensibility Mystery

## The *Austen Echoes* Series

All the Wrong Notes: A Modern Pride and Prejudice Improvisation

The Matchmaker's Melody: A Modern Emma Improvisation

The Second Ending: A Modern Persuasion Improvisation

Made in United States
North Haven, CT
28 July 2025